The Peace We Are Given

By Peter J. Murgio

AUTHORSUNITE

Dedication

This book is dedicated to my loving wife, as we celebrate our fiftieth anniversary. Although this book is not about her or us, there would be nothing without her inspiration and unconditional love.

And to those who dedicate their lives to peace...do not let your hearts be troubled.

Peace I leave with you; My peace I give to you. I do not give to you as the world gives. Do not let your hearts be troubled; do not be afraid.

—John 14:27

CONTENTS

Chapter Twenty-Two

CHAPTER ONE
Welcome Aboard

April 10, 1912, was a somber day, overcast with a light drizzle. Agatha's mood mimicked the weather. She had been in mourning for almost four months over the death of her young husband, Lord Prescott Dasher-Hornsby. It was a heartbreaking loss, not only for her but also for their only child, Lawrence.

"This way, my lady. Allow me to introduce myself. I'm Walter, your steward." He walked down the corridor. "Welcome to the Queen Victoria parlor suite, named after the lady herself, God bless her soul. Madame is lucky indeed. Only four other parlor suites aboard all of the *Titanic*, very posh if I may say so myself."

Posh indeed, thought Agatha. *It should be. It cost £670, a small fortune.*

"Thank you," she said.

"Come through, and I'll show you the private promenade deck. It's for your exclusive use, one of only two aboard."

Agatha entered the suite and took in the *Titanic's* ambiance. The cabin was indeed lovely. Window drapes made from the most luxurious fabric opened to let in the sea view. A charming settee and pair of Queen Anne club chairs had been deftly placed around an innovative tea table that raised to accommodate dining. The plush carpeting had geometric patterns in tones of beige and burgundy, and the intricately paneled walls were dark chestnut with brocaded fabric insets. Agatha recalled reading in the *London Times* that *Titanic's* price tag was a staggering £7.5 million. It was the most technologically advanced sailing vessel in the world…unsinkable at that.

"Through that door is the lavatory,–only nine other private ones aboard," Walter proudly pointed out. "It has a flushing Johnny, too. The bed dressings will be pulled down for you by Millie, your room attendant. There's a trundle under the bed for the lad."

When she booked passage, Agatha chose to forgo the upper-class custom of having children sleep in separate quarters with nanny nearby. No, she reasoned, be damned tradition; her son and she needed to be near, be close, as close as possible for he was now the most important thing in her life. She shuddered when she thought that she had almost lost him to a tyrannical grandfather, and now she was not about to let her beloved boy out of her sight.

Walter looked at the little boy holding Agatha's hand. "And who is this little gentleman?"

"This is Lawrence Dasher-Hornsby. Say hello to the steward," Agatha said.

The two-year-old, who was just beginning to speak, simply smiled and mouthed an indistinguishable word while clinging even closer to his mum.

"My, you are a big chap, aren't you, laddie? My name is Walter, you can call me any time, and I'll be there to help you out. You know, there are only 107 children aboard, so you are a very special cargo." Reaching into his uniform pocket, Walter produced a sweet. "There you go, laddie."

"Walter, can you tell me about Nanny? Where is she?"

"Yes, madame. Your nanny is two decks below and has very satisfactory staff quarters."

Walter figured there would be no daddy joining since Agatha was dressed in a widow's black garb.

"So, it's the two of you in this lovely suite, is it?"

"Yes, just the two of us."

"Well, fear not. God willing, I will be there for you both, day or night. Now I'll be on my way if you please." Pointing to the bell pull, Walter continued, "As I said, call anytime. I'm at your service."

The accommodating steward turned to leave but paused. "Will madame be making a booking in the Grand Salon dining room tonight? Chef has a special bon voyage dinner planned. Quite smashing."

"No, Walter, we will be eating our meals in the suite. Please bring tea at five and dinner at 7:45. Lawrence needs to be in bed by nine."

"In your room, madame? The *Titanic* has the world's poshest floating dining room. You wouldn't miss it, would you?"

"No, Walter, we prefer to be alone. We will eat at 7:45 right here."

"As you wish, madame. Seven forty-five, it will be. Would it be all right if I have a special little treat for Master Lawrence? Something from the dessert trolley?"

"That would be lovely, wouldn't it, Lawrence?"

As Walter opened the door, the baggage crew arrived with Agatha's two steamer trunks and twelve valises. A chambermaid and Millie, the room attendant, came directly behind them and asked permission to unpack her ladyship.

"Thank you, but you need not unpack the steamers, just these two black valises. The rest of the luggage is for New York. I'm relocating."

"As you wish, madame. I'll have the other bags collected and stored for you."

Within minutes, the efficient Millie and her assistant were stowing away the contents of the bags in ingeniously hidden wardrobes and bureaus.

"Will, that be all, madame?" the young woman asked.

"Yes, thank you…what did you say your name was?"

"It's Millie, madame."

"Yes, Millie, that will be all. Oh, would you have Nanny come up?"

"Of course, madame, it would be my pleasure."

Exhausted, Agatha turned to Lawrence. "Look, Lawrence, I have a massive sack of toys for you. Now you sit right over there and play quietly. Nanny will be here in just a moment or two, and she will take you for a little walkabout."

As soon as Lawrence and Nanny left the room, Agatha collapsed on the bed and cried herself into a grief-stricken sleep.

Nanny returned with Lawrence and was admitted to the room by the hall porter. Agatha woke suddenly. "Gracious, I must have dozed off. What time is it?"

"It's teatime, madame, just past five. The steward is outside waiting to deliver the tea, but I told him to wait."

"Oh, of course, have him come in."

Walter entered, pushing a large brass tea trolly fitted out with all the necessities. The silver tea service was fashioned in a new design by Elkington, with cutlery done in Du Barry, a pattern commissioned by the White Star Line bearing the engraved White Star flag emblem.

"May I serve you, madame?

Cream? Sugar?"

Agatha nodded to both.

"And some sandwiches? Or perhaps a sweet?"

Lawrence, eyeing the colorful pastries, marched right up to the cart and grabbed a green and white petit four.

"Lawrence, mind your manners. Come sit, and Walter will serve you."

Dinner arrived precisely at 7:45. They were served consommé en tureen, haddock with sharp sauce, and parsley potatoes. Walter raised the tea table for dining, and with the elegance and formality equal to that of the grand dining room, dinner was served. Afterward, as promised, Walter delivered an exotic dessert for the charming little chap: baked ice cream with chocolate sauce, a specialty from the American White House that was originally served for Thomas Jefferson in 1802. Walter even added a bright red candle just for the fun of it!

"Lawrence, eat up for Mummy, it's almost bedtime. Nanny will be up shortly to tuck you in, and after I kiss you goodnight, Mummy will get some air on our promenade."

Nanny left after dutifully tucking Lawrence into his trundle bed. Agatha walked out to the private promenade adjacent to her cabin for some fresh air. *Titanic* was now out to sea and speeding toward New York.

"New York," she thought. "A new home." New York was far, far away from the grief and despair of Briarcliff and the snowy grave where her beloved Prescott was buried alive. But most importantly, New York was her escape from her in-laws, Lord and Lady Dasher-Hornsby.

"I shall raise Lawrence as I see fit," she promised herself. Then panic grabbed her. Deep within her, she felt something gnawing, was it fear or a sense of peril? She wasn't sure. "Oh my God! How will I manage in my new world alone? Thank God, Prescott provided for this kind of tragedy. Lawrence and I will live comfortably in New York. It will be a new start and a new life for both of us. But perhaps I was too hasty running away. Leaving everyone and everything I know behind. Is this going to be a new life, or the biggest mistake I've ever made?"

The moon's reflection on the cold and unwelcoming ocean cast an eerie spell. She turned her head skyward: "Oh Prescott, how could you have left me? Why? I don't understand. My beloved, I shall grieve till the day I die." Agatha peered down at the cold, menacing sea and thought, "If it were not for Lawrence, I would welcome death. I would jump into the sea, and it would be all over."

A steady breeze swirled around her, and she suddenly grew chilled. Clutching her fur wrap closer, Agatha wiped her tears away and opened the heavy cabin door. Lawrence was fast asleep, and Nanny was dismissed for the night, so Agatha retired to the inviting bed.

Sleep came with difficulty. She closed her eyes and laid in bed, praying. Then, like every other night since her precious husband Prescott had died, she quietly sobbed. Eventually sleep would find her, and so would the recurring nightmare she had night after night, of where it all began in St. Moritz, just a few months ago.

CHAPTER TWO
TURNING HEADS

St. Moritz, Switzerland, December 1911
Four Months Before the Sinking of the Titanic

"LOOK, LAWRENCE, SEE THE PRETTY SNOW! IT'S SO COLD, isn't it? Come, make a snowman with Daddy," Lord Prescott called out to his son.

"Come on, Lawrence," he said, encouraging the little chap, "Daddy will show you. First, we'll roll a big ball. See, watch Daddy… that's a boy…good job. It is going to be the biggest bloody snowman ever! What shall we call him?"

Lawrence, too young to talk, seemed to mouth the words: "Mo-man."

"Brilliant! We shall call him Mo-man."

Bundled up only steps away, Agatha watched in delight. It was their third day after Christmas at the Badrutt's Palace Hotel. Her precious son looked so happy and healthy. She thought, "Just the three of us. We will celebrate this winter holiday as a sweet little family."

Lawrence was so important to her and her husband, after previously suffering two miscarriages. When Lawrence arrived, it was a blessing for which she would forever be grateful. The cherry on top was that the child was a boy, a male heir for the family dynasty.

"Honey, do you think it's too cold for Lawrence or for you too?"

"Not a chance, he's a real trooper. As for me, I love the cold. The colder, the better. I can't wait to take that mountain trek on Friday when Rodgers arrives."

"Of course, Rodgers." Sir Malcom Rodgers was Prescott's old school chum at Oxford and, like Prescott, a peer of the realm and descended from royalty. But more relevant, Rodgers was Prescott's best friend who stood up for him when he and Agatha married.

"Well, you can take all the treks you want. Lawrence and I will be toasty warm in the parlor in front of the roaring fire."

"Oh, Aggie." He used his endearing name for his beautiful wife, one that she loathed. "You're going to miss out on an adventure. The sights from the top of the Albula Alps are breathtaking."

"So is the howling wind and bone-chilling cold. And besides, I'd never leave Lawrence in the hotel alone with anyone, including Nanny. No thanks, dear husband, I will suffer. It shall be tea and sweets in front of the fire. When you and that crazy Rodgers come home, frozen solid,

Lawrence and I will thaw you out. I may have to have a hot water bottle for you in bed."

"Don't worry, Rodgers is as hot-blooded as they get. He'll be fine. As for me, you can be my water bottle..."

"Stop such talk; Lawrence is listening."

"I don't think he will mind. After all, it's how he got here…one of those cold evenings at Briarcliff. We didn't need a hot water bottle then."

Briarcliff, she thought.

That massive rambling country estate, an abbey at that, and the place Prescott called home. A place she dreaded from the first. One filled with antiques, portraits of nameless ancestors going centuries back, and, worst of all, Sir Sidney and Lady Penelope Dasher-Hornsby, Prescott's intrusive parents and Lawrence's overbearing grandparents. Over a hundred rooms in the manor house, each one filled with haunting memories that had no sentimental meaning to her whatsoever. Ignoring Sir Sidney's strenuous objections over leaving Briarcliff the day after Christmas was the best present ever. Coming to a winter wonderland filled with intriguing international guests and the finest cuisine in Europe and staying at the Palace Hotel was just what the doctor ordered.

"Now stop that kind of talk. It's indecent, especially in front of a child."

"I don't think Lawrence has the foggiest idea about such matters at his age." Prescott snuggled up and kissed Aggie's long, aristocratic neck.

As evening fell, Prescott and Agatha prepared to attend dinner in the hotel's grand dining room. It was to be a special night at the hotel: black-tie formal with dancing to a society orchestra brought in from Zurich for the night. The ambiance was elegant, and the dining room filled with European upper crust and even an odd lot of Americans. A majestic, curved staircase from the mezzanine dining level allowed guests to make a spectacular entrance. Descending the stairs enabled one to be noticed by the other dinner guests who might whisper: "Isn't that so-and-so?" or "I knew his family, dastardly scoundrels all of them. I hope they don't come over to our table."

Prescott admired his wife as she prepared to make her entrance. "Good God, Aggie, you look like a queen!"

Agatha blushed and felt as regal as she looked. Her gown was a creation from the Paris avant-garde design house of Paul Poiret. It was champagne-colored silk sewed with pearls and glass beads. Gratitude swept over the stunning Agatha as she said, "Thank you, my dearest husband."

"Thank you for what?"

"For this extravagant evening frock, for taking me here to this marvelous place, for being so handsome, for giving me Lawrence, the love of our lives, and most of all for being you, the most perfect man in the world!"

"In the world?"

"Well, in my world. You are the light of my life. Never leave me. Never."

"Don't fret Aggie; I'm here to stay. You are my world too. I'm in heaven with you, and if I travel more than two inches away, surely I will be homesick."

As the stunning couple descended the stairs, the room seemed to hold its breath. Agatha's train followed her down the staircase like water cascading over river rocks. Heads turned.

"Who are they?" voiced a prim and proper-looking older fashionista. "Look at that gown—it's a Poiret, I'm certain."

"It's Sir Prescott Dasher-Hornsby and Lady Agatha," chimed in another know-it-all socialite. "His father is Lord of Lancaster, Sir Sidney. He owns the largest fine-china factories in all of

Europe…fabulously wealthy, you know, and a peer of the realm at that."

"He must be rich!" chimed in a rather short, stout woman dressed in a puce lace gown that made her look more like an eggplant than a lady.

"Her tiara must be worth a fortune," gossiped yet another woman.

"I've only seen one as fine at the court of King George, at the coronation. It must be a family piece. Indeed, a young man would not have the means to buy anything like that, no matter how successful he is."

The tiara had belonged to Prescott's grandmother, the Duchess of Flemingham. It had been given to her by Queen Victoria when the Duchess left the Queen's court. The rumor was that the tiara had been confiscated from the Prussian royal treasury. According to lore, it was given to the Queen, who never wore it as she detested Prussians almost as much as she hated the tiara because, in her opinion, it was a "vulgar and gaudy Germanic design."

"Prescott, I think everyone is looking at us."

"Right. Of course, they are, my dear. It's because you are the most beautiful woman in the room."

The couple strolled down the steps,

"Good evening, Sir Prescott and My Lady," greeted the maître d', Marcel.

"Thank you, Marcel, thank you."

"It's my privilege, sir. Your table awaits."

A few finger snaps later and the couple was escorted to a table for two in a premier spot just under an enormous crystal chandelier.

"Sir, can I interest My Lady and you in the foie gras tonight? It's fresh from Saint-Marceau," offered Marcel.

"That would be lovely, Marcel, for both of us, *s'il vous plaît*. And then the Dover sole almondine. Grand Marnier souffle for dessert."

"Perfect, monsieur! And the wine?" He gestured to the sommelier, who was hovering like a moth around a candle directly behind the waiter.

"Would the cellar have Chateau Lafite 1904?"

"*Oui*, monsieur," echoed the impressed sommelier. "At once, *choix magnifique*."

Their dinner was perfectly prepared, no detail overlooked, and as usual, they could not take their eyes off of each other. Later, as the waiter cleared away the espresso cups, Agatha closed her eyes. "That was divine, darling. And thank you for making our Christmas holiday so special. Being here is so extraordinary.

"Now I want to go upstairs and peek in on Lawrence and Nanny before retiring."

"Right. And when you get back to the room, I have a special surprise for you."

Agatha blushed. "The only surprise I want doesn't come from a shop."

"Well, dear, that's exactly what I had in mind."

Agatha quickly returned to their suite after checking on Lawrence to find Prescott had lit some romantic scented candles, each giving off a delicate aroma of roses. "How lovely! It smells like spring, and it's the middle of the winter. Now I'm going to slip out of this lovely gown and then—"

"And then I'm going to slip into you!" Prescott interrupted.

Agatha blushed again. "Oh, you are just too—"

"Too what? Depraved! If wanting you desperately is depraved, then I'm as guilty as sin."

Prescott pulled Agatha to the bed and gently removed his remaining undergarments. He stood in front of her, naked and ready. Even after years of marriage and countless sexual encounters, Agatha still felt a bit reserved about looking at her handsome husband naked. Prescott moved ever so close and pressed his fit and excited body into hers.

"Aggie, I love you so much. I never knew I'd feel this way about anyone, never in my life. You make me feel complete and cherished. I'll never love anyone but you, never! We are one till death do us part."

"And I too. You are my world," whispered Agatha. "Kiss me again and again."

Even the lingering Victorian modesty soon vanished as Agatha pulled Prescott deep within her beautiful body. She thought: "I am blessed."

*****

Morning

The doors of the hotel suite opened as two servers delivered a breakfast trolly filled with fresh juices and eggs Benedict. Still in bed, Agatha reached for her robe to cover her nakedness. As she walked across the room, Prescott could not resist taking in her hastily covered body.

"Ring for Nanny, won't you, dear? I'll be just a minute, and the three of us can have breakfast in the sitting room. You must have a good breakfast for that hike you and Rodgers will be taking."

Nanny soon appeared with the child.

"Be a good lad and come see Daddy."

Little Lawrence stumbled and wobbled his way toward his daddy. Prescott scooped him up into his arms and kissed his little feet, which were a bit unusual. Lawrence was born with syndactyly, a rare but not serious condition when one or more toes are joined by a flexible skin bridge.

"What a big chap. Daddy loves you so much. Now let's eat that scrumptious breakfast 'cause Daddy is going on an adventure."

CHAPTER THREE
SERENDIPITOUSLY ENCOUNTERED

St. Moritz, Palace Hotel, December 1911

WHEN THE ROOM SERVICE PORTER RETURNED TO retrieve the breakfast trolley, he delivered the morning hotel bulletin.

"Aggie, it looks like it's going to be a brilliant day. Sun and blue skies. A bit warmer than normal too...plus-3 centigrade. Perfect for our hike."

"Plus-3 degrees isn't exactly warm to my way of thinking. I'd say it borders on Arctic!"

"Please, you are exaggerating. It's just fine. I heard it snowed another twelve inches at the top. It will be perfect for snowshoeing."

Agatha picked Lawrence up from his highchair and placed him on the plush carpeting. Nanny, just a step away, was ready to take charge: "Madame, shall I take Lawrence for his bath now?"

"Please do, and put his blue jumper on him, it's a wee bit chilly."

"As you wish, madame."

"Prescott, dear, where are you meeting Rodgers?"

"In the lobby, quarter past ten. We will be meeting the guide there, and then we'll have a go at it. It will be a spectacular experience. We are going to start on the top and work our way down the north face."

"When will you be back?"

"Should be back in time for tea or a bit later, depending on conditions."

"Lawrence and I will hold tea for you. Do try to be on time."

"No, don't wait tea, just have the two of you." Prescott threw Lawrence a kiss as Nanny escorted the little tyke out of the suite and toward the adjoining room where they both slept.

"Bye-bye, my big man. Take care of Mummy while Daddy's out."

The hotel lobby at the Palace Hotel was a triumph in Tudor design. The soaring ceilings and artifacts dating back centuries had been meticulously collected by decades of hotel historians. Even the most seasoned traveler or visiting royal was taken aback by the architectural brilliance and unabashed elegance of the Palace Hotel, which was the ideal backdrop for the Swiss's expert service.

Rogers's rendezvous with Prescott took place in the reception hall just adjacent to the concierge's desk.

"Well, there, old man, are you ready for that hike about? We are in for a treat. A glorious day, with fresh snow and lots of sunshine. Are you all settled in?"

"Right, they sorted me out, found me a room—and Bob's your uncle."

"Well, Champ," Rodgers said, using Prescott's nickname at Oxford. "Let's get going."

Seeing the pair ready to go, the concierge summoned the sports coordinator, who appeared within minutes.

"Sir Prescott?"

"Yes, I'm he."

"Right then. I'm Andrea, the chief sports coordinator. If you are ready, I will escort you to the men's locker room so you can get your equipment and meet your guide."

"Brilliant. I'm pleased to introduce Sir Malcom Rodgers, my best friend."

"Of course, a pleasure, sir. Now, if you please…"

Soon after lunch, the sunny skies turned gray with dark clouds. Agatha and Lawrence lunched in the informal dining room and later established themselves in front of a roaring fire in the hotel's pleasant parlor. Nanny appeared a few moments later to collect Lawrence for his nap.

"Nanny, please have Lawrence ready for tea. Sir may or may not be back by then, so it will be tea in the lobby with Prescott and Rogers if they arrive in time, otherwise it will be just Lawrence and myself."

"Of course, madame. Now off with you, Lawrence."

Agatha strolled across the lobby, admiring the room. A small but exclusive shop next to the entrance featured a limited but lovely array of merchandise. Spotting an especially attractive selection of tie pins in the window, Agatha thought something like that would be a perfect surprise for her husband. She figured it would be a great memento of this fabulous vacation. She'd call it a belated Christmas gift.

"*Guten tag, madame, wie kann ich ihnen helfen? Ich bin Fredrick.*"

"I'm sorry, but I don't speak German. Do you know English?"

"Pardon me. Of course, I speak English. What I said was, 'May I assist you? My name is Frederick.'"

"Yes, thank you so much, Frederick. I appreciate you speaking English. It makes things so much easier. Now, then, I'd like to see the tie pins in the window."

"Immediately, madame. It would be my pleasure to show you them all."

The clerk quickly walked over to the show window, unlocked the enclosing doors, and reached deeply into the window, seizing the tray of pins.

"Madame, these tie pins are incredibly special. They are made in Italy, by Venetian artisans. They are eighteen-karat gold, and the center is hand-blown Venetian glass. The colors are rich, captivating, and most vibrant, wouldn't you agree, madame?"

Agatha carefully selected one and lifted it out of the velvet tray. "I fancy this one, it's beautiful."

"*Ja, ist es.* Pardon, I mean to say, yes, it is. The center bead is called the 'eye of the raven.' It is widely believed in Italy to have the power to change lives. But who knows? Those emotional Italians are likely to believe anything."

"Change lives, how intriguing. That's something I'd be most interested in doing. How does it work? Do you make a wish or something like that?"

"Well, I really don't know, but my guess is that just owning it will do. There is no hocus-pocus about that."

"Right, then." Without another thought, Agatha told Frederick to wrap the tie pin up. "I shall present it to my husband this afternoon at tea."

"Smashing, madame. Undoubtedly he will love it."

After her shopping trek, Agatha decided to sit in the solarium. The sun had disappeared, and some dark clouds hovered over the majestic mountain peaks. Perhaps a bit menacing, but nonetheless, the view was captivating. She sat and took a retrospective inventory of her blessings. Her mind took her back to when she first met Prescott. It seemed a long time ago, but it was only six and one-half years from the spring of 1906.

*****

The Court of King Edward VII
Spring Presentation, 1906

In London, May was the height of the social season, and no one was more excited than Agatha. She had just come of age, and the anticipation of the debutante balls had every eligible young girl and her mother in a tizzy. The young daughters of the aristocrats were in a fierce competition to have the most stunning ball gown. But even more fierce was the quest to grab a suitable mate. Lord Byron had dubbed these "coming out" parties as marriage marts because it was one of a few opportunities for proper young ladies to encounter a fitting suitor, with a proper pedigree and social standing. The only other way was, of course, an arrangement between two families, which was not uncommon, but certainly less romantic.

Agatha Birmingham Clark fretted at the thought she would not have the best frock. Her mother, Sarah, was even implicated in a scheme to spy on the two leading dressmakers in London to make sure that her "little girl's" dress was the best and most spectacular. After all, a lot was at stake.

To Sarah, the idea that Agatha should be presented to society in anything less than the best was abhorrent. Coming on the last

Saturday in May, Agatha prepared for the most important cotillion of the season. It was to be held at the Queen's drawing room, St. James Palace.

"Mama, I think I will not be able to meet the man of my dreams unless I have the most perfect gown."

"Don't be absurd, darling, of course you will. You will not only have the most spectacular dress, but you will be the most beautiful of all the debutantes."

"Do you promise, Mama?"

"I promise."

*****

Later that evening, as Agatha entered the queen's drawing room at St. James Palace, Hall Master Gray barked, "Agatha Birmingham Clark of Mayfair and Stratford-upon-Avon!"

Agatha entered at the far left of the hall. The protocol dictated that each debutante was to walk across the room and join the others already lined up in front of the orchestra stage. Being presented last was desirable, a position every parent vied to get for their daughter, which usually required a handsome remuneration to the Hall Master.

The group of debutantes moved across the room past the orchestra and toward the dais where the new king, Edward VII, sat next to his queen, Alexandria, the former Danish princess, scarcely a few months older than the young women being presented.

"Your Majesties, Lords and Ladies, Gentlemen and Madams," cried out Hall Master Gray in his most official-sounding voice. "And now, the young ladies of the Court of King Edward are presented." Gray nodded to His Majesty, and the king rose. The long line of white-clad eligible young ladies waited to pass in front of the king and dutifully curtsy, paying respects.

Standing among the assemblage were the kingdom's finest eligible young men, ogling and eyeing each young maid as she passed in front of them. From the corner of her eye, Agatha caught a glimpse of a dashing young man, well over six feet tall. She could not take her eyes off of him. She thought: "Whom could that be? I've never seen him before. I must ask Mama."

The music began for the first dance, led by King Edward and his young wife, followed by a crowd of young men hustling across the floor to find a deb who they fancied for a dance.

The handsome stranger Agatha had noticed approached and began to introduce himself. "Good evening, I'm Prescott Dasher-Hornsby and—"

A brazen young man pushed Prescott aside and grabbed Agatha's dance card. "Good evening, my name is Percy Gaylord Wallace, and you are?"

Disappointed that this fellow had elbowed his way in, Agatha sighed and replied, "I'm Agatha Clark."

Agatha could not help discerning the difference between Percy Wallace and Prescott. Percy was a good two inches shorter than she, and his almost portly build was not what she dreamed about in a man. The overwhelming use of a men's cologne that smelled like disinfectant enveloped Percy.

"Agatha, you say? That's funny...my mother has a pet monkey named Agatha, and the blasted animal never stops grunting and squeaking. So tiresome!"

Although Agatha was not skilled or experienced in keeping men's company, she thought it odd, maybe even insulting, to say there was a monkey with her name—and it was tiresome. "I see," she said. "I hope your mother enjoys taking care of her pet monkey."

"Who knows what she thinks of the bloody animal? Both of them are twits."

"You think your mother is a twit?"

"Blimey yes, but she's a sweet twit. My father says she's limited, and that the monkey is smarter than she. He's probably right. As for me, I think she's just plain simple. The fairer sex is never, well, you know, bright."

Agatha recoiled at that remark and listened as Percy continued.

"I'm at Cambridge, you know, second-term man, fifth in my class," he said. "I'm going to be a barrister. My family is from Sissinghurst. We have thousands of hectares of land out there and a rather successful enterprise exporting and importing. My father is Lord Manchester and was an MP until just last year. I'm going to be one also, someday. My father says he can fix it."

Percy stepped back to get a better look at Agatha. "Nice dress, but it makes you look a little fat, I would think you'd want to wear something more slimming. But like my father says, a little meat on the bones never hurts, and when the lights are out, who cares if there is a pound or two extra. Hahaha."

Agatha gasped in disgust.

"Enough of the talking, Agatha," Percy said. "Let's do it."

"Do what?"

"Dance. Don't tell me you're a twit too. Now come on."

She rolled her eyes.

The couple walked to the center of the dance floor and began the waltz. Percy reached to clasp Agatha's hand. His hand was clammy and sweaty. He placed his right hand on Agatha's back, and when they danced, he began to slowly move it up and down from her shoulders to her buttock. He pulled her close and whispered in her ear, "You fancy that, don't you? I got a lot more you're going to like. You can't see it right now, but if you're lucky and a good girl, you will."

Percy's offensive remark was the last straw for Agatha. She pulled away and attempted to leave the dance floor. Percy pulled her back into his arms.

From across the room, young Prescott kept his eye on the couple. When he realized Agatha was in distress, he raced over to intervene.

"May I cut in, please?"

"No, get lost, she's with me."

"No, I'm not, Percy. I'm with no one. And least of all you."

Prescott towered over Percy as he said, "I suggest you move on, or there is going to be a problem."

It was indeed a chance meeting for the young Prescott Dasher-Hornsby. He had not planned to even attend that night because he was finishing up his spring program at Oxford and was thoroughly exhausted. At the last minute, urged by his best mate, Rodgers, Prescott donned his tails and tagged along. It took only one dance for Agatha and Prescott to connect, starting what was to become a whirlwind romance.

CHAPTER FOUR
JUST PLAIN GONE

St. Moritz Palace Hotel, December 1911

TEA WAS IN THE MAIN LOBBY AT PRECISELY 4:45 P.M. AT THE Palace, tea was a grand event. Several trollies maneuvered by elegantly attired butlers floated throughout the room, allowing the discriminating guests to choose from the wide variety of treats.

"The Swiss know how to entertain, perhaps not quite as formally as the British, but always to exacting perfection," thought Agatha.

"And for the little master, madame?" asked the server as he pulled the trolley next to Agatha's table.

"Lawrence, darling, what strikes your fancy?"

Lawrence pointed to a very extravagant pastry filled with whipped cream and berries.

"*Ja, hunger mann!* Good choice."

Turning to his assistant, he continued in German, "*Beerentarte mit schlagsahne für den jungen mann,*" ordering a berry tart with whipped cream for the young man.

The butler plated Lawrence's choice and then turned to Agatha. "And for you, madame?"

"Tea, Earl Gray if you have it, if you please."

"Of course, madame. Something else?"

"Oh, you tempt me. Perhaps a petit four, the lovely pink one with the precious flower."

Agatha organized a little tea table in front of Lawrence's chair. "Now, when we finish here, we must go for a little rest since you will be joining us for dinner tonight. Daddy should be back any time now. He probably will be all tuckered out and may need to rest also."

Lawrence, now covered with *schlagsahne*, was licking his fingers in delight.

"Oh my, we better get going. Daddy's coming. Nanny will have to bathe you … just look at you."

Agatha and Lawrence walked through the splendid lobby toward the staircase for a walk up to their second-floor suite. There seemed to be a bit of a commotion. A couple of uniformed policemen were talking to a group of men, which she ignored just like the newly installed elevators. Agatha wasn't quite ready to trust them, especially with her prized cargo, Lawrence. "Stairs can't get stuck," rang in her mind as she recalled the first time her mother had dared to try a lift. Sure enough, the contraption got stuck, and she needed to be rescued after an hour of being "imprisoned."

Nanny put Lawrence down for a nap in his room, and Agatha decided to lie down herself, "just for a few minutes." It would give her a second wind for their late-night dinner reservation.

"Madame, madame, are you there?" The furious knocking on the door startled Agatha awake. "Madame, madame, please!"

"I'm coming, just a moment, I'm coming."

Not waiting for Agatha, the door swung open. Jacques Moxhet, the hotel's general manager, his assistant, and the two uniformed police officers from the lobby along with a plainclothes detective crowded the opening.

"What on Earth is it? Is the hotel on fire?" Her heart dropped. "Where's Lawrence? I must get him!"

"No, no, madame," explained the general manager. "Let me introduce myself; I'm Herr Jacques Moxhet, the general manager here at the Palace."

"Yes, but what is this all about?"

"May we come in, madame?" the detective asked.

Agatha looked around, still half asleep and dazed. She nodded for the men to come through.

"Please sit down, madame," the detective urged.

"For heaven's sake, please gentlemen, I must get ready for dinner. My husband will be here any minute now, and he will be quite annoyed if you detained me from getting dressed."

The men looked at each other and paused. Finally, the detective began: "I'm Inspector Danial Bodmere. I'm here to tell you that there has been an accident."

"An accident? Where?"

"*Ja*, madame, an accident. On the trail, the hiking trail."

Agatha almost stopped breathing. "Go on, tell me what has happened. Where is Prescott?"

"You see, madame, there seems to have been a very unusual, how you say, event."

"Event? What do you ever mean, event?"

"Well, for this time of the year, it is extremely rare, but there has been a *lawine*."

Now quite annoyed and agitated, Agatha snorted: "Lawine? What the devil is that, and why should I care?"

"So sorry, madame. *Lawine* is an avalanche. Yes, an avalanche on the mid-mountain hiking trail. There were several guests and a hotel sports center guide who seem to have been overtaken by the *lawine,* sorry, avalanche. At this time, their whereabouts are unknown."

Agatha clutched her chest. "Oh, God, no."

"Madame, let me assure you that we have dozens of men searching at this very moment, dozens. "

"Are you sure Prescott was one of the missing guests?"

"Quite sure. You see, we have several eyewitnesses who saw them on that very trail just a few moments before the *lawine*…avalanche."

Agatha slipped into the loveseat and held her head in her hands. "Where is Lawrence? Call Nanny; I must have Lawrence with me—now!"

The assistant manager slipped out of the room and headed toward the room where Nanny and Lawrence were resting.

*****

Three days later

In an almost dream-like trance, Agatha approached the manager.

"Mr. Moxhet, it's been three days now, what can you tell me?"

"I am so sorry, madame. There is nothing new from this morning."

"But you don't understand. I can't go home without Prescott. I must take him home."

"I understand Madame, but the weather is bitter cold, and more snow has come since and…so recovery may not be feasible for a long time…maybe in the spring."

"Spring! You can't be serious. Spring? What am I to do until then? Just sit around and wait for you to dig my dearest Prescott's body out of a pile of snow? You must be mad. Please, there must be something you can do! Please! Please!"

"Calm yourself, madame, the authorities are doing everything they can. Search parties are exhausted; they have been at it for days."

*****

On the fifth day, Agatha reluctantly prepared to leave St. Moritz without her beloved Prescott. She closed the last of the valises, the one with Prescott's belongings. The box containing the tie pin that she bought for Prescott just a few days before was sitting on the dresser. She opened it and stared at the raven's eye. She recalled the shop clerk's words: "It is said to change lives." The legend was right, this seemingly benign piece of glass had changed her life forever. Then, as if it were red hot, Agatha tossed the tie pin across the room.

Just as Agatha thought there couldn't possibly be any more tears left, her eyes filled, and she wept again. She thought, "Thank God Lawrence is too young to understand what has happened: his daddy is gone…gone forever. He is somewhere in a frozen unknown grave."

There would be no good-byes. He was just plain gone, and she had no idea what came next.

CHAPTER FIVE
FAREWELL TO HARM

SOON AFTER AGATHA AND LAWRENCE ARRIVED BACK AT Briarcliff from St. Moritz, she realized she had to escape. When she arrived, she found the manor house covered with yards and yards of black crepe. On the massive entry doors hung a pair of solemn, black-feathered wreaths proclaiming that Briarcliff was in official mourning.

Each day, Sir Sidney locked himself in his study, so grief-stricken that he refused to receive Agatha or his grandson. Agatha could hear him from the corridor screaming and ranting at his wife, Penelope.

"That horrible woman! She took him to a frozen hell and saw to it that he died. My son, my heir, has been stolen from me. Prescott should have listened to me and stayed here. But no, she had to talk him into leaving Briarcliff and missing one of the most significant holidays, Boxing Day, and you know how important that day is to the lord of the manor and his heir. It's a day we celebrate with the staff and tenants. It's a tradition that should never be broken. How dare Agatha interrupt that! And what has she left me with?

Nigel, an utterly disgusting example of a human being, inept, and probably worse. How can I feel comfortable with him as the heir to Briarcliff and the factory? I shall hate her till the day I perish."

Agatha soon had heard enough. She knew if she stayed, Sir Sidney would make both Lawrence's and her life miserable, just as he did Nigel's.

Sir Sidney wasn't the only one grieving Prescott's loss. His younger brother by some nineteen years, Nigel, was devastated. He loved Prescott, and he considered Prescott a father figure, especially since Sir Sidney was hardly anything close to paternal. As a member of the peerage and born to the manor, Sir Sidney expected perfection from all, with only one exception—himself. He was a man of the times. His land, drink, horses, dogs, treasure, and women crowded his myopic world.

And then there was Nigel, the spare to the heir, never permitted to forget that Sir Sidney clearly favored Prescott in every respect, grooming him to take the title, the family business, and the reigns at Briarcliff. But all that vanished on an icy mountainside in Switzerland.

On a damp January afternoon after Agatha and Lawrence returned from St. Moritz, Nigel sat in a dark corner of the conservatory. Nigel was joined by Agatha, who silently sat next to him on a bench. Agatha broke the grieving stillness with a question.

"You miss him, too, don't you?"

"Oh, Agatha, desperately. You have no idea how much. He was everything I'm not. Strong and handsome and brilliant."

"He was the love of my life, Nigel."

"You know, Agatha, this is going to be hell for me now that he is gone. My father will never give me a moment of peace."

"I can only imagine. Will you go back to university?"

"I hope so, if he lets me, that is. I want to finish and become a chemist. I think it's in my blood. But knowing father, he'll keep me here like a prisoner to play heir apparent."

Agatha and Nigel sat for a few moments, their thoughts all over the place. "Do you like school?"

"Yes, I do, very much so. I love studying, and chemistry is fascinating. I think I could be helpful in the family business too. The future lies in science and change."

"Chemistry, that's a complicated subject, I would imagine. How do you ever manage?

"It's all about focus and effort. I have this condition which means I have to work extra hard. But when you have a passion, a labor of love, you can accomplish just about anything you want."

"Condition? Is that something you caught somewhere? Can you die from it?"

"Oh, Agatha, certainly not. They aren't quite sure what it is, but I kind of see things differently. The ailment was first studied at the end of the last century. I've learned all I can about it. One is born that way. And no, you can't die from it."

"Well, you certainly look normal to me."

"The condition is one that is manifested in the brain. You see, simply put, somehow the pathways in your brain get crossed or something like that. And when you read and write, things can be backward or mixed up, upside down, or even jumbled. With hard work, focus, and extra effort, I can manage it. It's just a bit harder for me than the average chap. My father calls me simple-minded, but the condition has nothing to do with intelligence. Many very successful and brilliant people have this condition, one being

Nikola Tesla, the chap who established the transatlantic telecommunications network. At least that is the whispered rumor. He's a genius."

"I see. … How interesting."

"Many experts believe a lot of gifted people suffer from some form of what I have. They say Leonardo da Vinci and Michelangelo both showed signs of it. A lot of their work was done in reverse, which is a characteristic manifestation. Not that I consider myself anywhere near their league, mind you."

"You know I'm very proud of you. Without a doubt, you will be the most brilliant chemist."

"Well, I'm glad someone is proud of me."

"Prescott was proud of you too. He loved you."

"And I loved him. Taking his place as the heir of Briarcliff is nothing short of a life sentence. Now that Prescott is gone, the old man will be insufferable."

Agatha nodded in agreement. "I know how cruel he is. Merciless."

"Father has always looked upon me as inadequate from the beginning. It's true, I don't have the panache that he expected for his son, much less that of a titled aristocrat. Prescott was always the one that my father admired. And he did have it all: he was tall and fit and a leader. Father only allowed me to go to university to get me out of the way so he could groom Prescott."

The two sat deep in thought. Nigel's memory brought him back to one of the most humiliating incidents in his life. It had happened on his eighteenth birthday. He could still hear his father's words.

*****

"Come on, boy, we're going to the village. There is someone special I'd like you to meet."

"Special, how's that, Father?"

"You'll see, get mounted."

On the way to the village, Sir Sidney and Nigel passed estate tenants who showed due respect to the lord with a slight bow and tip of the hat. When they arrived at a small cottage just on the edge of the village, Sir Sidney slowed down. He leaned into Nigel's ear to impart his instructions.

"Listen, boy. You are eighteen today, and it's about time you became a man. There are some lovely little fillies in that cottage, and they are all waiting to show you a good time, if you get my drift."

"A party?"

"No, you twit, not a party. You really are daft. They are going to…well, you'll see. Now get off that horse and knock on the door. Katey and her friends are expecting you."

"Katey? Do I know her?"

"Not yet, but you will get to know all of them pretty well. When you're finished, meet me at the Bull and Pig. I'm going to have a pint with the peasants. You know they expect that now and again."

Nigel dismounted and cautiously approached the door. A lavender sign read: "Primrose Cottage." He was pretty sure what this place was but was petrified to buck his father's plans. Nigel removed his riding glove and knocked. The door swung open almost instantly. "Good evening, madame, I'm Nigel—"

"Ah, yes. No need to introduce yourself, you're the spare," Katey replied, laughing. "We've been expecting you. Come in."

The cottage seemed a bit bizarre to Nigel. Candles and a sweet-smelling fragrance emanated from every corner. Provocative paintings of women lined the walls. A large chaise lounge covered in dark red velvet dominated the front room, where several young women were sprawled. At first glance, Nigel thought they were in various degrees of undress. With a closer look, he confirmed they were indeed partially naked. Already he was dreading what lay ahead.

"Come on, young man. I want to introduce you to some of my girls. They are dying to meet you. Now, this here is Gisele, she's French, and this one is Delizioso, she's one of our best, and over there, standing on the staircase, are Alicia and Mitzie. So, take your pick."

"Pick?"

"You really are daft, aren't you? Your father warned us. So, let's have a start of it. Pick one or two of the girls out, they're all very friendly and would love to get to know you better…a lot better."

Nigel was becoming more uncomfortable by the moment. Sir Sidney had set him up. One of the girls grabbed Nigel's hand and put her other one in his trousers' pocket. and said, "Come on now, your Lordship, let's go upstairs. I'm Mitzie, and this is my friend Delizioso, we're going to show you a good time."

The women were pretty in a common way, with a bit too much rouge. Delizioso was half-naked with her more-than-ample breasts bobbing for all to enjoy. Her exaggerated lips were painted crimson red, and she had a beauty mark on her left cheek. She leaned in and whispered: "I'm from Naples. In Italian, my name means 'delicious.'" She chuckled and continued, "And I am…"

Nigel flushed redder than Delizioso's painted lips. Katey laughed aloud.

"Ladies, it looks like we got ourselves a virgin here. We're going to have to work extra hard to make his lordship remember his first time!"

The threesome walked up the stairs, Mitzie half pushing Nigel. "Step in, this is my favorite room. I call it Fantasy."

Mitzie called over to a young man named James, also half-naked. He was about Nigel's age and a rather handsome local chap. "James, help his lordship with his clothing, be sure to handle it well, they are of the finest."

"This way, sir, allow me."

James, who towered over Nigel by several inches, took Nigel's jacket and waistcoat and folded them neatly. "And your trousers, sir? The ladies are waiting."

Nigel didn't know what to make of the situation. He was totally mortified and wanted out. But would he shame his father once again if he fled?

"Miss Mitzie, I'm not really—"

"Don't fret, your lordship," Mitzie whispered, guiding the now-naked Nigel toward an enormous featherbed.

"First of all, I'm not his lordship, that's my father. Second, I have a far different vision of romance than this."

Mitzie, laughing raucously, pushed Nigel onto the massive bed. "Just lie still. We will give you more romance than you could ever imagine."

Mitzie joined Delizioso, who already provocatively spread across the lavender sheets. The two women began the age-old ritual of seduction. Delizioso ran her fingers over Nigel's naked chest and down into his pubic area, exploring as if seeking a prize. Mitzie kissed and licked the young man's neck, occasionally plunging her tongue in and out of his ear. "Do you like this, your lordship?"

Nigel lay totally exposed, embarrassed and frightened. Following even more provoking advances, Mitzie blurted out: "It looks like his lordship has got some pretty lovely equipment, but it seems to be out of order."

The women pointed and laughed uproariously.

Delizioso joined in the conversation. "Maybe this is a job for James? We could have a Nancy boy here."

The two women looked at each other, shrugged, and abruptly walked to the door. Mitzie called out: "James, help his lordship. I think this is a job for you. You know, sometimes they like bananas instead of cherries."

Looking down at Nigel, she explained, "That's why we keep James around here. Some of our clients like to watch others rather than do it themselves, and still others prefer *ménage à trois*. And then there's the client who prefers the more, shall I say, masculine experience. Our James is a beauty, just look, so flexible. The world is full of all kinds, and we're here to please them all!"

James unbuttoned his trousers as he had so many times before and approached Nigel, clearly stirring something hidden within the young "spare." As he came closer, James, clearly ready to please his lordship, smiled.

"You'll like this, sir, I promise. I've never had a complaint."

Mitzie and Delizioso watched, both clearly amused. "He better not have complaints. James's mum's boyfriend will beat him blind. It wouldn't be the first time. James is a good lad.... He does as he's told, and he's bloody good at it."

"Blimey!" declared Mitzie. "It looks like his lordship's equipment works after all. Pretty impressive too, but what a waste!"

Suddenly Nigel bolted from the bed, pushing James aside, dressed quickly, raced out of the cottage, mounted his horse, and galloped back to Briarcliff.

Nigel heard that when he didn't show up at the Bull and Pig, his father went to the cottage and found the women in hysterics. Sir Sidney soon learned of the embarrassing show that his son made and stormed back to Briarcliff, enraged. He burst into Nigel's room and bellowed, "I want to talk to you, young man. Come out to the stable, immediately!"

Nigel obediently followed his father to the farthest stall in the stable. It was a place far away so no one could hear them. It was a place not unfamiliar to Nigel, for it was there that Sir Sidney had, on numerous occasions, delivered corporal punishment.

Grabbing Nigel by the scruff of the neck, he threw his son to the floor: "So, you made quite a fool of yourself tonight, didn't you? You always get it backward, don't you? You can't even write properly, letters all over the place. Is there something wrong with you? They called you a Nancy boy. Are you? If you are, do you know what shame it would bring to this house? My house! There will be no Nancy boys here at Briarcliff, do you understand?"

"Yes, Father, I understand. And I'm not that. It's just that I feel there is a lot more to romance than a cheap roll in the hay with a common tart."

"What kind of man are you anyhow? Romance? Are you serious? That is pure rubbish, something for books, not real life."

Sir Sidney felt as if his whole reputation was at stake. What would the people think? That the lord of the manor's son was a shameful degenerate? Sir Sidney reached to the wall and grabbed an enormous horsewhip.

"Listen here…you disgust me. I'm going to beat every ounce of Nancy boy out of you. You will be a man, and you will never, ever think about being anything less than that."

Sir Sidney ripped off Nigel's pajama top and began thrashing him. With each blow, he screamed, "You twit, this will teach you."

When Sir Sidney finished, he turned to leave. "I'm telling you right now, you do anything perverted to disgrace this house, and I'll have the stablemaster make you a gelding."

Sir Sidney left in revulsion, leaving Nigel lying on the floor covered in dung and whimpering like a beaten mule. His back was raw and bleeding, but the greatest pain was in his heart. Once again, he had disappointed his father.

*****

Nigel's painful recollection ended when Agatha spoke: "I'm going to leave Briarcliff, you know? Lawrence and I can't stay here. Sir Sidney blames me for Prescott's death and will ruin Lawrence and crush me with his disdain and resentment."

"You mean like he is trying to do to me?"

"Maybe, but I have no intention to subject Lawrence to anything like that. The solicitor told me that Prescott's estate was generous and will allow Lawrence and me to start a new life without dependency."

"He will never let you go. Lawrence is Prescott's son and, after me, the heir to Briarcliff."

"True, but he doesn't own us, or you either for that matter."

"Do you have a plan, Agatha?"

"While we were in St. Moritz, people talked about a new ocean liner. It goes to America. I think it will be a perfect way to get there and start a new life."

"You know, from the moment Prescott brought you to Briarcliff, I loved you too, like a sister. My brother made the right choice when you two married. And of course, I adore Lawrence. He's such a beautiful child and so much like his father. I'd give him the world if I could. Leaving Briarcliff is a wise decision. I wish you the best and will keep you forever, dear. If there is ever anything I can do to help you or the boy, please do not hesitate."

"Thank you, Nigel. You are the dearest brother. You take care of yourself. Follow your heart. God willing, you will find peace."

"Agatha, thank you for your advice. I don't know what lies ahead for me, and whether I will ever find happiness and contentment. The road is a crooked one filled with twists and turns. What happens to me remains to be seen."

CHAPTER SIX
THE SPARE

LADY PENELOPE USUALLY REMAINED IN HER BED CHAMBER until noon. Upon rising, Mavis, her maid, would help her dress from head to toe in black mourning clothing. Around twelve-thirty, she would take a tray into the sewing room, where she would eat her lunch in solitude. Sir Sidney and she grew more distant. Her relationship with Nigel also suffered for no particular reason other than she feared retaliation from Sir Sidney if she were openly kind to her son.

Sir Sidney usually rose early, dressed, and walked from his bed chamber down the massive stairs, through the great hall, and out the front door. He was on his way to see the stablemaster, like he did each day. It was an unsurprisingly chilly morning for mid-April, but sunny and bright. A few days earlier, Agatha and Lawrence had left Briarcliff after a monumental row. Despite threats and intimidation from an incensed Sir Sidney and his high-priced solicitors, he could not prevent Agatha and her son from traveling to America.

As a last-ditch effort, Sir Sidney had sent two solicitors and a burly hired thug to the Liverpool hotel where Agatha and Lawrence were staying before their departure. A last-minute confrontation in the hotel's lobby transpired.

*****

"Lady Agatha, I'm Martin Avondale, Sir Sidney's solicitor. May I have a word?"

"There is nothing to say, Mr. Avondale. Now, please step out of the way. Come, Lawrence."

"Lady Agatha, you don't seem to understand. Sir Sidney will not tolerate you taking his grandson. The boy has obligations… he is a future heir. Now you wouldn't want to deny him of such a vast fortune. Why would you want to deprive the lad of a life of great affluence? And considerable influence? Sir Sidney is prepared to be generous, very generous. You just have to leave the boy and be on your way."

"Sir, are you serious? I'd take Lawrence to abject poverty before I'd let that pompous ass get anywhere near my son. Sir Sidney is a despicable, intolerable bully. It is unimaginable that he could produce a son as admirable and loving as my late husband, Prescott. And to permit my son to spend his life rambling around that old dusty manor house, living a make-believe life with a debauched grandfather as a role model, is unthinkable. So, step aside and leave us be."

"Madame, this is a massive mistake, and Sir Sidney will not have it."

Agatha briskly moved toward the stairs, pulling Lawrence along with her. Mr. Avondale signaled the burly accomplice to make his move.

"Look here, gentlemen, if you take one more step toward us, I will have you arrested for assault. I don't think Sir Sidney would like that in the papers."

Seeing the confrontation from some twenty feet away, the hotel manager approached the party.

"Is there a problem here, madame?"

"Yes, it seems these gentlemen are harassing me. I'm Lady Agatha, and these men are threatening my son and me. "

"I see, madame. That won't do at all, would it?" The manager snapped his fingers, and a

hotel security officer and two muscular bellmen appeared. "Now gentlemen, we need not cause a ruckus, need we? My colleagues and I would be pleased to escort you to the door. And should you return, I would be obliged to notify the authorities that you have shown malicious intent toward this woman and her son. I'm sure the authorities would not look kindly at that."

The trio heeded the manager's warning and turned toward the hotel exit.

"By the way," Agatha warned the departing trio, "tell Sir Sidney that he will never see his grandson again. He has been liberated from a life in hell! Now be gone with you."

Nigel had returned to university in early February, coming home only for holidays. He was glad to be away from Briarcliff and delighted to put distance between him and his father. In April, he traveled to Liverpool to see Agatha and Lawrence off to America. When he arrived at the White Star first-class departure parlor, Lawrence raced over and gave him a huge hug.

"How's my favorite little chap doing?" Nigel asked as he picked the boy up high into the air.

"He's fine, and so is his mum."

"How was your trip to Liverpool?"

"Horrid. The train was crowded, the noise was deafening, and the seats as hard as nails. But it was worth it to come and see you and Lawrence one last time. Agatha, I—"

"I know, Nigel, this isn't easy for anyone. Thank God Lawrence is so young and unable to comprehend the enormity of the loss and the uncertainty of the future."

"Agatha, you are the bravest woman I've ever met. I know you will be fine. And someday, maybe Lawrence will learn to talk and tell me all about your wonderful adventure."

They both laughed at the prospect. "He'll probably be a chatterbox once he gets started. Nigel, I have something for you. I want you to have this. It's a portrait picture of Prescott that we had taken in St. Moritz."

Nigel waved the gift away. "No, no, I want you to keep it."

"We had two made, so this one is for you. I shall have the other one. Prescott sat for it two days before….. " Agatha chocked up. "Before the accident."

Nigel looked at Prescott's handsome face, filled with confidence and vibrant with life, looking back at him. A tear rolled down his cheek. "Oh, Agatha, I wish it had been me on that frigid mountain."

The gong rang, signaling the last call, and the announcement came: "All aboard that's going aboard."

Tearfully, Agatha, Lawrence, and Nigel embraced, fearing it could be their last for a long time or maybe even forever.

"Bon voyage!" Nigel whispered into their ears. "Godspeed."

The first-class passengers entered the special gangplank leading them to the world's most spectacular ship for its maiden voyage. The chicest of the chic, the richest of the rich, and the most elite of the elite, all dressed to the nines, walked the steep incline ready to make history.

Agatha waved at Nigel, now looking up from the pier. Both were uncertain of what was yet to come.

CHAPTER SEVEN
A Night to Remember

The first two afternoons onboard, Agatha took advantage of the private veranda that came as part of her suite, allowing her to take some fresh sea air without mingling with other passengers. Still dressing in black, everyone knew she was in mourning, and she would have to tolerate those sympathetic glances and the whispered comments: "How sad, she seems so young, and look at the poor, poor child…fatherless."

One afternoon, a small clock on the dresser struck three, and Agatha sat at the writing desk in the sumptuous cabin. When she had embarked on this journey, she had decided to keep a journal. It would be her way of talking to Prescott, giving him an account of her life. In years to come, she would read it to Lawrence, reminding him of their quest. She wrote:

> *Today is April 14, a bright and calm Sunday morning. The sea is almost like glass.*
>
> *Two days ago, we docked at Queenstown, Ireland, but I did not disembark, just not up to it. The day before, many*

passengers came aboard in Cherbourg, France. It was a gala bon voyage send-off that Lawrence and I watched from afar. I do believe the sea air is doing Lawrence a world of good.

He doesn't speak yet, so it's hard to know what he is thinking. Once in a while, he seems to say, "Da Da," but maybe I just imagine that. So, heartbreaking!

Lawrence also seems a bit off, not in a bad way; he's certainly bright enough, but an occasional mix-up with toys and such. Nothing to worry about, I'm sure.

Only a few more days and we will be in America. Our new country with a fresh start. It was thrilling to read what is happening over there. According to all reports, an atmosphere of optimism prevails everywhere. A place to begin over, without the smothering old aristocratic system where women were nothing more than pretty collectibles and obedient paramours. When I arrive in New York, I will be free from all of that baggage.

Sleeping comes with such difficulties. I asked the ship doctor to give me some powders to help me. One each night for a good night's sleep, he said. I close this journal entry with a prayer: May God see us through our journey and provide a new life for Lawrence and me, one that will be blessed. Good-bye for today, sweet Prescott. I love and miss you.

"Madame, Lawrence seems a bit tired this afternoon, shall I put him down?" Nanny gently interrupted from the doorway.

"Yes, Nanny, I'll tiptoe around the room while he naps. Meantime, why don't you take the rest of the day off? Find something to do on the ship. Lawrence and I will eat in our room and retire early."

"Very well, madame. It's Sunday, a beautiful day. I will take some air on the forward deck. Perhaps I will dine with a friend I met below. Just a few more days and we will be there.

I'm so excited, madame, the New World."

Agatha put her book down around ten P.M. and looked over at Lawrence, who was already in for the night. "Dear little fellow, how sweet he is, sleep well, my cherub, and dream of Daddy."

Agatha changed into her bedclothes, reached over to the sideboard where the steward had left an evening snack and fresh decanter of water. Next to it was a package of sleeping powders the ship doctor had dropped by her cabin the first night out.

"Let's see," she thought. "Last night and the night before, I didn't get a full night's sleep, so maybe I'll take one and a half powders tonight. That should do it." She unwrapped the first powder and stirred it into a glass of water. A knock on the door interrupted her. "Yes, who is it?"

"It's Walter, ma'am. I have a wire for you."

Agatha opened the door, took the telegram, and removed it from the distinctive yellow envelope.

It was from Nigel, wishing her a pleasant journey and sending his love to Lawrence. "How sweet of him to think of us, now so far away," she thought as she poured the second powder into the glass and drank it down.

"Oh, what a fool. What have I done?"

Agatha rang for the steward, who appeared almost instantly.

"Walter, I hate to disturb the doctor, but I accidentally took two sleeping powders. Please ask him if I am in danger."

"Not a problem, ma'am, I saw the doctor in the card room just a bit ago. Poor chap, it looks like he is a bit down on his luck, and I'm sure he would be most agreeable to be interrupted."

Within minutes, Walter returned.

"Ma'am, the doctor said not to worry. Two powders are not harmful; however, expect to sleep soundly, very soundly. In the morning, you may be a bit groggy, but it will pass before lunchtime. He said, sleep well."

*****

On the bridge

First Officer William McMaster Murdoch's responsibility was the navigation of the *Titanic*. He glanced at the time and noted: "Twenty minutes to twelve, my watch is almost finished."

Outside, perched high above the forward deck Fred Fleet, a curly haired twenty-five year-old junior seaman from Wales, peered through a crystal clear frosty night as he stood his watch.

As he scanned the horizon, his thoughts raced toward home. This was his first time away since he met his "delicious" Rosy Anne. He remembered how she had grasped him so tightly that last night before he sailed. The very thought of her aroused him, but like all young sailors, so did almost anything remotely romantic. His loose trousers accommodated his increasingly aroused state. Despite the freezing temperature, Fred felt the warm glow of desire as he recalled Rosy Anne's parting words over and over again: "Freddi, when you get back, I'm going to make you feel like a man of the world, if you get my drift. I'm ready for you, just see for yourself." Rosy Anne placed Freddi's hand between her legs, which totally excited him.

"I'll have some of that now, lass, if you please. Why wait until I get back? Don't you see, I'm as horny as a toad."

Rosy Anne, the quintessential tease, continued to torture him. "Freddi, I know you'd like to…but maybe it's not the right time."

"Bloody hell, not the right time, blimey. Just feel this, and you can readily see it's a perfect time." Fred grabbed Rosy Anne's hand, guiding it to his noticeable protrusion. He then attempted to unbuckle his pants.

"Stop that this minute, you're not being a gentleman. Ladies don't touch those things."

A cold wind brought Fred back to his perch high above the forward deck, and a broad smile raced across his face as he peered into the black abyss. He swore he was about to peak when it appeared. He blinked several times as if to clear his vision or prove what he saw was a mirage. No, it was real enough. Fred shrieked the blood-curdling warning over and over again: "Iceberg, starboard side!"

As the ship neared the floating mountain of ice, Freddie prayed, "Holy mother of God. Iceberg, iceberg! Sweet Jesus, save us!"

Within seconds, a soft but noticeable groan broke the night's silence as the iceberg sliced *Titanic* open under the water line like a tin of sardines.

"Full turn, 180 degrees port, NOW!" screamed First Officer Murdoch to the ship's pilot. The color drained from his face as the reality of the situation became apparent. He rushed outside to the deck, now covered with icy particles, and stopped just below the lookout station.

The decks glistened, and what looked like diamonds were everywhere, thousands of them sparkling in the moonlight—an eerie, almost magical sight. The cold was biting, and the sound of the rolling sea seemed to be beckoning. Murdoch turned and called back to the bridge: "Wake Captain Smith! Now! Get an assessment immediately from below. Check the engine room and the lower starboard side."

"Aye-aye, sir."

Speaking into the ship's communication horn, the helmsman relayed the orders: "All hands, begin ship inspection for iceberg damage. The starboard side first and account immediately to the bridge."

It only took a few minutes before the crew reported what would be *Titanic's* death sentence.

At 11:45 P.M., the second officer banged on the captain's stateroom door. "Sir, it's Commander Charles Lightoller. Please!"

"Enter."

Within seconds, Lightoller had briefed Captain Smith, who hastily donned his uniform and headed toward the bridge. "Damn cold out here, Lightoller, damn cold." The thermometer next to the bridge door read 28°F.

The crew came to attention as the captain arrived. "What the hell is going on, Murdoch?"

"Captain, here's the situation," Murdoch began. "Sir, with all due respect, first reports are concerning, very concerning." Sweating profusely, the officer continued: "It appears that the iceberg sideswiped the starboard side for some three hundred feet or so. Water is flooding six of the sixteen major watertight compartments, and the vessel is beginning to list starboard. It is bloody grim, sorry to say."

"I see." Smith stroked his aristocratic white beard as he pondered his next move. "Exactly when did it happen?"

"Sir, the lookout called the warning at approximately 23:40 hours. We turn hard to port, but it was too late."

"Your speed?" questioned Smith.

"We were steaming at 22 knots."

"Twenty-two knots, you say?"

"Yes, sir,"

"A bit excessive, I'd say. What were you thinking?

"Sir, the order of the day was to maximize speed."

Captain Smith knew precisely what the first officer was talking about. The officers had been given very specific instructions by Mr. Bruce Ismay, chairman and managing director at White Star: "No one would be upset if *Titanic* broke transatlantic crossing records, arriving hours or perhaps even a day early. Such a feat would be a public relations triumph."

"So, Captain, what are your orders?" asked Murdoch. Smith paused and then replied: "Summon Mr. Andrews. He's aboard and knows more about this ship than anyone alive. After all, he is the naval architect who built the bloody vessel."

"Aye-aye, sir."

When Thomas Andrews arrived at the wheelhouse, he was already in an ill-tempered mood. The thirty-nine-year-old shipbuilder was managing director of Harland and Wolff in Belfast, Ireland, where *Titanic* was built. Being handsome and accomplished at such a young age was the perfect formula for arrogance, which he pleasured in demonstrating at all times.

"I say, Captain, this better bloody be important to wake me out of a sound sleep, bloody important indeed."

After Andrews was briefed, he stood stunned. "Buggers, buggers. Where are the drawings?"

"Mr. Murdoch, fetch the blueprints for Mr. Andrews."

"At once, sir."

The three men unrolled the drawings on the chart table and studied them. Captain Smith broke the silence. "What say you, sir?"

Thomas Andrews remained quiet for a full minute, his gaze fixed on the prints. The *Titanic* was his baby. He knew every inch of her on paper, and being able to see her in action on her maiden voyage was a pinnacle in his life.

"Mr. Andrews, what say you?" pleaded the captain again.

"Based on the reports from below and my calculations, I say *Titanic* incurred a catastrophic incident."

"Andrews, please be more specific."

Fighting off tears and choking on his words, Andrews answered Captain Smith: "I can't be more specific, but I know for sure that *Titanic* has been mortally wounded. I see no path for her survival."

"Bloody hell! Are you saying what I think you are, sir?"

"I am afraid so."

"How much time do we have?"

"Hard to say, Captain. Maybe an hour or two, the most."

Captain Smith's life flashed before his eyes. He thought of his darling daughter, Helen, who just days before had celebrated her fourteenth birthday. He worried he would never have the joy that every father lives for, that of walking his only child down the aisle at her wedding. Nor would he ever see his grandchildren or celebrate his twenty-fifth wedding anniversary, just weeks away, with his beautiful wife, Eleanor. Eleanor, the love of his life. How she stood by him all these years. How proud she was of him when the White Star Line chose him to be the captain of *Titanic*, the pride of their fleet. Picked over seven other eminently qualified masters. He remembered how they celebrated at his club, where he was treated like a celebrity. For months, wherever he went, men would stand up and shake his hand, offering to buy him a drink.

His fear and panic were soon replaced by concern. Concern for his family and, for that matter, apprehension for every person and every family aboard this floating colossus. Unsinkable, they told him. How bloody wrong they were.

Snapping back to reality, Smith turned to his first officer and, in almost a murmur, mouthed the words that every captain dreads: "Abandon ship. Give the order."

The startling announcement came at 12:13 A.M.: "This is First Officer Murdoch. Ladies and gentlemen, for the sake of safety, please proceed to your lifeboat stations. I repeat, please move to your lifeboat stations. This is not a drill. Please follow the crews' instructions. Do not panic. I repeat, proceed to your lifeboat stations, with immediacy."

Most of the passengers were at first confused and then frightened. The shrill sound of the ship's horns, and the terrifying message repeated through the ship's PA system, unnerved Nanny. Her heart raced as she filled with fear. She recalled that she had never really wanted to sail on a ship, not just *Titanic*, but any ship. She couldn't even swim. When Agatha offered her a new life in New York, she made a decision that required her to put her life-long aquaphobia aside and travel to America.

Pushing past the scrambling passengers, many of them in panic, Nanny rushed to the first-class section and found Lady Agatha's cabin. "Madame! Madame! Open the door." After no response, a passing cabin boy unlocked it.

"Lawrence, get dressed, put on a warm coat," she said as she rushed in. "Now! Hurry, let me help you. Don't cry; everything is going to be all right, Nanny's here."

Nanny ran to the large bed where her mistress slept. "Madame, wake up. Please, it's an emergency." She shook Agatha to no avail. "Madame, I must get Lawrence to a lifeboat. I will return for you. Wake up, please."

Nanny finished dressing Lawrence warmly, put on his life vest and grabbed his frightened little hand. "Come with me, Lawrence, we must hurry, I will come back for your mama."

Arriving center-ship, Nanny found pure panic. People were screaming and pushing while crewmembers shouted orders to out-of-control passengers. From a distance, Nanny spotted Grace, a woman she had met in the third-class dining room. "Grace, are you all right?"

"I can't find my son, Gregory! He slipped away from me in the crowd. Can you help me find him?"

"Yes, but I must first go back and get madame. She is in a deep sleep; I think she took a sleeping powder. Here, take Lawrence. I'll be right back. I'll keep an eye out for your son too."

"He has a red cap on!" Grace shouted after her.

Grace clutched Lawrence's hand and pulled him along as Nanny disappeared. "Come on, lad, stick with me, and help me look for my Gregory." Grace hung her leather pouch around

Lawrence's neck to free up her hands, tucking it under his coat. "Here, lad, hold on to this for Grace."

One of the crewmembers seized Grace and pushed her toward the lifeboat. "You must get on NOW. Please."

"No, no, I need to find my son."

"This may be your only chance. Get into the boat."

The boat began to descend into the bitter, cold, dark sea. The crew manned the ropes as the craft started its treacherous journey into the black water filled with large chunks of ice, some almost as big as the lifeboats themselves. A crew member grabbed Lawrence from Grace and threw him into the descending lifeboat at the last second. He landed in a lady's lap with a thud.

Nanny rushed up to the Promenade deck and headed to the first-class cabin where Agatha slept. She had left the door unlocked and entered breathlessly.

"Madame, Madame, you must wake up, please!"

Agatha did not respond. Desperately, Nanny reached for the water pitcher on the bed stand and threw the water into her mistress's face.

Startled, Agatha screamed: "What are you doing?"

"Please, madame, you must wake up. It's an emergency!"

Still dazed, Agatha demanded: "Where is Lawrence?"

"He's on deck. Madame, the ship is sinking; you must come and get onto a lifeboat, NOW!" demanded Nanny.

Agatha didn't know if she was dreaming or if this was really happing. As reality set in, she shook her head in disbelief and asked again, "Where's Lawrence?"

"He's OK. He's on deck. Now please, you must come with me." Nanny put a fur coat on Agatha and pushed her towards the door. Abruptly Agatha turned back. "Wait, I must get Pookie. Lawrence can't sleep without him." She searched and found the teddy bear under the trundle bed. The pair raced towards the cabin door and suddenly *Titanic* listed another six degrees causing the steel door to warp.

Agatha and Nanny froze in fear. "Pull!" Nanny yelled. "Pull the door open." The two women, with all their strength, couldn't open the door. A few seconds later, the ship shifted another couple of degrees, and Nanny was able to pry the door open, barely enough for the two women to slip by. The passageway was now deserted, and the lights flickered like candles in the wind—from light to darkness. As they ran toward the glass door at the end of the hall, bone-chilling, ankle-deep, ice-cold water rushed over their feet. They could see passengers and crew in chaos through the glass. "Quickly, open the door," shouted Agatha. "We must get out of here and find Lawrence!"

*****

At 2:20 A.M., survivors on eighteen lifeboats witnessed the unthinkable: *Titanic* breaking in half and gently slipping into the frigid Atlantic Ocean, stern first. The survivors were almost as numb from the cold as they were from the catastrophe as they circled some two hundred yards away. Many of them prayed, and all wondered if they would be saved.

CHAPTER: EIGHT
HUDDLED MASSES

Aboard SS Carpathia

CAPTAIN ARTHUR ROSTRON, THE MASTER OF *CARPATHIA*, steamed at full speed toward the last known whereabouts of the *Titanic*. It was four A.M. when the first crew members began to rescue the 706 almost-frozen survivors. More than half of them were first-class passengers and among the wealthiest people in the world. But rank and position were for naught aboard *Carpathia*. Everyone huddled on the open decks, issued the same woolen blankets, and served whatever the ship's cook could conjure up.

Mrs. Landon Richmond walked toward one of *Carpathia's* young officers, saying, "Young man, I insist on seeing the captain."

"Sorry, madame. He's otherwise engaged. As you see, this is utter chaos. Captain Rostron is trying to sort matters out and is not to be interrupted."

"Really, young man. Apparently, you have no idea who I am."

"No, madame, and it wouldn't matter in the least. At the moment, we are in a life-and-death struggle. So, frankly, if you were the Queen of Sheba, which you are not, it would make utterly no difference. So, please take your seat and mind your manners."

"But you don't understand, I have this boy here, I have no idea who he is or where his parents may be. The boy was snatched from some domestic and handed to a crewmember. The fool threw the lad into my lap aboard the lifeboat. I saw the whole thing, and now I'm stuck with him. Can't you please sort this out for me? I'm sure his parents must be frantic, and I barely can fend for myself, much less a child I don't even know."

"I understand, madame, but all will be sorted when we get to America. I'm sure immigration will be able to resolve the matter. Now, please be seated, both you and the boy will be attended to in New York."

For three days, *Carpathia* endured rough seas, fog, and ice, as she steamed toward New York. Pier 59 was her first stop, where the *Titanic's* lifeboats were dropped off. On Thursday evening, April 18, 1912, at 9:25, the survivors arrived at their final destination, Pier 54. Despite a dark and rainy night, the pier was filled with huge crowds of reporters, immigration officials, and loved ones desperately looking for their kin.

Mrs. Landon Richmond pushed her way to the front of the gangplank, pulling the little boy who had landed in her lap. Once on land, the determined lady assailed the first immigration officer she sighted.

"Excuse me, I'm Mrs. Landon Richmond, and this boy, here, is lost. I'm not his mother, and I never saw him before. Can you help me?"

"Sorry, I'm unavailable. I suggest you go stand on that line over there, and someone in Passport Control will assist you."

Mrs. Richmond looked at the officer as if he spoke the unthinkable. "Stand on a line? You can't be serious. Do you know who I am?"

"No, and it don't matter one bit to me. The line is over there."

In a huff, Mrs. Richmond strutted over to a seemingly endless line of survivors. "What a moronic twit; he can't even speak proper English," she whispered under her breath.

The line was long, snaking around the dock. Cold rain and windy gusts coming off the water made matters worse. Mrs. Richmond noticed a young couple standing two spaces ahead of her in line. Elbowing her way forward, she approached the couple.

"Good evening, I'm Mrs. Landon Richmond, of the Park Avenue Richmond's."

The couple stared at each other. Were they supposed to know this woman wearing a most ridiculous hat, which had amazingly survived the rescue? Plumes of yellow feathers bobbed up and down as she spoke, like a strutting cockatoo.

"How do you do, madame?" the husband said. "I'm David Manning, and this is my wife, Ellen. We were on our honeymoon when this awful tragedy happened."

"Isn't that nice?" Mrs. Richmond said, then realizing how that sounded, she attempted a clarification. "Oh, not the tragedy, I meant that you were on your honeymoon was nice."

"We are on this line because my wife is British, and I'm American, so she must pass through immigration. The line for American citizens is much shorter. It's over there."

"Exactly, that's why I need your help. You see this boy here? Well, he's not mine. I mean to say, I was just sitting on the lifeboat, and some domestic handed him to a crewmember who threw him onto my lap, if you can imagine! It's just pure luck I wasn't seriously hurt. Now I'm stuck with him until I can find his parents."

"Oh my God, David, the poor chap, he's a cute little fellow, isn't he?" Ellen cooed over the boy.

David nodded. "Very cute. So, Mrs. Richmond, what is it that you want from us?"

"You see, I need to get out of here as soon as possible. I'm traumatized by all this. I need to get back to my penthouse and…well, recover from this frightful ordeal. So, would you mind taking the lad and sorting out getting him to his parents?"

Mrs. Richmond picked up the boy and handed him to Ellen. "There you go. Now, I'm off." She turned and briskly walked away, calling out: "By the way, he doesn't speak, not a word…Bye-bye."

"Next," shouted the immigration officer. "Step lively

David Manning introduced himself and his wife.

"And the kid?" asked the officer.

"Well, officer, that's a bizarre story. Let me explain."

When David was finished, the officer said: "So, some snooty lady just handed you this kid and walked off?"

"That's exactly what happened, officer. She thought the authorities might be able to find his parents. He looks to be about two years old, and he doesn't speak."

"English?"

"Probably doesn't speak a word of anything, officer. Too young, I would say, Sir."

"You are probably right. So, what now?" The officer leaned over to take a look at the boy, now comfortably sleeping in Ellen's arms.

"Cute kid, very cute. Let's see if he has anything on him that would help identify the lad.

When the officer opened the boy's jacket, he found a well-worn leather pouch not much bigger than a medium sized envelope.. "Lookee here, this might be helpful."

The officer opened the pouch to find two passports and two third-class tickets for the *Titanic along with several silver coins*

"Looks like the kid is named Gregory, Gregory Alkins from Scotland. His mother is Grace Alkins. She lists herself as a widow."

"So where is this Grace Alkins?" Ellen asked.

"Not sure. If she was a third-class passenger, likely she didn't survive. Only about 25 percent of them did. I'll check the list that the shipping line sent over, give me a minute."

The officer pulled out a manifest of survivors. "Alkins...let's see." His finger ran down the list of 706 names. "I don't see any Alkins."

Ellen covered her mouth to muffle a gasp. "Oh God, no."

"Look, I have to be honest with you. This list is preliminary, but the fact is that there were virtually no survivors other than those on *Carpathia*. It doesn't look promising that this kid's mom made it."

"What's to happen to him?" Ellen asked.

"The boy will have to be put into a home until someone claims him. The paperwork says his mother listed herself as a widow, but I've seen this a million times. The truth usually is that there is no father, or that the father is long gone, and the woman was on her own. Probably coming to America for a new start. Happens all the time. It's unlikely anyone will ever claim the kid."

"David, this is awful. You know what those homes are like. I read about them. Dreadful places, not fit for animals."

"I've heard that too, but there is no alternative."

The officer looked around to see if anyone was listening. "Look, you two seem like decent folks. If you are willing to take the boy, I will look the other way. It would cost me my hide if anyone ever found out, but surely the kid being with you would be a better alternative than an orphanage."

Ellen remained silent for a moment, then said, "David, this is the only solution. We must take the boy. It's the right thing to do."

"Are you kidding, Ellen? We just got married. We are barely off our honeymoon and certainly not prepared for anything like this. It's just too much to expect. And besides, I'm an attorney, and taking him would most likely constitute a crime. I could be in real trouble, disbarred or worse for not knowing better. This isn't like going to a pound and picking up a cocker spaniel. We can't do this. Absolutely not."

The officer, hearing David's decision, leaned toward the nearby phone. "Very well. Then that's that. I'll call my superior officer to arrange for the orphan asylum to come and pick up the kid. Just put him over there on that bench. I'll try and find him a blanket on my break."

Ellen raised her hand to the officer: "Wait. Look, David, this isn't at all what we planned. Nor is it ideal for a newly married couple to be thrust into parenthood. But consider this: God spared us a watery death just a few days ago. He gave us the chance to live our lives, and now God is asking us to save another life in return. It is his will and our fate that we take the boy."

"But Ellen—"

"No, David, there is no 'but.'" Turning to the officer, Ellen nodded. "We will take the boy, and we thank you for your compassion. You are a good man."

The officer nodded. He stamped their passports and placed an entry into the official immigration log, adding a note for the record: "Traveling with minor child Gregory Alkin."

"Here you go, missus. You made the right choice, and I know this boy will come to love you as his own parents. Good luck."

"Thank you, officer." Ellen walked away, but then turned back to ask: "Officer, what is your name?"

"My name? It's Officer Owen O'Toole."

"Owen, we shall rename this boy, Owen."

CHAPTER NINE
GONE BUT NOT FORGOTTEN

Briarcliff, April 1913

SIR SIDNEY'S PROFOUND DESPAIR WAS RELENTLESS. HE AND Penelope barely spoke. For years there had been distrust and doubt between the couple. After Prescott's death, the walls of separation, thicker than Briarcliff's ancient abutments, kept the lady and his lordship apart. The couple ate, slept, and grieved separately. It seemed almost impossible for things to get worse until the letter arrived at the breakfast table that bright morning.

"Yes, Thompson?"

"Begging your pardon, Sir Sidney, but a courier arrived from London with this letter."

"Right. Well, hand it over, man, don't be a slacker." Sir Sidney took the envelope and ripped it open. As was his custom, he read the signature first. "Martin L. Avondale, Esquire." Sir Sidney instantly focused on the letter's content, hoping against hope that the letter would have the answers he sought. He read on:

Dear Sir Sidney:

As you know, my attempt to dissuade Lady Agatha's intentions of removing your grandson, Lawrence from the country, failed. Regrettably, I am saddened to report further that Agatha and the boy traveled on the Titanic.

By now, I am sure you have read in the papers of the ship's fate. My office has tried on your behalf to ascertain Agatha and Lawrence's whereabouts. Unfortunately, the White Star Line cannot confirm their rescue or their arrival in America. According to the shipping line, both Agatha and Lawrence are presumed lost at sea.

If you would like further to engage our firm in a more comprehensive investigation, please advise in writing by return post. Quite frankly, sir, I think it would be a foolhardy endeavor.

I will consider the matter closed if I do not have your positive reply to proceed.

With respect to your late son, Prescott's affairs, he did not direct beneficiaries beyond his now-deceased wife and son. Therefore, it is anticipated that his entire estate would directly flow to his next of kin, which would be you. We will be in contact as soon as a proper death certification and mandated probate occurs.

Your loyal servant,

Martin L. Avendale, Esq.

Sir Sidney sat back in his chair, once more smothered by the devastating clutch of grief. "God, no, not the boy, not the boy too!" he muttered. "I hoped one day that we would find the lad, and he would return to Briarcliff. Then, after that reprobate Nigel goes to hell, Lawrence would become the lord of Lancaster and inherit Briarcliff." Sidney took a deep breath. "Damn it all!"

Sir Sidney immediately reached out to his solicitor, and despite Avendale's advice, instructed him to spare no expense in finding Lawrence. After months and months Sir Sidney's solicitor advised him of the futileness of continuing with the search for Lawrence, calling it counterproductive and a waste of money. In the solicitor's final letter, the closing line read: *"It is beyond doubt that Lawrence and his mother were lost at sea on April 15, 1912. Please accept our deepest condolences. May they rest in peace."*

Nigel returned from Oxford to Briarcliff for Lawrence's memorial service. His father had planned the event personally. Nigel arrived to find the manor draped with black crepe, just as it was when Prescott died. Most of the villagers and all of the tenants filled St. Albans High Episcopal Church. The assistant to the Archbishop of Canterbury traveled from London to officiate. Even the Prince of Wales representing the King attended.

Flowers graced every nook and corner of the gothic church, and the sun streamed through the ancient stained-glass windows, flooding the altar. The entire community, from lowly farmers to the high and mighty, sat shoulder to shoulder, commemorating the loss of an innocent young life.

Other than Nigel's silent prayers, there was not a word or a mention of Lady Agatha. She was persona non grata, and her death was never acknowledged. After the services, the family lined up in the narthex, where hundreds of mourners paid their respects.

Penelope dressed for mourning. Sir Sidney, gray-faced and grim, and his disappointing heir-apparent Nigel diligently shook hands and nodded to well-wishing mourners. One of the mourners approached the receiving line and shook hands with Sir Sidney and Lady Penelope. When he reached Nigel, there was a glimmer of recognition in each of the men's eyes. The mourner spoke very softly so only Nigel could hear: "May he rest in peace. He is gone but not forgotten."

Nigel clasped the mourner's hands, first one and then the other, lingering for just a moment as he looked into the other man's sad eyes and tearfully said, "Thank you, thank you."

CHAPTER TEN
BASKET OF CLOVES

ELLEN AND DAVID MANNING LIVED IN A LOVELY RESIDEN-tial area just off Sutton Place. David's hard work and drive were rewarded with a partnership at the prestigious law firm of Hancock, Hardgrave, and Martin.

Owen, now nearly six years old, was a rambunctious little tike. He kept both his mother and his new nanny, Bonnie, busy all day running after him—it was a joyful life filled with small adventures.

Even after four years, Ellen dreaded every knock on the door. She often worried that someday, someone would come and take Owen away. She knew the sympathetic immigration official was clearly out of bounds when he turned Owen over to them without official approvals and proper papers. Would his unlawful act be discovered? What would be the consequences? For sure, she thought, Owen would be taken away from them. It would be the very least punishment for their actions; perhaps it would even be considered kidnapping.

More nights than not, the terrifying memories of the *Titanic* filled Ellen's dreams. The cold, bitter night still stung her subconsciously. She dreamed of the horror and panic as the passengers and crew scrambled for the lifeboats. Her husband was one of the lucky ones to be assigned a seat early on, before it became apparent that there were not enough boats, and the order rang out: "Women and children only." David was unaware of his good fortune when the lifeboat reached the sea. Later, on the *Carpathia*, he hung his head in guilt, only to be consoled by a vicar, a fellow survivor, who described David's fate as "God's will."

Ellen remembered the hours of waiting, cold and wet, for a rescue ship. How chunks of ice, like sharks, surrounded the small boats that rowed in circles some hundred yards from the *Titanic*. She still heard the screams of those who jumped or fell into the sea as the ship sunk into the icy waters. At first, it was deafening, but in time the screams stopped altogether as the victims froze to death, their bodies floating like discarded trash. Then she evoked the most compelling image of all: she and her fellow passengers watching in shock as the mighty ship yielded to her providence. The sound of explosions breaking the eerie silence of the bitter cold. The final vision rushed into her dreams: *Titanic* slipping almost gracefully to her final resting place under the Atlantic's dark waters.

Ellen's prayers always began with her gratitude: "Dear Lord, thank you for our miraculous rescue and our precious gift, Owen, who has become our life. I beg, dear Lord, that our beloved Owen will be able to spend his life with us and never taken away."

Sometimes her survivor's guilt compelled her to include a prayer for Owen's real mother. "The poor woman," she thought. "Dying without knowing her son's fate."

Every afternoon, Ellen raced to the front door mail slot to check what had arrived. Furiously, she'd rifle through the mail, looking for the letter she most feared—something from the Department of Immigration, or maybe the shipping line who had new information. Day after day, she repeated her routine. Even after four years, she still could not let go of her fear and anxiety. David assured her that what they did was the right thing given the alternative of a heartless orphan asylum where the children were nothing more than inmates, often abused and neglected. Further he reminded her that, after all these years, she should not be concerned. People in immigration were hardly chasing down cases like this. They had far more critical things to do, and most of them were useless bureaucrats who rarely put in a full day's work.

"Ellen, darling, you don't have to worry, really. I've done some investigating, and there is no active interest in this. Trust me; I'm a lawyer; I know things like this. And besides, I've taken steps to make sure Owen is ours. I have my ways, so don't fret another second. Everything is just fine, really, just fine."

*****

The summer of 1918 was hotter than usual. New York City boiled by day and barely cooled from thundershowers in the night. But the storm that hit New York that August was not one of weather. Headlines in *The New York Times* screamed: "Death Toll Growing As Influenza Claims Many Score Victims."

David Manning lay in bed the morning of August 21. He was feeling ill but fighting it. "Ellen, I'm going to stay home today," he said. "I'm feeling a bit under the weather."

"You're not well, David. Let me call the doctor. He should check you out. With all this flu business going around, you can't be too careful."

"No, no. I'm fine. Don't be such a pessimist. You always think the worst. Just have Colleen bring up some juice and a jug of water. I feel very parched."

"You must have a fever. Let me feel your forehead." Ellen placed the palm of her hand on David. "Not too warm, maybe a little."

"See, Ellen? I told you I was fine. Now be gone with you and have Colleen bring a tray up."

David had a restless night, and by the next morning he had clearly deteriorated, giving Ellen much concern. "David, I have called Doctor Cunningham. He is overloaded at the hospital but promised he would stop by on his way home tonight. Meantime, he told me to keep you cooled down and give you lots of liquids. Also, he wants you to stay away from Owen. He was quite resolute about that."

"Don't worry, dear, I'll be fine. Ask Nanny to take Owen down to her quarters and keep him there for now."

Ellen relayed the doctor's instructions to the maid. "Of course, missus. I do hope the mister is going to be just fine. I understand that death is knocking on everyone's door. I'll put some cloves on the front stoop."

"Cloves?"

"Yes, of course. Back in County Cork, we always did that to keep the devil away. By Jesus, they say it works."

Ellen nodded in agreement. "Yes, do that, by all means. It can't hurt."

"Right then. Holy Mother of God, I'll pray for the mister."

"Thank you, Colleen. I will too."

Every thirty minutes or so, Ellen checked on David. With each check, his fever was up, and he was becoming disoriented.

Dr. Cunningham arrived at 6:45 that evening.

"Good evening, Ellen. It has been a grueling day. Hundreds and hundreds of patients everywhere. The hospital is so stacked up they had beds in the hallways, some even in the chapel. A nightmare!"

"That's awful!"

"Grim, I'd say. Now, let's have a look at your husband." After he examined David, he only said, "Hmm."

"What is it, Doctor? Will he be all right? Does he have the…?" But Ellen couldn't mouth the word.

"I'm afraid it looks as though David has influenza. His lungs are filling, and his fever hasn't broken."

"Oh my God. Should he go to the hospital? "

"I wouldn't recommend that, Ellen. First of all, hospitals are so overcrowded that he won't get any attention. And even if we admit him, there is little that they can do. The flu has to take its course. We don't have much in the way of medicine that works. I'll give him this powder, which in some cases helps with the fever. Let's keep him here; it's just safer."

"I can't believe this!"

"Keep the boy away from him, the maid and the nanny too. You will have to do the nursing. Wash everything often; don't put your hands on your face, and…" Dr. Cunningham paused.

"And what, Doctor?"

"Pray. That's about all we can do."

When Dr. Cunningham left, Ellen rushed to David's side. She felt his forehead to find he was burning up with fever. As the evening progressed, the powders the doctor had given David seemed ineffective. Every half hour, Ellen changed the damp washcloth she placed on David's forehead. She remembered that Dr. Cunningham had said to keep him cool. Colleen would leave a bucket of ice by the bedroom door every so often so that Ellen could give David sips of cold water. She pulled a chair close to David's bed and sat holding his hand. From time to time, she read to him from *The Magnificent Ambersons*, a best-seller he had just begun. The author, Booth Tarkington, a recent Pulitzer Prize winner, was David's favorite, and he was hell-bent on finishing the book before the summer ended and his busy season at the office began.

Ellen thought she must keep talking; he needed to know she was there. In between the readings, Ellen spoke of their beautiful life.

"David, our Owen has grown so, just in the past few months. I had to buy him new shoes twice since Christmas. Saks Fifth Avenue came through just in time. He loved them too. He said they make him run faster! He's so cute."

Ellen moved a bit closer to be sure David could hear her.

"Remember last August, how much fun we had at the farm we rented? Where was it again? Rockford, something like that. Oh, and those donkeys. I thought I would die laughing watching you and Owen trying to ride them." Ellen looked over and sensed that David, although non-responsive, was hearing her. She grasped his hand and held it close to her. "And on the last night at the farm, we sat out on the wraparound porch and held hands, like two kids in love. Remember? Owen slept just inside, and we made love on the glider, trying ever so hard not to wake old Mrs. Farkus, that funny old housekeeper who came with the farm."

Ellen smiled and continued, "I suspect she might have heard something because the next morning, she gave me the wickedest glare and practically threw my breakfast at me. I felt like a harlot or worse. But I didn't care; I was the happiest woman alive. You made me feel so special, showing the kind of love that comes but once. David, I loved you so much that night and still do, every second of every day."

A slight smile appeared on David's feverish face, and he whispered. "Darling Ellen, thank you for being the love of my life and the best mother to Owen. You and the boy will be fine; I've seen to it. We were spared that dark night at sea, but now my time has come. Kiss Owen for me and keep me always in your heart."

Ellen was now softly sobbing. She felt David slowly slipping away. His color was pale, and his chest heaved as he fought for each breath. His hand was burning up. Around ten that evening, David took a turn for the worst. He had not eaten, his temperature soared to 105, and his breathing was even more labored. Just past midnight, Ellen was desperate. David briefly regained consciousness but incoherently thrashed about in the bed.

Ellen sent Colleen to fetch Dr. Cunningham while she knelt and prayed at David's bedside. The doctor came and left, unable to do anything. Sometime around four in the morning, David Manning gasped, took his last breath, and passed away, becoming another Spanish flu statistic.

Owen never saw his father before he died. It was a crushing blow to a six-year-old to lose him without having the opportunity to say good-bye. The burial mass was at St. Andrew's church just a few blocks away from the Mannings' penthouse. Mourners—the few that dared to venture out because of the epidemic—streamed by the casket and offered their condolences to Ellen and Owen. Many of them remarked how ironic it was that, after surviving the rigors of *Titanic*, a microscopic germ would steal his life so prematurely. After the funeral, Ellen returned home knowing life ahead without David would be filled with unknowns and loneliness.

CHAPTER ELEVEN
Rot in Hell

Briarcliff, 1922

Sir Sidney and Lady Penelope rambled around Briarcliff as the years went by, passing like strangers with little contact. Penelope bore such bitterness over the loss of Prescott, and her guilt over Nigel overwhelmed and consumed her. Nigel graduated from university, and as demanded by his father, he returned to Briarcliff. Sir Sidney had grown tired of operating the family's luxury china business, spending less and less time at work, resulting in lagging sales and uninspired new designs. The factory's production methods became outdated and less efficient.

Sir Sidney wandered far and wide for sexual adventures of all sorts. His philandering was the only endeavor he fiercely pursued. One day, Sidney summoned Nigel to his office at the plant for a discussion.

"Boy!" barked Sidney. "You completed all the education one could possibly need, and to be honest, I'm surprised given your shortcomings that you actually graduated. So now it's time you earn your keep. I am appointing you managing director of Devonshire Enterprises. In one month's time, you will take it on. I am tired of running the bloody place. You know, you never have done much of anything, so here's your chance. Don't bugger it up."

"Are you saying I will have free rein to run the company, or are you just looking for someone to follow your never-ending orders and be the scapegoat for failure?"

"Mind your mouth, and don't take that tone with me. You're never too old for me to take you out to that stable to teach you a little respect."

"Well, Father, if you are not truly prepared to step down and relinquish the authority along with the responsibility of the job, then I'm not interested."

"Who the bloody hell do you think you are? Look, this place was supposed to be your brother's. He was born to it, and by all accounts would have done me proud. You're not worthy of shining his boots for Christ's sake. Look at you, an excuse of a man. I'd probably be better

off and turning the reins over to some dolt rather than you. Surely, you are no Prescott and never will be, and don't ever forget it. But you are all I got, and it will have to do."

When Nigel didn't respond and looked hurt, his father continued, "Take it. You can take it all. But remember, you may be the director, but I own the bloody company until the day I close my eyes for good. And I'll bet that wouldn't be soon enough for the likes of you and that mother of yours."

For the next eighteen years, Nigel ran Devonshire Enterprises. His training in chemical engineering gave him a keen edge to accomplish a company-wide rejuvenation. New products, production methods, and even his artistic design ability elevated the once sleepy firm into an industry leader.

When Devonshire Enterprises received a Royal Warrant commission to design and provide the new china for the twelfth-anniversary reign of King George, the company's popularity skyrocketed. Orders flooded in from all over the world.

All along, Sir Sidney managed to ridicule and demean Nigel's otherwise significant accomplishments. But in the end, he stayed away, as promised, content to whore his way through life. In the middle of Devonshire's rebirth, Sir Sidney passed away. It was an ugly death suited to an ugly person. Doctors would never disclose to Lady Penelope the exact nature of Sir Sidney's demise. Rampant rumors swirled about that he suffered from syphilis more than likely contracted from his nefarious and reckless behavior. The symptoms were all there: headaches, altered behavior, diminished muscle movements, and increasing dementia. Near the end, parts of his body were covered with chancres, and his swollen, almost disfigured face was a mirror into the soul of a mean, evil-spirited brute.

The last days of Sir Sidney's life were filled with physical pain and resentment. His hatred for everyone around him never subsided. The night before he closed his eyes forever, he summoned Nigel to his room.

"Boy, I want you to listen to me carefully. I have but one regret. That is not having someone who makes me proud to receive my legacy. I loathe the thought of passing my title on to someone like you, a spineless, retarded excuse for a man. You disgust me."

Nigel sat next to the dying man's bed and listened to his father spew bile for the hundredth time. Each word assaulted his very essence. The verbal attack ceased momentarily while Sir Sidney huffed for yet another breath and then continued with venomous words. "And that mother of yours, she's a bitch. She revolts me almost as much as you. Cursed, that's what I am, cursed. You and your mother not worthy of breathing the same air as our forefathers; you are two despicable excuses for human beings. You both deserve to reside in the gutter."

Nigel sat and listened, saying nothing perhaps out of respect, or maybe because down deep, he felt the beratement was justified. Self-doubt had always plagued him. Sir Sidney dismissed Nigel with one final salvo.

"Boy, my end is near, but before I leave this earth, I want you to know that your brother Prescott was the one who owned my heart. As for you, I never loved you and never could. You are retarded and a sod. You disgust me, so now go, get out of my sight."

Nigel's rage was barely containable, but he thought, "I will not give this man the satisfaction of knowing that I care what he thinks. I will, with every ounce of energy I can muster, give him the respect he rightly does not deserve. I will be a better man than he."

Nigel walked out of the room with his head held high. "Goodbye, Father. Godspeed."

The end came soon after. Sir Sidney labored in death. His body began to reject itself. His open sores oozed and emitted a foul odor, and his mind became less and less coherent. At night, they could hear him screaming in agony as the disease literally ate him alive. The doctors fed him more and more morphine until he eventually lapsed into unconsciousness. On Friday the 13th at midnight, with torrential thundershowers pelting the manor, Sir Sidney took his last painful breath, alone in his chambers. In the morning, Nigel was called to his father's chamber to view his remains. He whispered: "The gates of hell have opened to welcome you."

The funeral was quick and without much ceremony. Vicar Graham, knowing Sir Sidney's reprehensible behavior and the nature of his disease, refused to grant him a Christian burial. The family did not object. They agreed with the vicar: Sir Sidney was anything but a good Christian.

Less than twelve people gathered at the gravesite to commend Sir Sidney to eternity: a few servants, William the groundskeeper, his faithful butler, the stablemaster, and some curious passersby. The few flowers that surround the deep hole in the earth came from Sir Sidney's solicitor. It was difficult finding someone who was willing to eulogize Sidney, so no one spoke a word as a tearless Nigel and his mother watched them lower the casket into the open grave.

Later that evening, Lady Penelope and her son sat quietly in the garden. It was a cool but clear night, and the pair held hands.

"It's been an ordeal, one that has finally ended," Lady Penelope said. "I can't tell you how sorry I am for everything."

"You have nothing to be sorry for, Mother. You have always been kind to me."

"Not always. After Prescott died, I fell into the ugly rut that your father dug. At times, I know I took my anger and grief out on everyone, even you. That is why I am apologizing."

"No need, I understand. Father was, well, what he was. In the end, he got his due."

"I suppose you're right, but my heart aches for all his misdeeds and hatred."

"Mother, do you know why he detested me so? I tried so hard to be the son he wanted. I have completely put aside my personal life and needs just to satisfy him. I stood silently as he both physically and verbally abused me. I resurrected his business from near bankruptcy. Yet he never once said a word of thanks. He never even acknowledged that I was his son. To him, I was just 'boy.' It was always about Prescott, and no one else would do. No matter what, I was still a day late and a pound short."

"Nigel, darling boy, you know that Sidney was a hater, and his hatred was like cancer. It grew and grew over the years. After Prescott, his hatred metastasized throughout his entire being. He hated everyone and everything."

"But why would he not treat me like his son? I did all that he asked for all these years."

Nigel's mother, squeezing his hand even tighter, answered her tormented son's question while choking back tears: "He never treated you like his son…because…because you are not."

Nigel gulped. "Not his son? What do you bloody mean? Of course, I'm his son. I may not be the son he wanted, like Prescott, but I am his flesh and blood, regardless of who or what I am."

"No, Nigel. You are not his flesh and blood. You see, many years ago, I learned that your father was chronically unfaithful, and in the end, it was the cause of his demise. He had this illusion that just because he was the lord of the manor, rules did not apply to him. Especially when it came to fidelity."

Nigel sat stunned and motionless.

"I was young and foolish and desperately hurt by your father's debauchery," she continued. "He slept with everyone but with me. So, in an act of defiance, I had a casual affair."

"With whom?" demanded Nigel.

"It's unimportant. He's long dead and never was in our lives after that brief encounter. When your father figured out that you were not his, he went mad." Penelope's eyes streamed tears. "From that day forward, he never had anything to do with me. He loathed my very existence, and by extension yours too."

"Why are you telling me this now? Why now?"

"I'm telling you this now because I was afraid to tell you while he was living. He didn't hate you because you mixed up letters now and then, or because you weren't the he-man Prescott was. "No, he hated you because you were the living proof of my infidelity and his hypocrisy."

"So, for all these years, I thought he loathed me because of something I did or something I wasn't, while all along those things had nothing to do with it. I blamed myself for not measuring up to the kind of son he wanted, but the reality is that I could never really be his son, no matter what."

"That's right, dear boy. And it broke my heart to watch his cruelty toward you. He scarred you forever, not just physically with that horsewhip, but emotionally. For that, I am eternally sorry. So many times, I wanted to kill the sod. But I am a Christian and knew God would never grant me eternal peace."

Nigel did not speak his thoughts. But if he could, he would have said, "I would have killed him too, but feared it would break your heart, not because of his death but because of the consequences. I would have to face the law for committing such an act. They would put me at the end of a rope. I would not allow you to lose another son."

Lady Penelope patted Nigel's back and drew him close. "You are a good son; never forget it."

Around midnight, Nigel walked to the churchyard and stood alongside Sir Sidney's fresh grave. Villagers and tenants dutifully placed wildflowers on the raw earth. His emotions ranged from rage to pity, but in the end, hatred won out. Nigel shouted at the top of his lungs into the night: "You miserable bastard. You are a disgrace to all of us. You wrecked my life for all these years and tortured my mother. You weren't man enough to face the truth. When Prescott died, you died too. You never loved anyone since and took out your anger and frustrations on all that you knew. When you whipped me, I refused to cry because I did not want to disappoint you by not being manly enough. When you pub-licly ridiculed me, I turned the other cheek because you were my father, and I felt I had to respect you. What a sham!"

The tears finally came—not for Sir Sidney, but for himself and his mother. The notion that he had allowed this man, who was not even his father, to dominate and humiliate him for his entire life was devastating. They were also tears of joy. A tremendous burden lifted from his shoulders. He felt ten years younger, and for the first time since Prescott's death, optimistic. At last, he was free from the tyrannical rule of a sick and depraved fool. He knew from this day forward that he need not live under a shadow. Nigel smiled at the prospects that lay ahead and could barely wait to live life his way, being himself and doing what pleased him.

After a few more moments, Nigel decided to leave but abruptly turned back. "Your reckless whoring got you just what you deserved, a miserable and painful death."

Then Nigel walked up to the fresh dirt and spit on Sir Sidney's grave. "You bastard, I hope you rot in hell."

CHAPTER TWELVE
WINNEY THE WHO

Cambridge, Massachusetts

MATRICULATING IN THE DOCTORAL PROGRAM AT MIT AND working eight hours a day in the lab were serious business. Advanced courses in physics, chemistry, and calculus were not for the faint of heart. Long hours and pressure were served up daily, along with the inedible food in the commons.

Owen worked like a trooper and was almost daily recognized for his incredible abilities. He was heralded as a prodigy by his professors, especially for his advanced work on Albert Einstein's Law of the Photoelectric Effect, a pivotal step in quantum theory physics that defined the physical properties of nature at the scale of atoms and subatomic particles.

Attending school alongside Owen was a dashing Brit named Winthrop Barrington, affectionately known as "Winney the Who." He helped put a light side on the rigorous curriculum. Winney was a native of Great Britain and considered a foreign student, one of many. But what separated him from all others, foreign and otherwise, was Winney's unconventional, raucous behavior. He was brilliant like Owen, but unlike Owen he burned the candle at both ends, mainly when it came to partying and women. He was a flamboyant sort who looked like a celebrity footballer despite never spending a second in the pursuit of sports. His thick, dirty-blond hair hung over his right eye, and he brushed it back constantly. That, along with his tall, fit frame, was a proven magnet for women of all sizes, shapes, and ages. When Winney spoke with his upper-class English accent, people turned to listen. And if that wasn't enough, his family was fabulously wealthy and thought the sun rose and the moon set just for him.

Winney, with all his glitz and glamour, was a show horse. Despite having it all, he was a fearful and reticent child, a "mama's boy," and never changed as a young adult. His outward bravado was quite different from the real him, and he often thought that God played a trick by blessing him with everything that anyone would ever want, except the one thing that matters most, at least to him…self-esteem.

Winney often thought back to his childhood and the years that followed. The day before he left for MIT, his father called him into his study.

"So, son, off you are. Your mother and I will miss you terribly."

Winney sat in front of his father's impressive Chippendale desk and gazed out the palladium window. Acres of green lawn rolled out, reaching the broad river that dissected Dumford Hall, the ancestral family estate. It was the only home that not only he but his father and his father before him knew. When he left for public school, where England's ruling class sent their sons, it was a hard transition, especially being separated from his devoted mother and the slew of servants who catered to his every whim. Later, it was off to Oxford where he lived in a lovely flat belonging to his parents, who frequently visited. His father's words broke his drift.

"You know young man you have been given a very rare opportunity. To travel abroad and to be able to study at one of the world's most prestigious universities. This is why your mother and I are so happy for you."

"Thanks, Father."

"But as your father, I must give you some sobering advice."

Winney rose to leave. "Thanks, but I really don't need advice. I'm fine...."

"Sit down, Winthrop, I'm not done."

"Very well."

"You see, you have led a charmed life, and your life has always been pretty much perfect. But the world is changing, and things will not be as they are. You need to take stock and begin to realize that every day is important, and not to be frittered away in ways that are well known to you. You have been given many gifts, and now it is time to use them."

Winney squirmed in his seat as his father concluded. "MIT is a lifetime opportunity. Make a go of it, son."

Despite being almost polar opposites, Winney and Owen struck up a fast friendship and decided to room together their final year at MIT. Winney was left in charge of not only choosing the flat but organizing the move. To him, money was no object, so while Owen was away on a field trip to Princeton, Winney called in Boston's best department store decorators for, as he put it, "a thorough fitting out." His first encounter with Brown Brother's lead decorator Dana French turned into a lot more than picking out fabrics. Trading on his good looks, British charm, and aristocratic accent, Winney made short time of it with Miss French. It was on a Saturday afternoon when the intercom phone rang.

"Cheerio, who's there?"

"It's the doorman, Tom. I have a Miss French, from Brown Brothers Department Store here to see you. May I send her up?"

"Blimey, I almost forgot. Tom, give me a minute and then send her up. I have to find my trousers. I haven't seen them since last night."

Winney opened the door after the third ring of the bell. "Come in, come in. I'm Winney Barrington."

Dana walked in and gaped at the half-naked Winney. "Would you mind? Please put on a shirt and some shoes. Do you always receive guests like this?"

"Not really, it usually takes a couple of whiskeys and sodas before we both get like this."

"Really, Mr. Barrington, I think I better leave."

"Wait, please." Winney looked at the large leather bag Dana was carrying. "Whatcha got there?"

"There are samples and some pictures of furniture I gathered for you to look at."

Winney grabbed the bag and started to dump it on the floor of the vacant apartment. "Let's have a look-see, sweetie."

"Please, I spent a lot of time pulling this together, so don't get them all mixed up."

"Right, then. Why don't I pour us a couple of drinks, and you can show me what you got...samples, that is."

"Wow, you are really boorish. I thought I was going to meet a professional. They told me a gentleman from MIT, not a tenth-floor Casanova."

It only took two drinks and a lot of sweet-talking before Miss Dana and the tenth-floor Casanova were in the sack, which was the only stick of furniture in the place.

Winney decided that hiring interior decorators was a great way to meet pretty women. So, after Miss French came Miss LaRoach, Miss Hillard, Miss Marchetti, and lastly, Brown Brothers sent a fellow named Bruce, who didn't make it past the door.

Owen called Winney to check in on the status of the apartment late one Tuesday night.

"Winney, how are you doing?"

"Good, same old stuff here."

"How's the apartment going?"

"It's going, mate. So far, I had four or five designers in to help out, but for some reason, we never got passed the bedroom."

"You mean picking out the bedroom furniture?"

"No, you sod, I mean the bedroom."

Owen got the feeling that he was going to return to Boston to an empty apartment. "So, are we ever going to get settled in?"

"Yea, mate. I'm working on it. Meantime, don't worry, Uncle Winney is in charge, and he won't let you down."

Mrs. Northrup, the fifth decorator, was the charm, and as luck would have it, one of her old clients was in the process of getting divorced and moving back to New York, shedding all her almost brand-new furniture along with her husband. Dealing with Mrs. Northrup was uncomplicated since Mrs. Northrup was pushing sixty, and as Winney would say she was a daft cow, and he wouldn't do her with yours.

The furniture arrived on the same day that Owen returned from New York.

"Where do you want this table?" asked the burly mover.

Mrs. Northup, who was on hand to supervise, pointed to the large dining area. "Over there, if you please."

Owen walked through the apartment, checking things out. "Hey, Winney, where the hell did you get this stuff? It's a little bit frou-frou for a couple of guys."

"Foofoo? What's that supposed to mean?"

"I don't know, but I was expecting a little more leather and a lot less chintz."

"Don't worry, you'll learn to love it. And besides, the decorator told me that it's the kind of stuff our lady friends will love. It will make them feel less threatened than some stuffy men's dormitory room filled with stained furniture. It will be like getting to first base without even trying."

The movers and Mrs. Northrup left, and Owen and Winney walked around the apartment, checking it out. When they arrived in the second bedroom, the one for Winney, they both busted out laughing.

"Hey, Winney, are you serious, they gave you your grandmother's bed? It's a canopy one."

"Bloody hell, the only canopy I need is under the bed in case I get caught short."

The two of them ended up in the spacious living room overlooking the Charles River. They sat on the somewhat delicate love seats facing each other. Their large frames barely could get comfortable.

"So, how was Princeton?"

"Great, I actually met Albert Einstein, and he loved my work. He invited me to dinner at his home, a simple cottage on a quiet street near the campus. We talked for hours. We met his stepdaughter, Margot."

"Stepdaughter? Tell me, mate, is she a looker? Maybe I need to visit Princeton?"

"Cut it out, Winney. She's married and is a bit older than you."

"No woman is too old for me. Is she a pretty bird or cow?"

"Please! She's very nice, and smart too. They're not US citizens but are hoping to become one. You know he left Europe because of that Hitler fellow and his brownshirts. Had no choice, really, if what they're saying is to be believed. God forbid they drag the world into another war." Owen opened his satchel and took out a handful of papers, placing them on the coffee table. "But Dr. Einstein is truly a genius. Look, Winney, he actually made some notations on my papers. He said I was onto something significant, maybe even breakthrough science, and he would like me to keep him in the loop. Wait until the guys at the lab see this."

"See, I told you. You are a genius; even a genius thinks so. I'm jealous."

"Don't be. And besides, he didn't say I was a genius. He just liked my work."

"Don't be daft. When the most important physicist in the world says your work is breakthrough science, he thinks you are a genius. So, you are a genius, just like I always knew."

Owen carefully arranged his papers on the table. "After Princeton, I dropped by my mother's. I hadn't seen her in a while."

"Yeah. When I get back to the UK, I must go see my mum as well. Dutiful son and all that. My father, meanwhile, is pulling strings to get me a deferment. I'm not the fighting kind."

"Well, apparently, Uncle Sam doesn't think I am either. I flunked the physical. I'm 4F. They said I had syndactyly."

"Crap, that sounds serious. Does that have anything to do with your willy? Is it catchy?"

"No, you twit, it is the medical term for webbed toes."

"Toes? Let me see them."

"No way. I've always been self-conscious of them, and I just as much prefer to keep them to myself."

Winney would not take no for an answer and jumped on Owen, throwing him to the floor, sat on top of him, and forcibly removed his shoes and socks.

"Bloody hell, look at that, you have duck feet!"

From that day on, Winney nicknamed Owen "Duck."

CHAPTER THIRTEEN
I Got a Hunch...

December 1938, Cambridge, Massachusetts

THE ORCHESTRA BEGAN PLAYING "POMP AND CIRCUMSTANCE" as the PhD candidates gathered at the back of the MIT's Barbour Field House, a yellow brick structure that could hold thousands. It was a bit unusual to have a December graduation, but as with many advanced degree programs, they did not generally follow the traditional academic year. Family photos on the campus's lawn, now covered with a thick blanket of snow were moved to pleasant areas set up in one of the ante rooms. The weather, although quite cold, cooperated by providing a bright blue, sunny sky. Owen Manning sat on the dais next to the keynote speaker, Henry Louis Stimson, a Washington dignitary. Stimson was a well turned out bureaucrat with a worried look on his face as he walked to the podium to address the Class of 1938.

Just hours before arriving on campus Stimson had plowed through a pile of official US government reports, many of them top secret.

There was a September assessment report that analyzed the implications of British Prime Minister Chamberlain's appeasement of Germany's, Adolf Hitler. This capitulation was worrisome. Britain was the beacon of democracy in Europe. Would Chamberlin's actions give the wrong signals to the Third Reich? An August surveillance report spoke of the German's military mobilization, and in early November, the stunning coordinated attack on Jews all over Germany, Austria, and other Nazi-controlled areas. Shops owned by Jews were broken into, windows smashed and looted. The press dubbed it Kristallnacht – the night of broken windows. Synagogues were prime targets, burned and desecrated.

Soon after, tens of thousands of Jewish men were arrested and sent to concentration camps, many of them beaten and maimed.

*****

Stimson returned to his seat after delivering an address filled with optimism and hope, despite what he knew and the ominous war clouds over Europe and probably heading toward the United States. He concluded his remarks with a solemn thought: "So, as you go out into the world, remember your obligations, your values, and your duty. Make your life a journey well-traveled—waste not your collective God-given genius that we recognize and celebrate here today. Use it wisely by seizing every opportunity with gusto and conquering every mountain and then looking for the next. And lastly, I say with much regret, war is more of a probability than a possibility. The world is at a dangerous juncture. It will take all we have to survive. Good luck, Godspeed, and congratulations on a job well done."

When he was done, MIT President Karl Compton adjusted the microphone and continued the commencement program: "Hmm, thank you, Mr. Stimson. Honored guests, distinguished trustees, faculty, parents, family, and friends, ladies, and gentlemen, it is my great honor to introduce our 1938 valedictorian and soon-to-be Doctor of Philosophy. Today, this young man is graduating summa cum laude and receiving the highest honors in mathematics, physics, and engineering, a first for any MIT PhD student. This remarkable student maintained a perfect score of 4.0 for six consecutive years in every core subject. And even more impressive is our valedictorian has overcome the disability of dyslexia.

"Our recipient served as adjunct assistant to our own Dr. Bush, director of MIT's Office of Scientific Research and Development, and partner with the United States Defense Department. He served as an assistant professor at MIT's Radiation Laboratory, which accelerated the development of radar technology in conjunction with the United Kingdom."

Ellen Manning, along with her faithful housekeeper, Colleen, was sitting in the front row, and they couldn't be prouder. She thought: "If only David could have been here to see this, he'd be so pleased."

Compton continued, "Now, it is my great privilege to introduce MIT's 1938 valedictorian, Owen David Manning."

The audience rose and loudly applauded as Owen took the podium. Looking out at the crowd, he winked at his beaming mother. Owen began his speech, which he intentionally kept short and sweet. But he had a powerful conclusion: "And today we are on the brink—the brink of many things. Our technology is in its infancy, on the verge of incredible breakthroughs. Still, we have much to learn and much to share. We just heard from our distinguished keynote speaker, Mr. Stimson, that war is more a probability than a possibility, and that we are on the threshold of having to choose between war and peace, a decision that will not come lightly and one that our leaders will make for us. We can all hope for peace, even as we are forced to prepare for the worst. So, I urge my fellow scientists, go forward carefully and judiciously into the unknown with the knowledge that what we have learned and how we use it may very well impact mankind."

Following the commencement, there was a small reception at the president's residence for all the honored recipients. President Compton pulled Owen over to a corner of the room for a special introduction.

"Mr. Stimson, I'd like to introduce you to Owen Manning, our valedictorian."

"Dr. Manning, I am delighted to meet you," Mr. Stimson said. "I must say your valedictorian remarks eclipsed mine. But should I expect less from a genius? I read your credentials, and I must say I'm impressed. Summa cum laude and all three of the highest awards, simply astounding."

"Thank you, sir. I appreciate the compliment. I am most humbled."

"I'm the one who should be humbled! I'm just a government employee, hardly a genius."

Owen blushed. It was true that his IQ tested at 162, in Einstein's range, but for him, it was just one of those things. Hard work came naturally to him, as did exceptional good looks.

"You are so kind, but I think you are overrating me," Owen demurred.

"Handsome, smart, and modest too…you are quite the package."

Another blush. "Thank you, Mr. Stimson."

"Young man, you are impressive, as I said. What are your plans?"

"I've been offered a research position here at MIT. Nuclear physics, but I'm thinking maybe of going into medicine. It's far more humanitarian."

"Oh, good choices. But have you considered serving our country first? These are troubled times, and the government needs people like you."

"Of course, sir, I have thought about it. I'm afraid I couldn't pass the physical. I have syndactyly, which makes me 4F."

"You have syndactyly? What the hell is that?"

"To put it simply, it's a foot problem."

"Well, Manning, I don't think the military would be too interested in your feet. It's the brain they'd be after We have some extraordinary programs underway that would be of great interest to someone like you. You could be invaluable."

"Really, sir. Here at MIT, I know of several defense-oriented programs and research efforts. I'm peripherally involved in one of them. But thank you, sir. I appreciate your offer. For now, I'm all set." Owen was being careful in his remarks—Stimson was a high-ranking official, after all—but privately Owen had no desire to have his work turned to creating weapons.

"The world is a mess, Owen, and getting messier," Stimson said, as if he could guess at Owen's thoughts. "If you really want to do something for your country, there'd be a place for you. And for Christ's sake, don't worry about those feet. You'll be sitting on your ass most of the time. We don't let our geniuses get in harm's way."

The two men laughed at Stimson's joke.

"Well, Mr. Stimson, thank you. But I have a commitment here at MIT. I am bound for the next six months."

"Six months is a long time. But I appreciate your loyalty. It's what all good men have. So, is there a lucky girl in your life?"

"No time for that, sir. But maybe someday."

"With those good looks and a PhD to boot, don't waste your life in a dingy laboratory. There are lots of young ladies who would die to be on your arm or anywhere else."

"Ha, ha. So far, I haven't seen a long queue."

"So, Owen, I wish you the best, but I already know you will be a star no matter what you choose to do. You'll make MIT proud."

"Thank you, Mr. Stimson. I'll do my level best."

Stimson paused, reached into his pocket, and presented Owen with his business card: "Look, young man, here's my card. I got a hunch about you. I think our paths may cross again. Maybe not, but if ever I can do anything for you, give me a call."

Owen took the card and looked at it:

Henry Louis Stimson
Secretary of War
The United States Department of War

Stimson reached out and shook hands with Owen. "Like I said, I'll be seeing you; I just got a feeling about it. And don't be shy, call me anytime. And don't forget, your country needs you."

CHAPTER FOURTEEN
PASS THE MEATBALLS

WORKING AT MIT WAS TAXING AND OVERWHELMING BUT challenging and exciting. Owen eventually settled on a path of study in advanced thermonuclear physics. His department had received a War Department grant for more than $1.9 million, and the lab was humming. To Owen, who was still hesitant to become part of the war machine, it seemed like his lab might be doing work that could actually deter war, which looked inevitable at this point as the Germans and their allies, the Japanese, made their plans for world domination clearer by the day. Despite his strong feelings that war should be avoided at all costs, Owen was also a realist. If war was coming, at least his work might help end it. He often felt morally conflicted not knowing which was worse.

One evening, in a rare break from his grueling routine, Owen ventured into one of his old haunts, Simeoni's, where the food was spicy, portions heaping, and the price was right. Simeoni's was located on Cambridge Avenue, just past Harvard Square. The basement steps were hard to navigate, but the scent of fresh garlic bread and onions from home-cooked Italian food beckoned all who ventured past.

Simeoni's was way too basic for the nearby Harvard crowd. You'd be more likely to see a mechanic and his kids than "swells" in blazers with a yacht club emblem. Equally unlikely was seeing any fancy foreign sports cars parked out front. More likely, the diners arrived on foot.

The eatery attracted those more interested in food than form. A dozen or so rickety tables, with matchbooks under their legs and covered with colorful checkerboard cloths, filled the intimate dining room. Empty Chianti bottles with melted wax running down their sides sat in the middle of the tables along with shakers of red pepper flakes, Parmesan cheese, salt, and pepper. Posters of Italy lined the walls under bright fluorescent ceiling fixtures. Owen had once brought his mother here when she visited Boston. He and his mother were more than close. He had been the man in her life ever since his father died so many years ago. He loved her and her spunky personality peppered with wit and charm. Her comment about Simeoni's was clearly her at her best: "How quaint. They did it in early Depression." Despite the decor, Simeoni's was immaculate and the food memorable.

Owen stepped into the restaurant and was immediately recognized by Angelo, the owner.

"Hey, *Doctorie Owen. Quanto tempo! Sedersi, sedersi, mangiare!*" [Long time, no see! Sit, sit, eat!]

Owen attempted a reply in his pitifully meager command Italian, "Grazie, Angelo. It's great to see you."

"That's a nicea. You been good, yeah?"

"Yes, very well, Angelo, and you?"

From the corner of his eye, Owen saw Mama Lucia heading toward his table. He hunkered down into his chair in preparation for an Italian culture attack that climaxed in a juicy kiss on both cheeks, followed by a good pinch of each cheek.

"*Madre di Dio,* it'sa Doctorie Owen! Where you been *mio bella, bambino?*"

"Around."

"Around! Did you hear that, Angelo? Around. Around what?"

"You know, working, teaching, studying, just around." Cringing, Owen knew what was coming next.

"Look here, Mr. Owen, big shot PhD. You no need work so much, you need a woman to cook for you in a *bella casa.* You're too beautiful of man to be alone."

Owen began to regret not opting for Chinese and changed the conversation from him to her. "Mama, you look nice too. It looks like you lost some weight."

Running the palms of her hands along her sides from her watermelon-sized breasts down to her more-than-ample waist and hips, she blushed. "Momma mia! You think so, huh? *Forse un po!* [Maybe a little]. What you say, Angelo? You think?"

Wisely, Angelo looked Mama up and down while winking to Owen and delivered the right answer: " *Si, Si.* For sure it shows."

"Thanks God, ahh. Now, it's time to eat, Angelo. Pasta Lucia with meatballs for the handsome doctorie. Rapido! And don't forget the Parmigiano, a fresh one."

Owen looked around and spotted a young woman sitting across the restaurant with a white coat draped across her chair, the earpieces of a stethoscope protruding from the pocket. He was intrigued—and could see that she was trying to hide her amusement. Mama Lucia, catching wind of Owen's glance, followed his gaze and shrieked: "*Madre di Dio!*"

From her tone and the volume of her voice, Owen became alarmed. "What is it, Mama?"

"A gift from God! Look, Owen, she's a nice-looking girl all by herself. Go over, say hello. Make nice."

Owen looked over, this time more carefully. She was pretty, very pretty. "Stop. I don't know who that is. She's probably married or something, so drop it, Mama."

"She no married, I can tell."

"How?"

"How? Because I can tell. Mama knows things like this. Look at her, she doesn't look like she has a care in the world. For sure she's not married."

Before Owen could say another thing, Mama pranced over to the young woman. "*Ciao, bella mia.* Where's your husband?"

Swallowing a mouthful of meatball, the young woman blushed. "Well, to be honest, I'm not married."

"Ahhh, Mama knows these things. So, you gotta boyfriend, maybe?"

Beginning to get annoyed, the young woman reluctantly answered, "No, but why is it any of your business?"

"Molto Bene, Because, I'd got doctorie over there who needs to know a beautiful woman like you. But he's too stupido to know." Pointing to Owen, she said, "See him? He's gorgeous, no?"

Deciding to cut her meal short and get out of there: "I've really got to get going, ma'am. The Pasta Lucia and meatballs are the best, and you are the best too, but I must run."

"Aspetta, aspetta!" [Wait, wait!] Waving to Owen Mama, less than subtlety, yelled, "Doctorie Owen, you come over here. This *bellissima* wants to meet you."

"No, no, Mama. I'm just leaving. Really, I must go."

"Aspetta! Owen. Owen, you come over here."

Owen knew there was no escape. Mortified beyond words, he sunk his six-foot-five frame deep into the creaking wooden chair that Mama had pulled up to the girl's table.

"God!" Owen couldn't believe what she's doing. "I'm NEVER coming back here again."

"Come on, Owen, now you do what Mama say."

Almost immediately, Mama had Owen and the girl on a first-name basis. "I'm Owen Manning, and I'm pretty embarrassed right now."

"Me too, probably more. I'm Lonnie Quackenbush."

Mama hovered over the table, clearly delighted with her matchmaking efforts. "See, I told you, you'd like her. You a nurse, right?"

"No, ma'am. I'm a doctor, an intern to be exact.

"Mama mia, another doctorie! Now you two sit, eat, and when you finish, the cannolis are on me."

Innately shy, Owen attempted to make the best of an awkward situation. "Don't mind her," he said. "She's obsessed with matchmaking. I'm sorry for the intrusion. I'll leave as soon as she goes into the kitchen. I'm so sorry to ruin your dinner."

Lonnie, not missing Owen's boyish good looks, tried to soothe the apparent uneasiness.

"It's okay. ..." She smiled. "So, she says you are a doctor. What kind?"

"Oh, I'm not really a doctor, I mean a doctor like you, you know a real one."

"So, you are a…?"

"I'm a PhD. But to Mama Lucia, a doctor is a doctor, and if she had her way, I'd be making house calls. … And you? You said intern. Tell me more."

"I'm hoping to specialize in pediatric medicine, but it's hard in these medical schools. The medical establishment think women should empty bed pans rather than practice medicine."

"Yes, I see that at MIT too. Women scientists are often not taken as seriously as men. I personally find that ridiculous. Anatomically speaking, a women's brain is equally as capable as a man's, anything other than that is nothing more than a myth purported by men who feel threatened. "

Lonnie looked at him warmly. She liked this man. He was someone who understood. "Are you Italian? Related to Mama Lucia?"

"I should be so lucky. If that were true, I'd probably weigh a hundred pounds more. No, no, I'm not a relative, and I'm not Italian either. No, I'm just a regular here because I like their food."

"I suspected you weren't Italian. There aren't too many of them who are six-foot-four with auburn hair. Where are you from?"

"I'm from New York, and I'm part British and American and I'm not six-feet-four. I'm six-feet-five."

"Pardon me! I should have brought my tape measure."

The couple laughed.

"How about you?" Owen asked. "Quackenbush isn't exactly a common name, and certainly not one you'd find in Italy."

"Dutch. My family's still there. I'm a second-year intern at Mass General on a fellowship from The Hague. My late father always wanted me to become a doctor, so here I am. But I love medicine. Helping people is something that I find so rewarding."

Lonnie caught Owen eyeing the half-eaten platter of Pasta Lucia and meatballs on the table. "You hungry?"

"Actually, I didn't have lunch today, and I'm famished. Would you mind until my dinner comes?"

"No," she laughed. "Please. Help yourself."

"Great, pass the meatballs, and perhaps some of the pasta too." He ate the rest of her dinner—and then his own when it was delivered piping hot to the table.

Lonnie smiled as this six-foot-five man with the little-boy face smacked his lips as he devoured the last bite of the meatballs, leaving a smidgen of sauce on his chin. She leaned over and gently dabbed it clean. She thought, *You know, he's pretty adorable.*

Mama, wiping her hands on her apron rushed over to the table, with two freshly filled cannoli's. "See, I told you'd like her. Now eat."

Leaning into Owen's ear, Mama half-whispered her last instruction before returning to the kitchen: "Don't forget get her phone number, she's a bella, you too. You make beautiful bambini!" Ready to leave, she turned on her heels reached over and gave Owen one last pinch on the cheek. "Bella bella."

"Seriously!" Owen exhaled in humiliation.

Suddenly, Angelo appeared at the table. "Mama says no charge for Pasta Lucia and meatballs or the cannoli." Angelo blushed, uncomfortable being Mama's messenger. "On one condition. You give him your phone number. And Mama says, makea sure it's the real one!"

*****

The following Tuesday, the phone rang at 312 Boylston Street, Apartment A.

"Hello, this is Dr. Quackenbush. How can I help you?"

"Hi, it's Owen Manning, we met at Simeoni's last week."

Lonnie took a deep, pleased breath. When he hadn't called within the first few days, she thought she would never hear from him. "Owen, how nice to hear from you. Sorry about Mama Lucia. She's a character."

"Yes, a character is an understatement; I'm still red with embarrassment. That's why it took so long for me to call you. I didn't want to put you on the spot again. But I thought it over and gave it a shot. Are you okay with that?"

"I'm okay with that. In fact, I'm delighted that you called. How are you?"

"I'm pretty busy at the lab and a little strung out. But I'm not calling to gripe. I do enough of that with my roommate."

"Oh, that, that's not serious griping. That's just, well, life."

"Right. But I do have a reason for calling. I was wondering if you like to bike?"

"Well, I haven't for a while; there is never enough spare time. But I used to in The Hague. There, it's a major source of transportation."

"So, are you up to it?"

"Sure, when?"

"How about Sunday? Say around ten?"

"I have to cover at the hospital in the morning, but I'll finish by noon or so."

"That works. We'll do lunch first, and then we can work it off. You know Ralph's in Harvard Square?"

"Yeah, great sandwiches!"

"Perfect, meet you there, noonish, on Sunday. Do you have a bike?"

"No, but my next-door neighbor has; I'll borrow it."

On Sunday, Owen arrived a bit early and found a table by the window that looked out at the busy square. The Coop, Harvard's busy bookstore, was directly next door. Boston was such a great town, so young and filled with enthusiasm and promise. Even the mounting fear of war didn't seem to dampen the spirit of these young students.

"Hello there, how are you?" he heard her voice say.

"Great, Lonnie, thanks for coming."

"Thanks for the invite. I had to dust off the old bike that I borrowed from my neighbor. It's as rusty as I am."

"Well, it's not a marathon, just a ride. You'll do great. Have you tried the triple-decker roast beef here?"

"No. But could we share it?"

"Fries, too?"

"Well-done?"

"Perfect, just the way I like them, extra crispy and extra hot."

The afternoon got cut short when the skies opened up, and rain poured down on the bikers. Owen and Lonnie scurried back to her apartment to dry off.

"Nice place, Lonnie. Do you live here alone?"

"Yea, it's all mine. My mom wanted me to live alone, fewer distractions and more privacy. I often work twelve-hour shifts, and when I get home, I need peace and quiet."

"Pretty nice of her. I love these old townhouses. They're classics. Love how you did it too. Almost like a grownup's place."

Lonnie fumbled in the kitchen with an old percolator. "I never know how much coffee to put in, so most of the time it comes out either too strong or like weak tea."

"Let me help. I'm in charge of coffee at the lab."

"Well, I'm glad you learned something practical at MIT, most of the guys I've met there can't get out of the way of their own slide ruler. No offense, Owen. And besides, I'm not much better in the coffee department."

The couple laughed.

"Coffee is served." Lonnie poured two mugs filled with steaming black java. "I'm sorry, I don't have cream, but there's sugar."

"Black's great."

*****

Months Later

Moving in together wasn't Owen's idea. He longed to be near Lonnie, and he spent most waking hours with her if he wasn't at work. So, when Lonnie invited Owen to move in, he at first hesitated. Unmarried and living together was not looked upon with favor, especially in 1939 Boston. It just wasn't done. He loved Lonnie so much and never would do anything to hurt her or her reputation. What would people say? For sure tongues would wag. What would his mother think?

Lonnie explained that in Europe unwed couples living together was common especially among the educated. Often they had children together and never married. "It's what we think that matters, no one else's opinion counts." Lonnie said so persuasively.

Owen was reluctantly convinced. He wouldn't tell his mother, who conveniently lived hundreds of miles away. As for the rest of the world, like Lonnie said, who cared what they think.

Leaving his prankster roommate Winney was a big decision, but one he was ready to make. He felt it in his gut, but even more in his heart. Perhaps it was time for him to grow up.

Until now, Owen never had time for anything other than studying and working. Despite living with his perpetually horny roommate, his experience with women was limited. There were a couple of dates in high school and a senior prom at a girl's school in the city. It was arranged by his mother and Mrs. Kelly, their downstairs neighbor. Then there was camp one summer when he was seventeen and had his first kiss, which never progressed beyond a few kisses and a quick feel. As an undergraduate, there were a few meaningless romps in the hay but nothing more than that.

Moving into Lonnie's spacious, three-bedroom townhouse allowed plenty of space to navigate their new arrangement.

"Do you want me to use the guest bathroom, Lonnie?" Owen asked as he maneuvered a box of toiletries through the entrance foyer.

"I thought we'd share the one in the master. It is plenty large enough and has a great shower…big enough for two."

"Share it. Hmm. Well, if you think that will work, I'm good to go. I guess that makes sense—just one less to clean." Her shower comment never registered.

"Jeez, Owen. You are always so practical, the man of reason, relaxed, cool, and collected. The picture of efficiency."

"And you, Dr. Quackenbush? A woman so beautiful that you can steal a man's heart and have her way with it. A woman who makes this man smile whenever he's with her or even thinks about her."

Friendship turned to love. Lonnie knew first, and from the beginning she had loved Owen's naivete. More importantly, she loved his kind and tender manner, especially in bed.

As for Owen, he was becoming smitten. For the first time in his life, he couldn't wait to leave the lab and rush home and be with Lonnie. Between Lonnie's late-night shifts at the hospital and Owen's demanding workload at MIT, life was a balancing act. Career and new love seldom work, but Lonnie and Owen made it. They thought like scientists but made love with the passion and desire of teenagers.

On a cold blustering night in Boston, the temperatures hit a new low. Lonnie and Owen had returned home after a hard day's work. Bone tired, they cuddled on the sofa eating popcorn that Lonnie had just taken off the stove.

Owen wondered that bitter night on his way home from the lab: "Was Mama Lucia right that this would be a marriage made in heaven?"

CHAPTER FIFTEEN
THE CHRISTMAS GIFT

"LONNIE, NEXT WEEK IS THANKSGIVING, AND MY MOTHER has invited us to come to New York and spend the holiday with her. It would be a great chance for you two to meet."

"Meet your mother? That sounds like you are getting serious...are you?"

"Maybe just a little...just kidding. Just kidding...maybe a lot? Actually, I can't wait for you and my mom to get to know each other. I know she will love you as much as I do."

"Owen, I hope so. I really hope so. Let me check with the hospital. I think I can get off. I worked most holidays for the last year because I didn't go home, so it shouldn't be a problem."

"Great, let's do it. I'll call my mom. She'll be so excited."

Ellen Manning answered the phone on the third ring. "Hello?"

"Hi, Mom, it's me. How are you?"

"Owen, how nice to hear your voice. I'm fine, and you?"

"Great. I wanted to let you know that Lonnie and I will be coming for Thanksgiving. That is, if we are still invited."

"Oh, Owen, stop. Of course, you are always invited, and that young lady of yours is too. I can't wait to meet her."

"So, it's a date. We'll come the day before."

The train arrived in Grand Central Station the evening before Thanksgiving. Owen hailed a cab and gave the driver the address. The city was already decorated for Christmas. The cold, crisp November air put a bounce in the step of the crowds of pedestrians.

"I have never been to New York. It is so different from The Hague. Everything is so big and bright and busy, nothing like Boston either. It's wonderful. And the holiday decorations are everywhere. God, I love Christmas!"

"You haven't seen anything yet. There is this amazing Christmas tree in the center of Midtown. They started the tradition just a few years ago, and each year the tree gets bigger and bigger, as do the crowds."

"Owen, I'm nervous."

"Nervous? About the crowds?"

"No, silly, about meeting your mother and if she will like me."

"Who wouldn't like you? You're perfect: beautiful, smart, witty, and a doctor no less! Every mother's dream."

"But mothers often think their sons, especially an only child, will never find anyone good enough."

"Cut it out. She will love you."

"But I'm not an American and have this little accent."

"Accent? What accent? We just left Boston. I can barely understand practically anything they say. 'Park the car in Harvard Yard.' You just think you have an accent; no one else does. And besides, my mother wasn't always an American. She was born in Britain and became a citizen."

"That's right, you did say you were part British."

"Yeah. But I was born right here in New York City." Pointing toward the river, Owen said, "Look over there: it's the East River. The city is divided by two rivers, the East and the Hudson. I did tell you I'm going to be your tour guide, didn't I? If you get sick of it, let me know."

Lonnie leaned over and kissed Owen on his open lips. "I'll never get sick of you, never, and you can guide me anywhere."

The cab arrived, and the husky Irish doorman in his mid-fifties with a pronounced Irish brogue rushed to help the couple out of the car. "Happy Thanksgiving, Dr. Manning. Welcome home, sir."

"Thank you, Brian, and happy Thanksgiving to you and your family. Are they all well?"

"Yes, they are all well. My oldest is in the army, and my two daughters are studying to be nurses. It's pretty hard managing that, but we are working hard and keeping our heads above water."

"Of course. Well, say hi to them and the rest of the staff too. I'm sure I'll see them while I'm home. By the way, this is Lonnie Quackenbush. She's a doctor, the real kind, not like me."

"Nice to meet you, miss, I mean doctor. Welcome to the Riverview House. And happy Thanksgiving to you too. Anything I can do to help you, just ask. Anything."

Owen reached into his pocket and palmed a ten-dollar bill into Brian's hand. "Have a great night."

"Thank you, doctor. Let me grab your bags."

Brian grabbed the bags out of the cab and whisked them to the elevator on a shiny brass trolly. "Your mother is in. I'll announce you." Then Brian leaned over and whispered into Owen's ear, "Your lass is a beauty, doc. Lucky man, you are."

Owen and Lonnie entered the wood-paneled elevator and pressed the button marked twelve. When the door opened directly into the apartment, Ellen Manning was already waiting in the vestibule. Colleen, their long-time housekeeper, took their coats.

"Oh my God, I can't believe you are here. I've missed you so much. Come in, come in."

"Mom, this is Dr. Lonnie Quackenbush, the woman I told you about," Owen said. "And this is Colleen, my second mom."

Ellen Manning smiled at her son's love—she was certainly beautiful. Lonnie's long, silky blonde hair, blue-green eyes, and petite size were indeed pleasing. "Welcome, Lonnie, I'm so happy you came for Thanksgiving."

Ellen wasn't the only one sizing someone up. Lonnie was a great believer in first impressions, and Owen's mom made an excellent one. But what impressed Lonnie the most was not that Ellen was elegantly turned out in a beautiful suit. It was her smile and sparkling eyes filled with kindness and admiration. Clearly, she was a proud mother and, more importantly, one who truly loved her son.

"Thank you for inviting me to Thanksgiving. I brought you a little something." Lonnie handed Ellen a beautifully wrapped package.

"Oh, dear, how sweet, but you shouldn't have, really." Ellen hugged and gave Lonnie a kiss on the cheek.

"Mom, did you know they celebrate Thanksgiving in The Netherlands, where Lonnie is from? She told me all about it."

"No, I had no idea. Lonnie, dear, let's have some champagne to celebrate, and you can tell me all about your country's Thanksgiving."

Lonnie followed Ellen into the living room overlooking the East River. "Come, we'll sit by the window."

"Oh my God, Owen, look at all those lights," Lonnie said. "And the river, it's so busy. Is that a terrace? Owen, take me out there for a minute. I must see."

"It's pretty chilly for that, Lonnie. The winds make it feel even colder."

"It will be all right, just for a minute. Please!"

Owen grabbed his jacket, put his arm around Lonnie, and opened the door.

Ellen smiled. She looked at Owen and then at Lonnie and knew at that very moment that her son was in love with this enchanting young doctor. It was the way Owen looked at her, the way he smiled, and how he could not possibly say no to even this most chilly request. Ellen looked at the nearby smiling Colleen. She knew too.

The terrace provided a panoramic view of the East River.

"Owen, this is breathtaking. All the lights and boats and buildings. Amazing."

Lonnie shivered as much from the cold as from the thrill of seeing a city like none other.

"You're cold…here, take my jacket." Owen wrapped his jacket around Lonnie and then gathered her in both his arms. She drew him close and gently enfolded her body into his.

"You better watch out, Lonnie, I'm falling."

"Falling? Whatever do you mean? Isn't this terrace safe?"

"Of course, it is. I mean that I'm falling in love with you. I can't help myself."

"Oh, Owen. I know what that is like. It happened to me the day we shared that ridiculously enormous triple-decker sandwich at Ralph's. Now give me one of those superb kisses of yours."

Owen reached over and pulled Lonnie close. He felt her warmth and smelled the light, flowery perfume that she sparingly applied each morning—a dab here and there. His lips parted as he kissed her so intensely that it moved him.

"This woman," he thought, "is the one that I could love forever. She is a gift to be treasured."

Owen ran his fingers through her wind-blown hair and kissed her neck. When he whispered into her ear, she smiled and said yes to his provocative request.

Lonnie mentally recorded this moment. Being with Owen in this incredible spot was something she would never want to forget. Love was new to her, and she cherished every second of it. The couple lingered in the cold New York night air, enjoying the magic of lights and the wind off the East River.

Ellen had a fire burning in the fireplace and a tray of hors d'oeuvres ready on a coffee table when Owen and Lonnie came back from the terrace. "Look at you two, your cheeks are so rosy. Come, sit. Now tell me about Thanksgiving in The Netherlands. You know, I'm of British descent, so an American Thanksgiving was a new holiday for me when I came to this country years ago. But first, dear, try one of these canapes, they're Owen's favorite. When he was a child, I would have to make sure he didn't eat them all before the guests arrived. But the little sneak would find a way to get his fill." Ellen chuckled.

«I›m sure you know how charming he is," Ellen continued. "But more than that, he is one of the most exceptional people I know. Of course, being his mother, I would think that, but I think you probably have already made that determination. Now, Owen, open the champagne."

Owen blushed. "Oh, Mom, you're embarrassing me. Cut it out. And besides, a mother is hardly a good judge of how wonderful her child really is. There is very little objectivity…love is often blind."

"Perhaps. But now, Lonnie, tell me about your country's Thanksgiving."

"Most people don›t realize that Thanksgiving in The Netherlands has a similar origin to the American holiday."

"Really? You are right, dear, most people don't know that."

Lonnie went on, "You see, before the Pilgrims came to America to practice religious freedom, they traveled to The Netherlands and landed at a place called Leiden, where they settled for more than eleven years. They left because they didn't want their children to assimilate as Dutch, and because there were very few opportunities for them to make a living there. To the Dutch, they were outsiders, keeping to themselves, and rather zealous about their religion. From what the Pilgrims heard, America seemed to hold more promise."

"So, they came here?" Ellen asked.

"Right. The whole Plymouth Rock bit. But every year on the third Thursday in November, a celebration is held at the Pieterskerk, a famous old church where one of the Pilgrim leaders is buried. I can't recall his name, something like Roberts or

Robinson. We don't have turkey or anything like that, but usually we attend church services and have coffee and cookies afterward. It's a nice family day."

"Well, your Thanksgiving sounds a lot less caloric than ours," Owen said. "We sit around a table and fill ourselves with everything from turkey to pumpkin pie. Way too much. And by the way, Colleen makes the best stuffing you ever ate."

"Stuffing?"

"Yea, Lonnie, it goes inside the turkey."

Lonnie made a funny face.

"What Owen is trying to say is that we make what you might call bread-based filling and cook it inside the turkey," Ellen said.

By the look on Lonnie's face, Ellen could tell she still hadn't understood. "Well, dear, you will see exactly what this is all about tomorrow. I'm sure you will love it. And how long will you two be staying? I hope through the weekend."

"Mom, we both have to be back at work on Monday morning," Owen said. "So, we will leave Sunday after lunch. There is a two o'clock train with only one change in New London."

"So short," Ellen protested. "My darlings are going to eat and run."

"Hardly, Mother. We have three full days before Sunday."

*****

Thanksgiving Day

Ellen outdid herself. She invited old Mrs. Kelly, also a long-time widow. She and Mrs. Kelly spent a lot of time traveling together and playing bridge. This year, it was also Ellen's turn to invite Father Bethel, the Anglican priest from St. Elmo's, her church down the street.

Ellen set the table in the dining room, which featured a floor-to-ceiling bay window and a magnificent view of the East River.

"Mrs. Manning, I love your table," Lonnie said. "What beautiful flowers. And that view…spectacular."

"Thank you, dear. I couldn't do it without Colleen. She's lived with us ever since Owen was five. So, tell me, what do you think about the city?"

"It's overwhelming. So different from Boston and gigantic compared to The Hague. So many people and such tall buildings. I thought Boston was huge, but New York is … overwhelming."

"Hey, Lonnie," Owen interrupted. "How about after dinner I take you for a little walk? New York is all decorated for the holidays, and I know how much you love Christmas."

Later, the couple walked hand in hand down Fifth Avenue, enjoying the shop windows all decked out in holiday dress.

"Just around the corner is Rockefeller Center," Owen said. "That is where they have the big Christmas tree I told you about. Would you like to see it?"

"I wouldn't miss it for the world."

Owen steered them toward 51st Street, and the tree came into sight. "There it is, Lonnie, see it?"

"See it? You can't miss it. I've never seen anything like it before. How long did it take to grow that tree in that spot?"

"No, no" Owen chuckled "The tree didn't grow there. It is brought in from far away—each year from a different place. Too bad. We are a bit early. They don't light the tree for another week. You can't believe how gorgeous it is when it's all lit up."

Lonnie looked at Owen and saw a glimmer in his eyes. "You love Christmas, too, don't you?"

"Always have. Growing up, my mom always made our holidays memorable. It was just the two of us, plus Colleen. My dad died when I was only six, but Mom had magic and provided my fondest memories. You know, I sort of still believe in Santa Claus; at least I want too, and I'm almost sure my mom definitely does."

"You are too much, Dr. Manning. A kid at heart."

"Yeah, probably." Owen leaned over and kissed Lonnie.

"Well, I can tell you one thing," Lonnie said. "Kids don't kiss like that."

*****

Christmas Morning, Boston

It was early when the bells from Christ's Church in Harvard Square rang out, announcing Christmas Day. Rolling over in their king-size bed, Lonnie kissed Owen's forehead and softly whispered, "Merry Christmas, sweetie."

Barely stirring, Owen opened one eye and then the other. "Merry Christmas to you, darling." Then with a sly grin, he leaned into her side, pulling her closer.

Lonnie smiled a little smile. "Oh, looks like Santa Claus may be coming early. I think I'm going to get a little Christmas present."

"You could say that, Lonnie, but 'little' might not describe what I have for you."

Lonnie snuggled a bit nearer, enjoying the sensation of his closeness. Then, putting her arms around Owen, she kissed him, urging him to make the next move. Owen, in the habit of sleeping naked, pulled back the coverlet and rolled over on top of Lonnie.

"You good?"

"I'm better than good."

After showering, Owen and Lonnie dressed and shared a breakfast cappuccino with a couple of generous slices of banketstaaf. They were on their second helping when Owen asked, "This is delicious. What is it?"

"Banketstaaf, or Dutch Christmas log. A kind of breakfast cake, you know, like what they call Danish pastry. It's stuffed with a mixture of sweet almond paste and orange zest filled with nuts and rolled into a log and baked. My mother makes it every Christmas, and this year I tried."

"It's delicious...really delicious. So, you made this? Really. When?" Owen licked his fingers like a five-year-old boy.

Lonnie smiled at this giant kid she loved so dearly. "When do you think? My day off last Tuesday. I baked it while you were at the lab and froze it for a Christmas morning surprise."

"Let's have another piece if it's okay?"

"Owen, two is enough for now. You'll get fat. I don't think a big belly would become you."

"Well, okay. So, this is my second treat for the morning, I had my first one in bed with the baker."

"Oh, Owen, you are too much."

" I sure hope so..."

"Well, you know, Owen, they say things come in threes, so there is going to be the third surprise."

Owen gulped. "I hope it's not what just flashed into my mind. You know, a visit by the stork or something like that."

"God, NO. It's something much less complicated."

Reaching over to the presents under the tree, Lonnie picked one up and handed it to Owen.

"I think you might like this surprise."

"Whatever it is, it can't beat what I got earlier this morning from that baker."

Lonnie playfully poked Owen in his firm but full tummy. "You are incorrigible, but oh-so-loveable."

The package was wrapped in gold with a special ribbon tied in a perfect bow. "Oh, babe, this is too nice to open."

"Just open it, Owen."

Owen shook the box, weighed it in his hands, and then smelled it just for good measure.

"Let me see if I can guess what it is. Maybe socks or underwear? It couldn't be pajamas since I never wear them."

"Owen, for crying out loud, just open it!"

Owen enjoyed the banter and watching Lonnie, who was obviously dying for him to open the box. He slowly and methodically untied the ribbon and rolled it up. Next, he carefully peeled off the wrapping paper and folded it into a nice square. He knew this was driving Lonnie mad. At last, Owen cautiously opened the present.

"A box, great, just what I always wanted."

"Owen, you are torturing me and making me crazy. Just open it, you jerk."

Owen opened the box to find yet another box inside. This one was leather. "Oh, just what I wanted, another box."

"Stop, being so annoying, it's not another box—just open it."

When Owen opened the leather box, his eyes popped. "Wow, is this really for me?"

"Of course, it is. Do you like it?"

"It's beautiful…more than beautiful. Is it an antique? It looks vintage, but it also looks brand new."

Lonnie had taken a big chance giving Owen this gift. Their relationship was going strong, but so far, Owen hadn't made any serious gestures toward building something more permanent. There was always the possibility that things wouldn't work out. Living together was a big milestone for both of them. They had ignored tradition and let their hearts dictate. But living together did not come with a guarantee of permanence.

"It was my late father's Rolex," she said. "He left it to me. I had it restored for you."

Owen immediately recognized the significance of the gift. Lonnie would never give something so dear to just anyone.

"Wow, your father's. I'm honored. Are you sure you want to do this?"

A shiver of concern raced through Lonnie, and she worried: "Oh my God, have I've made a big mistake? He has doubts."

She said, "Owen, why do you ask me that?"

"Oh, I don't know, maybe it's because I'd expect you to give this to someone that you plan on spending the rest of your life with. Someone like…well, maybe me." Owen reached into his trousers pocket and pulled out another, much smaller box containing an engagement ring.

*****

At Thanksgiving when he was in New York his mother pulled him aside:

"And, so young man." She asked, "What are your intentions?"

"Intentions? Whatever are you talking about, Mother?"

"You know very well. I can see it on your face and hers too. It's love, isn't it?"

Owen meekly grinned, paused, and nodded. "Yea, Ma. Does it show? I got it bad."

"She's a marvelous person, and I love her to death. She is the real McCoy. Trust me, mothers know these things. So, Dr. Manning, what are you waiting for?"

"I don't know. Maybe I'm a little scared? Maybe I'm feeling a bit unworthy to have such a wonderful woman?"

"And maybe you're a fool! Honestly, they call you a genius, but you are really pretty stupid when it comes to love. Come with me." Ellen walked Owen into her bedroom and opened her dresser draw. "This is my engagement ring. I stopped wearing it after your father died. I really don't know why, actually. Maybe because it hurt too much to look at it and have all our memories rush back. I want you to take it and give it to Lonnie. When you are ready, of course. I can tell she's the perfect woman for you. I feel she is going to be the daughter I never had since your father died so young."

In the glow of their first Christmas tree, Owen raised to one knee, opened the box, and

and sweetly asked, "Lonnie, will you marry me?"

The ring was a modest one with a very modest diamond surrounded by small diamond chips.

"It's nothing like the watch, which I suspect is really valuable, but it's got sentimental meaning. It was my Mom's and she wanted you to have it. She said it's for the daughter she never had."

Lonnie took the ring out of the box and held it next to her heart. "Yes, yes, I will marry you. And, it has great value; it's price-less! Like you."

CHAPTER SIXTEEN
WHAT'S SCHADUWGAZON?

The Hague, Netherlands, January 1940

"HALLO, MOEDER, IT'S LONNIE."

"Hallo, lieve dochter, Mamma has missed you. You are well?" The phone crackled with intermittent static making hearing difficult.

Lonnie raised her voice. "I'm well, very well, Mamma. And you? Can you hear me?

"I can, but there is a lot of static. I'm just fine. And that young man of yours, he's good too?"

"Ja, he's good. Working hard at the university. He's working in a new type of science, having to do with nuclear physics. It's very exciting work, but I hardly ever see him it feels like."

"Oh, I'm sorry about that, but I can tell by your letters, and in your voice, you are very much in love, ya?"

"Very much."

"I'm sorry I missed Christmas with you, dear. You know it's getting harder and harder to travel these days. Travel papers and identifications are required to leave the country, and I'm afraid the Germans are preparing for war. So far, we are okay, but it feels like a storm is gathering, and no one knows when it will break. But enough of that. Pinch me, I can't believe you are engaged to be married! I wept when I read your letter. I can't wait to see you and your ring, too."

"Oh, Mamma, I missed you at Christmas too. But I have news. Good news. Now that Owen and I are engaged we decided to get married sooner rather than later."

"Married! Hoe geweldig! How . . . what is the word . . . wonderful! Tell me all about it. Details, please. How did he propose, was it romantic? Where you surprised?"

Lonnie filled her mother in with all of the minute details. "And yes Momma, I was surprised, and it was terribly romantic! My best Christmas ever. Being in love is special, but being in love at Christmas is magical. I looked out at the garden and there was a dusting of newly fallen snow. Like a white blanket; it reminded me of home.

"We sat by the fire in each other's arms, so cozy and close and spoke of our future. How happy we were going to be and how much we had to look forward too. But we worried too, about the troubling news coming from Europe and the hideous German war mongers. But we know come thick or thin, we will be together for the rest of our live and that's all that matters."

Lonnie could hear her mother sniffling. "Are you crying, Mamma?"

"Tears of joy, darling. And tears because your father won't be here to see this. He loved you so much, you know."

Now Lonnie was sniffling too. "I know…he was my hero. I remember all those wonderful days in the country when we would run and hide at the lake house. And how much he wanted me to become a doctor."

"Ja, and you did; he'd be so proud. I remember everything, too, such fond memories." Lonnie's mother paused and continued, "So, let's get down to business. When? Where?"

"When and where what?"

"The wedding, you silly *liefje*, my darling."

"Owen and I decided that it would be challenging for you to come to Boston, so we will come to The Hague."

"The Hague? Is that possible, or more importantly, is that smart? Things here are always changing depending on the rumors of war and troubles elsewhere in Europe."

"Owen checked with the State Department—he has connections because of the work they're doing in his lab. They said that The Netherlands is still open for US citizens. It should be okay. He will make sure we cross the Atlantic as safely as possible. Mamma, we would not want to be married without you there."

"Well, we must be sure of your safety before you come. But I will trust you and your soon-to-be husband. Both so smart. I know you will be careful. So, now we know where, how about when?"

"Next month, if that is good with you."

Lonnie's mother went silent "*Liefje*, is there something you are not telling me?"

"No, Mamma, why do you ask?"

"Well, a wedding so quick, sometimes, you know, accidents happen, dear."

Lonnie caught her mother's innuendo and smiled. "No, no, it's nothing like that. Owen and I want babies, but not at the moment. There is so much uncertainty in the world, you know, the war, his work, and a lot of other things. We don't want to waste a second waiting to be man and wife."

"I see. But next month…So soon? I couldn't get Madame Louise to make me a dress that quickly, much less one for you."

"Don't worry about that, Mamma. I could always bring a dress from here, and one for you too. They actually have stores that stock ready-to-wear gowns."

"No, no. I'm sure if I beg Madame Louise, she will *komen door* for us. I've been with her for decades, and I'm her favorite client. The best-paying one, for sure."

"Very well. By the way, Owen's mother, Ellen, will be traveling with us. She's the only guest on his side. His father died many years ago, just like Papa did. He has no other relatives. Owen's old college friend, a Brit, who lives in London and is a math professor at Oxford, will come to The Hague and be his best man."

"*Goede.*"

"And I will ask Katrina to be my maid of honor."

"I know your sister will be thrilled."

"How is she?"

"I'm worried about her. You know she's married a German. I'm not sure of his politics, but things are so unsettled between them."

"Mamma, he's only part German, and she swears he's different from the rest of them."

"Well, I know he says that, but I'm not so sure, Lonnie. To me, they are all the same…officious, and you can't trust them. He works here in The Hague. Some kind of government job and regularly goes back and forth to Berlin; he's away for days at a time. I just have a bad feeling about him, always have. But you know Katrina, she has always been strong-minded and willful. She's not one to listen.

"But I think he knows something about Germany's plans. I won't be at all surprised if he is working with them against our country. Probably behind the scenes so he will be aligned with the Nazis if they take over The Hague." She stopped and Lonnie could almost imagine her shuddering. "What are they saying in the States, dear? Are people worried?"

"Oh, Mamma, yes. Very much so. Everyone is worried here, but mostly they don't want to fight again and get tangled up in Europe's politics. But thanks to his work, Owen is in touch with the State Department. He says the government looks like it's preparing for war no matter what the citizens think, that President Roosevelt is solidly backing the Allies. What is happening in Europe is much too serious to ignore or look away. At least not any longer."

"I'm glad to hear that at least."

"Yes, but he's almost alone in that. Most people think it's another European problem."

"What does Owen think?"

"He's a patriot, Mamma, first and foremost. But he also doesn't want war. It is a dilemma the world finds itself in. And he's hearing things at work that are very frightening. He can't talk about it much, but it seems that Roosevelt is preparing for war, even pushing scientists to work on new weapons."

"New weapons?"

"Yes, but I don't know much, Mamma. We just hope it doesn't happen."

Her mother let a few seconds pass, then she exhaled deeply, and Lonnie wondered what her beloved mother was thinking. She was obviously holding something back.

"Mamma? What is it?"

"Nothing, Lonnie. Let's not talk any more of this! This is a happy call. Let's set the date!"

"How does the eighteenth sound, Mamma?"

"The eighteenth it is. I'll barely have time to ready the house. I'm going to open up the entire place up for a gala. Do you want a church wedding? Shall I call Reverend van Aarle?"

"That would be great, a church wedding. Owen will love that."

*****

The Hague, Netherlands

Owen, his mother, Ellen, and Lonnie traveled across the Atlantic on the three-year-old *RMS Queen Mary*. It was a long journey, and tensions were high, with the threat of German U-boats actively hunting passenger ships to torpedo. The trip was particularly stressful for Ellen, who had not been on an ocean liner since her tragic voyage aboard the Titanic. Old fears conjured up in her mind, and even after decades, deep inside she still worried someone would take Owen away from her.

Onboard, extra precautions were everywhere with double, round-the-clock lookouts and additional lifeboats. The normally light-hearted festive atmosphere of passengers making the crossing was replaced with worried faces and anxious anticipation for the trip to end safely—the sooner, the better.

On the way over, Lonnie thought frequently about the conversation she'd had with her mother. Back in New York, spending happy days and long nights with Owen, war really did seem far away. But on the cold, open ocean, with packs of U-boats roaming the dark waters like wolves, it seemed much more real. Is that what her mother didn't want to say? That war was coming no matter what? What would that mean for her? For Owen?

When she asked Owen about it, he was uncharacteristically glum and closed-mouth. She knew that Owen hated war but felt there was something else. When she pressed him, all he said was, "I'm afraid that if war does start, no one knows where this one will end. This won't be like any other war that's come before, and once we let the genie out of the bottle, it may not be possible to put it back."

"I don't like this kind of talk," she said. "What does that even mean?"

But Owen wrapped his arms around her and gave her a kiss. "I don't want to think about this now, darling. Not when we're about to get married, and you'll make me the happiest man in the world."

And it was true—the young couple could hardly wait, especially since they were deprived of each other's company on the way over. Lonnie had insisted on sharing a suite with Ellen since she and Owen were not yet married. No matter how modern she felt about their Boston cohabitation, it was not the same as being on a ship with hundreds of prim and proper ladies and gentlemen who would very well be offended. Not to mention what her future mother-in-law might think of such an arrange-ment. So, Owen took a single room adjoining their suite.

On the last evening at sea, the ship florist delivered a cor-sage of fresh gardenias to Lonnie's room. Pressing a dollar into his hand, Ellen thanked the steward, and she accepted the flowers.

"Lonnie, they are for you."

Lonnie undid the glittery silver ribbon and opened the transparent box. The enclosed card read: "To Lonnie, my true love and soon-to-be partner for life. Thank you for being you and thank you for loving me. Always, Owen."

She put the flowers to her nose and inhaled deeply. "How lovely! Gardenias! He knows they are my favorite. He's such a dear."

"You don't have to convince me on that idea. He's my son, and all mothers think their sons are more than dear, even when they don't quite act that way. Of course, that's not the case with Owen."

Dinner in the Queens Grill aboard the *Queen Mary* was reserved exclusively for first-class passengers. World-renowned chefs delivered extraordinary gourmet cuisine nightly for the select few willing to pay the price. Art deco crystal and brass wall sconces provided intimate lighting, casting shadows with the promise of more amorous encounters to follow.

Being the last night at sea, Ellen insisted that Lonnie and Owen dine alone together. She arranged with the maître d' for the young couple to have a window table for two. A dozen red roses in a hand-blown Waterford globe placed in the center of the small table, along with candle votives, added a romantic touch.

The Queens Grill was always black tie-formal, so Lonnie wore one of the new gowns from her trousseau.

Owen in his dinner jacket and she in her emerald-green velvet evening dress began the evening with French champagne. Clicking glasses, they toasted: "To us."

When they finished their dinner of poached lobster preceded by escargot and followed by profiteroles anglaise, Owen and Lonnie strolled the promenade deck for some evening air. They looked far into the night under a chilly sky filled with shining stars. Their lives together were just beginning, and although optimism filled their hearts, there was the reality that all the world soon could be at war. They did not know what was to come, but they did know they would endure it together. Owen held Lonnie's hand tightly and said, "I never thought I would find someone like you to be my wife. I'm truly blessed to have found a woman as kind and wonderful as you, and smart and beautiful all at the same time."

Lonnie, touched by Owen's sincerity and enchanted by the heartfelt words, simply tightly embraced her extraordinary man.

✳✳✳✳✳

Southampton, England

The liner arrived in Southampton, where the trio spent the night. The next morning, they traveled by ferry to Calais and then by rail to The Hague, arriving seven days before the wedding.

Lonnie's mother had arranged for her driver to pick them up at the train station. Their luggage was piled high in the boot, and the driver sped off in the Pierce-Arrow. As they passed through

The Hague, Lonnie pointed out the local attractions, just as Owen had in New York.

They passed a massive cathedral. "Look, Owen, that's St. James, the largest church in The Hague. And surprise, surprise! It's where Mamma has planned for us to marry."

"Some church. But I don't think we are going to fill it."

"Of course, we're not. But it's beautiful, and it's where I was christened. My mother and late father were congregants since before I was even born, and she still attends every week."

"Wow."

The sedan drove the twisted thoroughfares of the city and turned into a quiet residential area. At the end of an unpopulated street, about a half-mile down, the driver stopped at a massive wrought-iron gate flanked by stone pillars. A sign read: "Schaduwgazon."

"Lonnie, what is this place? What's Schaduwgazon?"

"It means Shadowlawn."

"Oh. But I thought we were staying with your mother, not at a hotel."

Lonnie laughed. "We are staying with Mamma. This is her house."

Owen shot a glance at his mother, who looked equally impressed. He emitted a low whistle: "Her house is a lot more than a house, it's a mansion. No, an estate. You never said—"

"There are a lot of things I never said. Don't worry, I'm going to explain."

A groundskeeper opened the gate, and the Pierce-Arrow glided down the lovely tree-lined drive.

"You see, Owen, our family, came from Amsterdam. They had a successful business there and in South Africa, too. The business was left to my father by his father, who worked really hard growing it, and when he died he had amassed a rather sizeable estate."

"Must have been some business. What was it?"

"Papa was a diamond merchant, and he owned mines in South Africa and cutting houses in Amsterdam. Along the way, he became a very astute investor, mostly in real estate and stocks."

Owen gulped, looking over at Lonnie's engagement ring. *Oh, God,* he thought, *look at the size of that diamond. I doubt if it will make much of an impression with her mother, who probably is dripping in jewels the size of eggs.*

Lonnie caught Owen's gaze and, as if she could read his thoughts, lifted her hand. "Owen, I wouldn't trade this ring for the Hope Diamond, never, ever. Love is not measured in carats; it is a priceless commodity but has no material value. And yet love is the most valuable of all things."

Bringing the ring to her lips, she kissed it. "See, I told you I love it."

The doors of the mansion flung open as the sedan maneuvered the circular driveway and came to a stop.

"*Liefje, liefje!* Welcome, welcome."

Owen, seeing his future mother-in-law for the first time, found it hard to believe she was old enough to be Lonnie's mother. She looked like European royalty. Her blonde hair was exactly the color of Lonnie's with the same blue-green eyes. Lonnie and her mother embraced and kissed each other's cheeks several times.

"Mamma, you must meet Owen. Owen, this is my Mamma, Maria Quackenbush. And Mamma, this is my Owen, and this is his wonderful mother, Ellen Manning."

"Welcome! Come in, come in. I have tea waiting."

They entered a grand foyer filled with Dutch paintings by well-known artists. Large vases of flowers filled the hall with a delightful fragrance. Chandeliers glistened as they shined down three stories. Although he was raised well, Owen couldn't help but be intimidated by all of this grandeur and wealth. But not being particularly materialistic, he let it go. Maria poured from the silver service and said, "Now, we shall have tea, and let's get this wedding week started."

On the day of the rehearsal dinner, Winney Barrington arrived to serve as Owen's best man. He had traveled from London, where he taught advanced mathematics at Oxford but was on loan to the British War Department. It was no surprise that he had on his arm a lovely young lady who soon proved her breasts were far more extensive than her brains.

The rehearsal dinner was a small affair: just the happy couple, their mothers, Winney and his date, Lonnie's sister Katrina, and her husband Hanz. As soon as he met Hanz, Owen felt that something was off. Hanz seemed to take a special interest in him, staring at him openly like he was sizing Owen up and giving Owen a smile that Owen thought would look about right on a sand salesman in the desert. Maybe, Owen told himself, it's just because Hanz spoke with a thick German accent, and already Owen realized he was thinking of Germans as enemies.

Hoping not to create an issue, Owen was disappointed to discover Hanz was seated next to him and across from Winney. It only took a minute after sitting down that Hanz leaned closer to Owen and started asking questions in a low voice.

"So, Herr Manning, I understand you work at MIT, *ja?*"

"Yes," Owen said warily.

"Very good university. What is it you do there?"

"I'm a researcher and part-time teacher."

"Interesting. You are in the study of nuclear physics, *ja*?"

Owen was shocked for a minute into silence before he could answer. "In the lab, yes. How did you know that?"

Hanz gave a small laugh that never reached his eyes. "We will be family soon, eh? No secrets in family!"

Owen glanced over and saw that Lonnie and her mother were deep in conversation and not paying any attention. Across the table, however, Winney was watching their conversation closely, even as he kept a steady stream of whiskey flowing into his glass and one hand almost indecently draped over his date.

"Oy!" Winney called out after Owen caught his eye. "You didn't mention, Hanz. What field are you in?"

Hanz's head swiveled around, his fake smile never slipping. "I'm just a lowly government functionary," he said. "My job is all paper shuffling. It would bore you."

"You work for the government, then?" Winney pursued. "Tell me, Hanz, are you in the party?"

From the corner of his eye, Owen saw Lonnie's sister Katrina stiffen and scowl.

"As a matter of fact, no," Hanz said smoothly. "I'm not important enough to come to their attention. Perhaps it is only a matter of time before they will no longer allow me to work there at all, *ja*?"

"Yeah. Sure," Winney said, obviously unhappy with the answer.

And Owen understood why. He was certain Hanz was lying, that he was a Nazi. And why would Hanz know anything about Owen's work in the lab? Owen knew that his name was known in certain circles, but he wasn't famous or well-known. He didn't even lead the lab he worked in—he was just another pair of hands.

He exchanged a look with Winney. He could read his old friend's face like a book and knew that Winney was thinking the same thing.

At that moment, Katrina leaned into the conversation. "Oh, let's not talk politics!" she said a little breathlessly. "We're not here to worry about the state of the world, but to celebrate my sister and her dashing fiancé!" She raised a somewhat shaky glass for a toast, and the attention shifted away from the men as everyone raised their glasses to the happy couple.

In fact, Owen and Winney's instincts about Hanz were right on the money—and it was even worse than they could have suspected. The Third Reich had expanded its tentacles in preparation for its worldwide dominance. Not only was Hanz a member of the Nazi party, but he was also a Abwehr operative and spy tasked with creating a network of informants in countries the Nazis planned to target and to recruit scientists and German-Americans to support the Third Reich.

In every significant research college and university in the United States and Canada, Nazi informants infiltrated faculty and administrative positions. Regular reporting on the activities and research of professors was transmitted to intelligence specialists in the Fatherland. The Massachusetts Institute of Technology was a treasure trove because of its noted scientists and their vast expertise. MIT's relationship with the War Department made it a prime target, rich with information. Hitler's master plan was a simple one: through intimidation, social and economic dominance, ethnic cleansing, and the military might of a superior army, Germany would conquer the world. But to implement it, the Reich need its enemies' secrets.

Before Owen's arrival, the Reich told Hanz that Professor Manning was a brilliant physicist, one they had been watching.

Hanz was also in a position of knowing something that Owen was yet to find out. The SS had gained access to the secretive Nobel Prize Selection Committee in Oslo. Norway was in the preliminary process of creating a pro-German puppet government, allowing the Nazis into all segments of the Norwegian establishment. Hanz knew that Owen was to be awarded a Nobel Prize in physics at the next awards ceremony. His application had been quietly submitted by his peers at MIT. No public announcement had yet been made by either the Institute or the Nobel Committee.

*****

The Wedding

The bride and groom mingled among the guests in the great hall. Joined by Katrina, the maid of honor, and her husband Hanz, the wedding party formed a reception line as the guests began to bid farewell.

Since the rehearsal dinner, Owen had done his best to avoid being cornered by Hanz, but it was obvious the German was trying to find a way to continue their conversation. A quick chat with Winney only confirmed Owen's misgivings. "That bloke's a Nazi as sure as I'm a libertine," Winney said. "Tough luck having him for a brother-in-law. You know, there is a lot of scuttlebutt about the Nazis taking over The Netherlands. It could be imminent, from what I hear. Those Krauts seem to be able to just walk in and take over any country they want. It looks like they have their eye on Poland, many say an invasion could happen any time now, who knows. The sooner you get out of here, the better."

Owen nodded and agreed, silently wishing away the war clouds that were reaching into his life and threatening the world.

He pushed these thoughts away and thought about the ceremony, which had taken place just a few hours before at St. James, a landmark Protestant church and one of the oldest buildings in The Hague. The cathedral dominated the Torenstraat town square with its high tower. Royal members of the House of Orange-Nassau had been baptized and married here for centuries, at the very altar where Lonnie and Owen exchanged their vows. Despite the pouring rain outside the enormous church doors, the scene could not have been grander when Lonnie walked down the long aisle on her mother's arm who dutifully took her deceased father's place. Owen, waiting at the altar's steps, accompanied by Winney, broadly smiled as his eyes shone with admiration.

Madame Louise had outdone herself when she created Lonnie's one-of-a-kind bridal gown. It was white lace covered in sea pearls and appliqued lilies, laid upon a silk bodice. Her train was a long veil affixed to Lonnie's beautiful blonde hair by an antique diamond clip. Reverend van Aarle officiated, ending his blessing with some ominous words, perhaps a veiled prediction: "This land and lands all over the world are in danger. Evil forces abound, and in times like these, it is vital that vows like yours bind you together. In good times and in bad, sickness and health, till death do you part, those were your vows, remember them always. Go now, live your lives, and pray for peace."

After the reception, Winney was one of the last guests to leave Schaduwgazon. He pulled Owen aside.

"Hey, Duck, you got yourself quite a woman there," he said. "She's beautiful and smart too—a doctor, not to mention loaded."

"Thanks, Winney. And thanks for standing up for me. It meant a lot."

"No problem, mate. I wanted to ask you, though, what's on tap for your honeymoon? I hear you changed your plans?"

"Yeah. Lonnie wanted to go to Italy. Rome and the Amalfi coast. But Italy is a mess with the National Fascist Party and Mussolini, Hitler's new best friend. Not exactly a tourist haven these days. So, in the name of good sense, we changed our plans and are going to London. Two weeks."

"Probably for the best. Europe is going to hell. I'd like to get out of London myself, but my work is pretty important. So, for now, I'm there. Hey, when you are in London if you can drag your arse out of the bedroom, give me a call. We'll have a pint or maybe two...or three!"

"Sounds good. But I'm a married man now, so I'll have to ask the little woman for a night out."

"Bloody hell, Duck. The ink on the wedding certificate isn't even dry, and you're already whipped. Well, if the boss lets you out, we'll make a night of it." They laughed together, and it felt like old times for a second, until Winney offered his last words: "And remember to watch out for that brother-in-law. I'll see what I can dig up, but better safe than sorry!"

After Winney was gone and the last guest had left, the driver took the happy couple along with Owen's mother, Ellen, to the train station, where they all boarded an express connecting with a ferry heading to mainland England. In London, Ellen bid the honeymooners a tearful goodbye and started her journey back to New York.

Over the next two weeks, Lonnie and Owen spent their honeymoon wandering around London, a city preparing for war. Sandbags replaced flower planters in front of shops, and restaurants draped black curtains ready to be drawn at a moment's notice. Each night, ominous sirens rang out announcing air raid drills. Blinding rays from giant searchlights combed the dark skies looking for the Luftwaffe. Anxiety and panic engulfed Londoners like the ever-present fog did Parliament and Buckingham Palace. Londoners worried, would the city survive?

CHAPTER SEVENTEEN
AND THE PRIZE GOES TO...

Stockholm, Sweden

THE CONCERT HALL WAS FILLED TO CAPACITY TO HONOR THE Nobel Laureates. The Stockholm Symphony Orchestra, some ninety strong, played the processional as King Gustav V and his wife, Queen Victoria of Sweden, along with their family, filed into the hall. All stood in respect as the royal family took their places. A robust rendition of *"Du Gamla, Du Fria,"* Sweden's national anthem, played, followed by the chairman of the board of the Nobel Prize Committee, taking the podium.

"Good evening, Your Majesties, board members, Nobel Laureates, family and friends. Today is December tenth, the anniversary of Alfred Bernhard Nobel's death. A day each year we set aside to honor those who have achieved excellence in a variety of disciplines..." He spoke for several minutes before concluding his remarks and presenting awards. After the first four laureates spoke, the chairman came to the next recipient: "I am pleased to present this year's Nobel Laureate in Nuclear Physics to Dr. Owen Manning of the United States of America. Please come forward."

Owen walked to the dais, opened a leather folder, and stepped up to the podium to speak: "Your majesties, fellow laureates, distinguished guests. Thank you for this great honor. The advances that my MIT associates and I have made over the years in nuclear physics have opened a previously unknown world, allowing a kaleidoscope of opportunities in science. Our journey is just beginning, and our progress is measurable. For that, I accept this award with humility and thanks."

Owen's mother and mother-in-law, along with Lonnie and her sister Katrina, sat in the fourth row, beaming with pride. Hanz was seated in the gallery with a large gathering of uniformed Nazi officers, a point that Owen noted with disdain. His brother-in-law wasn't even bothering to hide it anymore.

Given the situation in The Netherlands, Lonnie was pleased that her mother was able to attend and see Owen receive one of the world's most coveted awards. Getting Maria Quackenbush out of The Hague wasn't easy. Things there were getting tighter, with more and more restrictions on travel every day. At the last minute, Hanz pulled some strings and arranged for an exit visa. But it didn't come without strings and wasn't cheap. Maria had to agree to let visiting German dignitaries and high-ranking military officers stay at Schaduwgazon for, as Hanz put it, "indefinitely."

Owen finished his remarks. The Chairman commenced the presentation: "And now I ask Dr. Manning to step up onto the platform to receive this year's Nobel Prize in Nuclear Physics from the hands of His Majesty the King, Gustav V. Congratulations, Dr. Manning."

The orchestra played the "Star-Spangled Banner" as the Swedish king presented the twenty-three carat gold medal, along with a diploma and a check in the amount of $16,000. Owen had already pledged the cash prize to MIT's scholarship fund.

Lonnie and Owen stayed another day to make official appearances with the other laureates. However, Maria Quackenbush's permit required her to take the next train back to The Hague.

After a photographic session, Owen returned to his hotel. Hanz was standing in front of the building, waiting for him, and grabbed Owen's arm as he walked by.

"Herr Professor, a word please."

"Later, Hanz. Lonnie, is waiting for me."

"This will take just a moment, Herr Professor. I wanted to introduce you to some colleagues who are most anxious to meet you and offer their congratulations."

Owen wasn't excited about the idea of meeting a group of uniformed Nazi officers, but he was also aware that Hanz was technically family now, but more concerning was that he potentially was in a position to cause Lonnie's mother trouble. Reluctantly, he let Hanz guide him to the lobby, where a cluster of three Nazi officers waited in the corner. They were in full uniform, black on black, with the armbands that were quickly becoming feared all over the world. As he approached them, Owen noticed everyone else in the lobby watching surreptitiously and whispering to each other.

When he reached them, Owen was determined not to shake any hands, but he didn't have to worry about it as one of the officers stepped forward and gave him a crisp salute with a "Seig Heil!"

"Good afternoon, Herr Professor," he said in lightly accented by otherwise perfect English. "I'm Major Dinkendorf. Congratulations on your prize."

"Thank you," Owen said, hoping this would be the end of it. He also made a mental note to find out who Dinkendorf was.

"Yes, you must be very proud," Dinkendorf continued. "It may be of interest to you to know that we support your work fully."

Owen had been thinking of an excuse to walk away, but Dinkendorf had caught his interest. "Oh? How so?"

"Forgive my limited understanding of the exact nature of your work, but I understand from Hanz that you are working on a technology that may bring peace. Peace through strength is a German concept." Dinkendorf laughed at his own joke.

"Peace through strength, eh?" Owen said. "Seems the best way to peace is to stop aggression."

"We couldn't agree more," Dinkendorf said smoothly. "The German people have been victimized and are only interested in regaining their pride, reestablishing the natural order of things."

Owen didn't have any response for that.

Dinkendorf continued, "We'd love to learn more about your work if you'd be willing to share. We, of course, understand that science is expensive and would be willing to pay for your time."

"Oh, uh, well, of course I can't share any details," Owen said. "We're funded by the U.S. government. It's mostly theoretical anyway."

"Then surely there's no harm in taking a meeting." Dinkendorf said: "we can meet you anywhere, even back in Boston. Hanz can arrange everything."

Something about the way Dinkendorf twisted the word "safely" made the hairs on the back of Owen's neck rise.

"No, I'm sorry. I couldn't possibly."

"Come, come, Professor. We are not your enemies. And we don't wish to become enemies. Germans value the same things you do. Peace. Prosperity. Safety for our families and loved ones."

Owen felt the blood rising into his face. "If I didn't know better, I'd think you're threatening me."

"Threatening?" Dinkendorf sounded genuinely surprised. "By no means! I wanted to meet a man as accomplished as yourself, one who is working with what will surely be the future. And, of course, any family member to Hanz is a man we are interested in knowing."

Owen wasn't convinced and remained silent.

Dinkendorf reached into his pocket and withdrew a small card with the familiar swastika on it along with two lightning bolts and his name and rank. "You can call this number any time you like," he said. "If I'm ever in a position to help you, or your mother-in-law if she chooses to remain in The Hague in the days to come, you can please call me."

Owen took the card, sliding it into his wallet next to the card from Stimsom, the U.S. Secretary of War. The irony of it wasn't lost on him—two powerful men, mortal enemies and architects of the war machines rapidly being assembled on different continents, living cheek-to-cheek in his wallet.

"Well, I must be going," Owen said. "My wife is waiting."

"Surely," Dinkendorf responded from behind a wide smile. "I expect I'll be hearing from you before long."

Owen walked away, aware that every eye in the lobby was on him, feeling very exposed and unsettled. He decided the first thing he'd do was enlist Winney's help and find out who this Dinkendorf character was. He knew that his important work obviously had caught the attention of the wrong people and that he had to be concerned about this and his family's welfare.

*****

Boston, Massachusetts

Owen arrived back in his Boston lab to hearty cheers and applause. Dr. Karl Compton, President of MIT, was among those gathered to welcome him back and to congratulate Owen for his award. "Well done, Manning. You know you are MIT's first Nobel Laureate. You have distinguished not only yourself but the Institute."

"Thank you, Dr. Compton. I am just part of a team, you know. As far as I'm concerned, all these Fellows are equally worthy of a Nobel."

"Well, sir, I admire your humbleness, but in every team, there is a leader, and you are ours. So, take the laurels and allow yourself to bask in them for a moment."

"Thank you, sir."

"Also, Dr. Manning, on behalf of the board of trustees, I'd like to thank you for your generous donation of the prize money. It will go toward scholarships, hopefully to future Nobel winners here at MIT."

Champagne was popped and poured, and the president lifted his glass and gave his toast: "Here's to our first Nobel Prize winner, Dr. Owen Manning. A man of science and knowledge whose future is limitless!"

Owen enjoyed the applause for a minute, then smiled and waited for the lab to go back to normal. After a long trip to Europe, the wedding, and the constant tension and threat hanging in the air, Owen mostly wanted to go back to work and lose himself in the familiar rhythm of equations and algorithms, the world that made sense to him.

Spring was almost over by the time Owen finally heard back from Winney. He had sent Dinkendorf's information over to his friend and asked him to use his connections in the British government to enquire around. Owen could have just as easily done this at home—he was surrounded by military types all the time and carried the Stimson's card in his wallet. But the truth was, Owen didn't want it getting around that the Nazis were interested in him, that he'd met with uniformed Nazi officers in Europe. Mostly, he didn't want it getting around that he was related to a member of the Nazi party, even if by marriage. It was widely known that the Germans continued to build their army with frightening speed and already there was talk of spy networks penetrating government and university offices throughout the country. Owen knew the MIT lab would be a prime target—if anyone knew about his brother-in-law in Boston, he would likely lose his job, Nobel Prize or not.

"So old boy," Winney's voice came crackling over the transatlantic line. "That's some Nazi you picked."

"I didn't pick him, Winney," Owen said, annoyed. "He sought me out, remember?"

"Yeah, sure. Turns out your old friend Dinkendorf isn't just some regular bloke in the Wermacht. It was those lightning bolts that gave him away. Over the last few years, the Germans have been busy building a secret police force. They call them Gestapo. Spies, paramilitary. From what I hear, every so often one of ours goes missing and turns up in bad shape after the Gestapo is through with him. Some of them are beyond recognition if you catch my meaning. Dinkendorf is right up there with them. You'd best steer clear of that one, mate, and your brother-in-law too. If he's mixed up with the Gestapo, there's no good news."

Owen sighed. "Thanks. Not what I was hoping to hear."

"Wouldn't imagine so," Winney said. "But look, as long as you're on your side of the pond, you're beyond the reach of the Gestapo."

"Yes, but my mother-in-law is still in The Hague. She's refusing to leave."

Winney exhaled sharply. "That's a sticky business," he said. "These are bad characters, and it looks like they have designs on the continent. Hitler's not content with the concessions he's already been given. It doesn't look good, Duck. I've got some friends in The Netherlands. I'll ask them to keep an eye on the old girl, but if war comes to Lonnie's mother's doorstep, you'll need to get her out of there. Listen, old friend, these are serious blokes."

"Thanks, Winney. Maybe we won't have to worry about it after all."

"I wouldn't count on it, mate. Wouldn't count on it."

War was infecting Europe like the spread of a vicious storm. The thunder of hatred roiled the world, with columns of Nazi armor backed by the screaming planes of the Luftwaffe rolling over hapless Polish cavalry and turn-of-the-century cannons in a *blitzkreig* that swamped that country in days. Hitler immediately promised that was the end of Germany's ambitions, but no one believed the German appetite for conquest was satisfied. When they looked east, Owen and Lonnie thought mostly of Maria and Schaduwgazon and hoped that Hanz was as good as his word and would keep her safe.

CHAPTER EIGHTEEN
Devoted

Stoke-on-Trent, England, January 1941

NIGEL WAS A DECENT-LOOKING MAN, NOT HOMELY BUT WHAT one might call ordinary. Unlike his older brother, Prescott, he was rather unappealing to the fairer sex. Average height and lean but not strapping, he grew up self-conscious of his looks. Nigel's shyness and insecurities made him more comfortable rifling through science books rather than some lovely young lady's petticoat. His life had changed in so many ways over the years.

When he was a boy, he insisted on attending Oxford to study chemistry and engineering. At the same time, Prescott was pressed into learning the family business at the knee of their father and skipping university. That was the old man's strategy: Prescott was to get the title and all that went with it and Nigel was to stand by "just in case." Never did Nigel think "just in case" might actually happen.

"A bit frosty tonight, wouldn't you say, Marshall?"

"Indeed, sir," replied Marshall, Sir Nigel's faithful butler and companion. "I checked the thermometer in the hall, one-degree centigrade tonight but clear as crystal."

The master stood next to his devoted Marshall outside the manor house overlooking Stoke-on-Trent's picturesque village. "Sir, I see no lights; the village is completely dark," Marshall said.

"Right," Nigel, agreed.

It was the clear night skies that troubled the Lord of Lancaster, Sir Nigel Dasher-Hornsby. As the second son, he wasn't born to be the Lord of Lancaster, thanks to the tradition of primogeniture. But after the tragic death of his brother, the job fell to him. The job came with many privileges and even more obligations, not to mention the crushing burden of rank. The enormous responsibility for the massive baronial estate Briarcliff, with its many staff, required Herculean attention to detail. Devonshire Enterprises, the extensive family business, and the title Lord Lancaster could daunt even the most self-confident aristocrat.

"The village looks…a bit eerie, Marshall. Damn war. Even the factories' furnaces are shut down to avoid attracting the Nazi bastards and their bombs. It kills my production schedule. The war procurement people are breathing down my back to meet deadlines, and it's hellfully stressful. It's the clear nights, Marshall, that are the most worrisome, aren't they?"

"Indeed, sir."

In fact, Nigel knew that he was among the lucky ones, living outside of the city. The Germans had blitzed London, sending waves of bombers over the city every night with no end in sight. He'd heard stories of whole blocks being obliterated and terrified citizens hiding in the Tube tunnels to get away from the bombs.

It all made him sick to think about, but there was little doubt that the war had been good for the business.

"When we switched from making fine china to government work, I thought my life would be less arduous," Nigel went on. "I'd only have to worry about one customer. But the truth be told, I made a deal with the devil, a double-edged sword it is. Those heartless bureaucrats are more concerned with procedural correctness at the expense of the workers' needs. On the other hand, thank God for those contracts, because there aren't too many customers buying fine china these days. They are more concerned about survival."

"A mixed blessing, I'd say, sir."

"Yes, Marshall, a mixed blessing. As long as we have the contracts, we can keep the factory going. Stoke-on-Trent has depended on the factory for generations; without it, the village would dry up. You know … it's almost humorous. We went from catering to the gentry to making the ghastliest mess-hall dishware for the armed forces. My father and grandfather must be turning over in their graves, along with six generations of Hornsbys."

"I can only imagine, sir," Marshall said. "They all took such great pride in their business. Devonshire produced such lovely things, setting the bar for luxury not just in Britain but worldwide. But the times are what they are. You are doing the best you can."

"Yes, we are."

As they often did, Nigel's thoughts turned to a more troubling aspect of the war. He was thinking of the top-secret project commissioned by the War Office and placed under his charge. His chemical engineering expertise and the factory's commercial diversification into heat-resistant ampule development made

Devonshire a natural pick for the military's R&D laboratories. Devonshire was asked—rather, conscripted—by the army to join the war effort. Nigel was charged with the development of advanced ceramic materials for secret military use. Such technology, when combined with other war innovations, could affect the outcome of the war.

This endeavor presented a major ethical conflict for Nigel, who was worried about the morality of the war. The secret work seemed morally questionable. Yes, people often said the ends justified the means, but Nigel wasn't sure he was one of those people. In the end, he capitulated to serve God and country and held his nose to the stench of war. As a reward, Devonshire received a lucrative government contract to produce mess hall dishes, which as it turned out, was almost as repugnant to Nigel as the secret formulas.

The two men stood in the freezing night air and gazed down on the almost ghostly village. Nigel thought, "If those Krauts in Berlin every got wind of what was actually going on in this factory, there would be a bullseye right on the roof of that brand-new research center that cost us over 85,000 pounds. For as long as they think we're making dishes, they won't waste a bomb."

Breaking the silence, Marshall asked: "Sir, can I fetch you a heavier mackinaw? It's frigid out tonight. You look frightfully cold."

"No, Marshall, I've seen enough. Let's go in."

"As you wish. Shall I fix you a brandy? I have a fire going in the library. It would be quite toasty by now."

"Most appreciated. Thank you." He paused. "How long has it been, Marshall?"

"How long for what?"

"How long have we been together at Briarcliff?"

"Too long to remember, sir."

"Now seriously, how long do you suspect?"

"Well, we saw each other over the years in the village, and after a while, we became closer. Then, just after your father died, you asked me if I wanted to come to work at Briarcliff. I was green as an apple, but Mr. Homely, the head butler, God bless his soul, taught me the way of the house, polishing me as he did the precious family silver. When he passed away, I…well, sort of took his place. And all along, you have been so kind and respectful, and more."

Nigel smiled at the nostalgia and brushed off the compliment just as Marshall had gently brushed off the snowflakes now falling on his shoulders.

"Let's make haste, I'm getting cold out here." Nigel whistled for his faithful hound, Oliver. "Come on, boy, inside."

Later, Nigel and Oliver settled down in front of the roaring fire Marshall had stoked.

"Here you are, sir. I poured a brandy, a double. It will warm you up and make you sleep better. A blanket perhaps?"

"No, thank you, Marshall."

Marshall turned to leave his Lordship: "May I draw a bath? It would be very warming."

"Yes, Marshall, that sounds lovely. Let's make it special, one of your herb ones. But first sit here with me by the fire for a while and join me in a brandy."

The two men sat warming themselves, reminiscing about their years together and their close bond. Marshal finished off his brandy and asked, "Are you ready for that bath now?"

"Please."

It broke Marshall's heart when he wrapped a robe around Nigel and patted him dry. The dressing gown covered the deep scars inflicted by the vicious horse whippings delivered by his father's hand decades ago.

"Shall I turn down the bed?"

Nigel tilted his head, smiled, and looked over his shoulder to the devoted Marshall. "Yes, I'll be there shortly."

CHAPTER NINETEEN
GREGORY WHO?

Boston, 1942

"Come in, Dean Handover. Please sit down." Owen welcomed the dean into his office.

"Thank you, Dr. Manning."

"Now, to what do I owe the pleasure of this visit?"

"Well, it's not exactly a pleasure, more like business."

"Go on. I'm all ears."

"Dr. Einstein himself has written the Dean of Faculty and commented that your insight into his photoelectric effect law has opened new parameters to the nuclear development of atomic energy. As you well know, this is becoming more critical in developing military and civilian applications."

"Yes, Dr. Einstein and I have spoken many times. He is truly brilliant, and I learned so much from him."

Dean Hanover chuckled. "That's funny. Einstein said the same thing about you. For the last three years, you have distinguished yourself; your work has been…well, to quote Dr. Einstein, pioneering. Through your exceptional effort, you've elevated your lab into the premier one here at MIT. And winning the Nobel Prize is the icing on the cake."

"Just doing the job, sir."

"Right, and a damn good one at that. You know, the War Department has recently contacted MIT. They have been following your work closely."

Owen didn't raise an eyebrow, worried that the Dean was next going to ask him about any connections to the Germans. Owen hadn't heard anything else from Dinkendorf or even Hanz, and his mother-in-law was still safe in her home, but he had no doubt that the War Department was interested in his work for the same reason the Nazis were. "Well," he said in a neutral voice, "they're all over the place, so I'm not surprised."

"Yesterday I received a letter from them requesting a meeting with you."

"Me? For what?" Now he became really worried—Owen was sure he hadn't done anything wrong, but these were challenging times. Since the Japanese had attacked Pearl Harbor the previous year and the United States had entered the war, things had been moving quickly and there was no room any longer for equivocation about the war effort. Most of the country believed the United States was literally fighting for its life, along with the lives of the Allies in Europe.

But then most people didn't know what Owen knew. His lab was pushing forward into a new branch of science, one that would literally harness the power of the sun. If this could be used to develop weapons—and Owen wasn't really sure it was possible—he felt that humanity would cross into a new terrifying reality. If the early calculations were correct, a single atom bomb could be hundreds or even thousands of times more powerful than the most powerful bomb in the world at that moment. Once that genie was out of the bottle, Owen was convinced there would never be a way to put it back in.

"I don't know why they want to meet with you," the dean said, snapping Owen back to attention. "They aren't saying. But...we can make an educated guess. ... The meeting will be on Tuesday, 8:30, in the boardroom next to President Compton's office."

"Is this an order, or are they inviting me?"

"Just be there, please. Tuesday morning, 8:30 A.M. Sharp."

"I'll be there, sir."

Owen rose early on Tuesday. Lonnie did too. He dressed in his usual chino pants and hand-knitted cardigan sweater and raced downstairs for breakfast. Lonnie fixed him some strong coffee, a bowl of blueberries, and a slice of rye toast. "Owen, are you going looking like that?"

"Like what?"

"Like you're going to the lab. Like you look every day."

"I'm a professor, not a fashion plate. Besides, I'm not out to impress anybody, just going to some boring meeting."

Lonnie shook her head in defeat and moved on. "So, Owen, what's this all about? This meeting with the War Department. They aren't going to draft you, are they?"

"No. You know I'm exempt ...4F."

"So, what then?"

"Probably has something to do with my work at the lab. But I'll just have to wait and see, won't I? Wish me luck."

"Bye, sweetheart," Lonnie leaned forward and planted a huge kiss on Owen's lips. "I'm having your favorite tonight, lasagna, so don't be late. I'm picking it up on the way home from the hospital. Mama Lucia made it especially for us."

"Great, don't forget the garlic bread and a couple of cannolis too. It's going to be a feast."

Owen raced out of the house and jumped into his four-year-old Oldsmobile. The cold morning made the Olds hard to start, but after a few cranks, the well-used car chugged into action. He bucked the Boston traffic, crossing the Charles River bridge, heading into Cambridge. As he drove, he thought of Lonnie and how proud he was of her. Just last month, after seven years of schooling, she passed her final test and was now a board-certified pediatric surgeon, one of just a handful of women to earn this position. Lonnie's hard work had paid off. He had no doubt that Lonnie could handle anything that came her way, even in a competitive field where female surgeons were as rare as hen's teeth and faced blatant discrimination from their male counterparts. She was a strong and determined woman, something he greatly admired. He felt that they were both trailblazers in many ways, which he loved about their relationship. It made them a team.

The boardroom was on the third floor; Owen skipped the elevator and chose to work off the piece of rye toast and hike up the stairs. He prided himself on his exceptional physical fitness. Expecting to see three or four bureaucrats, or maybe a general or two, he was surprised to see a solitary officer sitting at the table. He knocked on the open door.

"Good morning?"

"Are you Dr. Manning? Owen Manning?"

"Yes, I am, and you are?"

"I'm Lieutenant Colonel Eric Martinson, from the War Department, please come in."

Colonel Martinson was forty-something and a picture of military bearing: a tall, lean, West Pointer, fit to fight. His hair was closely cropped to military standards, and his chest was covered with theater medals, including West Point's Superintendent's Academic Award. The colonel's shoes were shined to mirror brightness.

"Nice to meet you, Colonel. Can you tell me what this is all about?"

"Before we begin, could you provide me with some identification? Your license, or maybe an MIT ID?"

Owen shrugged impatiently, pulled out his wallet, and produced both. "Will this do?"

"Perfect, Doctor. Please sit down. Coffee?"

"No, thanks, had my quota already."

"Let's begin. Now let me ask you this. Can you identify who David and Ellen Manning are?"

Owen frowned slightly, his heart starting to race a little bit. Questions about his family could only mean the army had been investigating his past, and he knew that road led to Hanz and the Gestapo. "Yes, David was my father, now deceased, and Ellen is my mother. She lives in New York City. Why?"

"Thank you, Doctor, I'll get to that later. But first, we have become aware of some rather interesting things you are working on in your lab. Things that could prove vitally important to your country."

"Yes. As I'm sure you know, we're partly funded by the War Department, if you're interested in learning more about my work."

The colonel gave him a tight smile. "Yes, I've read the grant application, and of course we've been keeping tabs on the investment. I trust from your point of view that things are going well?"

"I like to think so," Owen said, "but I'm hardly the most senior person in our lab. You'd have to ask my superiors for the complete picture."

"Yes. Right. The good news is I'm not here to get your update on the lab work. Like you said, I can get that on my own. It's your family I'm more interested in."

Owen's heart sank, and his career flashed before his eyes. This was surely it; he was about to get fired, maybe even accused of collaboration with the Nazis. Just the mention of collaboration would be enough to get him blackballed from every major research lab in the country.

"My family?" he faltered.

"Yes. You may be aware that your name has been put forward by your dean and other supervisors at MIT as someone who might be able to help us at the War Department."

Owen frowned. "No, actually, I wasn't aware of that at all. Are you here…to recruit me? You know I'm 4F, right?"

The colonel laughed out loud, and it sounded too loud in the small room. "Dr. Manning, we don't put nuclear scientists in the infantry. Is that what you're worried about?"

Owen was thoroughly bewildered. If this was about Hanz, was the colonel just toying with him?

"No," the colonel continued, "they want you for something else, but before we could even approach you, we had to do a background check. For top-secret clearance, so you got the works. FBI, Office of Strategic Services, all the watchdogs turned you inside out."

Owen tried to swallow around a suddenly dry mouth. "And?"

"Well, they found some things that they felt we needed to address directly, in person with you. And asked me to come to talk to you, see if you could help us understand."

"I'm not sure I know what you mean," Owen said, preparing an answer for the next question.

"Of course. I'm sorry, not trying to beat around the bush here, but…this may come as a shock to you, or it may not. But we've discovered that your birth certificate is a fake."

Owen started to say something, already defending himself against charges of collaboration, when his brain caught up and registered the colonel's words. His mouth snapped shut in shock. "Excuse me?"

"Yes. Your birth certificate, the one listing David and Ellen Manning as your birth parents, is a forgery. We've looked, and it seems to have been faked when you were an infant. Judging from the look on your face, you didn't know anything about this?"

"I sure as hell did not," Owen said, sounding more aggressive than he meant. "What exactly are you saying, Colonel? That my parents aren't my parents?"

Martinson held his hands out, palms up, and shrugged. "Truth is, we don't know," he said. "What we do know is that the doctor who signed your birth certificate was a chiropractor, not a gynecologist or a pediatrician. And his license to practice was revoked years before he signed it. He was known for trafficking in fake documents, among other unsavory practices. He ended up in the slammer, doing ten plus, when they finally got the goods on him. He was virtually broke when they tried him, but he was fortunate to have a high-powered white-shoe attorney volunteer to represent him pro bono. And guess who that was? None other than David Manning, Esquire. Well, that was the first red flag with the boys in DC. Then there were the hospital records. Or should I say lack of them. We checked. The birth certificate stated you were born in New York General Hospital, but there were no records to confirm that."

Owen took a deep breath. "How sure are you of this? This is a hell of a thing to lay on a man."

"We're certain," Martinson said. "We've checked this twenty-five ways to Sunday. And, uh, that's not the end."

"There's more? What else could there possibly be?"

"Well, when all this came out, the obvious question is what David and Ellen Manning were up to when they had this faked. Why go through all this trouble? So, we looked into them."

"You investigated my parents?" Owen said, anger creeping into his voice as he forgot all about his concerns over Hanz. "I hope you have a good explanation why the government is doing this."

Martinson shrugged. "We're not in the business of leaving stones unturned, Professor. And yes, I'm sure you'd agree that, considering your position and the situation the world is in now, that extra caution is warranted."

When Owen didn't respond, Martinson continued, "You knew your mother was born in England? And that's she's a Brit?"

"Of course, I did. That's no state secret."

"Did you know that she and your father crossed on the *Titanic* in April 1912?"

"Well, that was family lore, but it never really was topic for discussion. I assumed my mother didn't like to talk about it. I figured it was too traumatic. And my father died when I was six years old, so it was not something a kid would discuss."

"Right. David and Ellen Manning crossed on the *Titanic*. We verified this with White Star Lines. Then we checked the immigration records. In the records, your mom, a British citizen, was admitted to the United States of America on April 18, 1912. As part of the journal entry, the immigration officer notated: 'With unaccompanied child, Gregory Alkins.'"

"Gregory who?"

"Gregory Alkins. Ever hear of him?"

"No."

"Well, here's where it gets interesting. We checked with White Star Line and found records that showed a Grace Alkins, a Scot, was a passenger with her son, Gregory. Apparently, Grace was from a small Scottish village called Arbroath and was immigrating to the United States but was lost a sea when the *Titanic* sunk. The assumption was that her two-year-old son perished with her. But then, ah, we discovered something else during the background check. Ellen Manning, your mother, never had children. We confirmed with her doctor. She was infertile."

Owen gasped, beginning to see where this was going.

"So," Martinson said, "here's where that leaves us. We believe that Ellen and David Manning booked passage on the *Titanic* from Liverpool to New York on their honeymoon. Young newlyweds with the world ahead of them. But we all know what happened then. The ship went down, taking more than fifteen hundred souls down with her. But 706 people survived, David and Ellen Manning among them. As I'm sure you know, the survivors were rescued by the *Carpathia* and taken to New York City, where they were processed, treated for medical needs as needed, and sorted out. At some point, we believe David and Ellen Manning found a boy alone, Gregory Alkins, who had managed to survive somehow but was on his own. And there's no record of this, but we believe something caused David and Ellen to make the decision to pass off Gregory Alkins as their own child."

Owen swallowed hard. "And you…you're saying that I'm this Gregory Alkins, is that where I understand you're heading?"

Martinson nodded. "Yes."

"Do you have any proof of this? You're accusing my parents of being liars, of tricking me my whole life."

"We can't speak to what they've told you or said, and we're not trying to. Professor, it's entirely possible they made this decision to protect that boy, keep him out of the orphanage. Who knows? They might be Good Samaritans. But there are several coincidences that we believe support this theory."

"Go on."

"When David and Ellen were processed through Immigration after the *Carpathia* landed, we have a clear record of them listing a two-year-old child accompanying them. We know for a certainty they had no children when they boarded the *Titanic*. And what's more, the name on the immigration form for the child was Gregory Alkins so noted to be traveling with your parents. Possibly, Gregory Alkins became Owen Manning when your folks left the harbor that night. And, interestingly enough, it just so happens that Owen was the first name of the immigration officer who stamped the papers."

Owen was dazed. His mind raced. For all his life, he had been Owen Manning, and now, according to this colonel, he was not.

"I'm not sure what to say, Colonel," Owen finally spluttered. "This is … just … unbelievable. I thought you were here because of my brother-in-law. Now I almost wish you were."

Martinson nodded slightly. "I can imagine, and I'm sorry there's no way to break news like this easily. For the record, we do know all about Hanz Weber. He doesn't exactly keep a low profile."

"You know he's a Nazi?"

"Of course. And we're aware of their professional interest in you, Dr. Manning. Like us, the Nazis believe that the work you're doing may just wind up ending this war, and they're doing their own parallel work. We're literally racing against them." Martinson leaned forward and gave Owen a hard look. "Are you saying Hanz has attempted to recruit you?"

"Hmm?" Owen's mind was still racing, memories of his parents now flashing through his brain. "Oh. Recruit me? It wasn't him, but yes. First at my wedding and then later at the Nobel ceremony, with Hanz and then later with a guy named Dinkendorf, they've approached me. I'm assuming you already know about this too?"

"No, actually we didn't." Martinson's voice was cold. "You didn't report this?"

"What was there to report? I told them I had nothing to say to them."

"Dr. Manning, I'm not sure you appreciate how serious this is. We know the Nazis have spy networks throughout the United States. They know the nature of your work. You have to assume they're watching you."

"First you tell me I'm not who I think I am, that my parents faked my birth certificate, and now you're telling me that the Nazis are spying on me!" Owen erupted. "Jesus!"

"My point is that you need to be aware, careful. You think it's an accident I'm here? The work that you're doing with your colleagues at MIT is important, and it's only the tip of the iceberg. The truth is, Dr. Manning, I'm here to make you an offer."

Owen slumped back, emotionally exhausted and needing time to process everything he'd just heard. "What kind of offer?"

"Let's face it, Dr. Manning, you're one of the world's foremost experts on certain aspects of nuclear physics. In addition to funding programs like the one at MIT, the Department of the Army has its own program. It's top secret, but it's years ahead of the work you're doing now, more focused. Vital to the war effort, you might say."

"What kind of program?"

"I'm not at liberty to say just yet, but let's just say there is a team of world-renowned scientists, the best of the best, who are working on something big, really big. Something that could turn the tide of the war. They need some help in an area in which you have unique expertise. I've been authorized to come here today and first debrief you on what we found, but also ask if you'd be willing to take a meeting and learn more about joining this project. It would be your patriotic duty."

"My duty?" Owen scoffed. "You just told me I'm not even a U.S. citizen."

"I also just told you the Nazis are most likely spying on you. We can offer you and your wife protection. You'd be working at a top-secret lab, completely beyond the reach of any German spies."

"A lab? Where?"

"I can't say."

"But…what about my job here? And my wife. She just—"

"We've worked it out with MIT. They'll grant you a sabbatical and pay your salary for the duration. As for your wife, military hospitals are always in need of good doctors. We'd accommodate her too."

"I not so sure that would be very welcomed by my wife. She has a specialty that is in demand at big-city hospitals, not remote military facilities. I'm not sure she is going to uproot her career after all she has invested, and I wouldn't dream of asking her to do so."

"Dr. Manning, I hope you understand, that this is a matter of urgent national importance. We're talking about ending the war, saving millions of lives, sir."

"Is that what we're talking about?"

"Yes. So, here's all we ask. Give us consideration. Talk to your wife and impress upon her how important this could be. And how we can protect you and your family as part of it. And then there's the bonus."

"Bonus? Money? I'm a scientist, not an entrepreneur, and my wife is a doctor, not a businesswoman."

"No, Dr. Manning I'm not talking money. The bonus I am offering is priceless, it isn't for sale and cannot be bought.

Manning gave the officer a perplexed look and listened carefully.

"You see, under an emergency war act, certain powers have been granted to the War Department for extraordinary circumstances, and this certainly qualifies. As part of the bargain, the government will grant both you and your wife immediate United States citizenship with all the rights and protections that come with it. And as a further inducement we will make all the potential charges against your mother for fraudulently taking you as her child disappear. We'll give you forty-eight hours, Dr. Manning, to make a decision."

Martinson abruptly stood up. "Think about it, Dr. Manning. We're all in this together, sir, and with all due respect, if I could make the kind of contribution you may be able to, I wouldn't hesitate."

He left Owen alone and bewildered, unsure of what to think. His whole life seemed like it had shifted and turned upside down. He wasn't even supposed to be Owen Manning anymore, but a lost child named Gregory Alkins. The subject of Nazi spying. And now this mysterious offer that seemed like it wasn't completely voluntary. What would he tell Lonnie? How could he tell her that the Army wanted them to move to some top-secret base, and she'd have to give up her new job to work in an Army hospital? And what exactly were they doing in this lab? Owen could only imagine they were creating a devastating new weapon—everybody knew the potential of nuclear power—and he wasn't sure he wanted any part in unleashing that on the world.

No, all he knew was that he needed to go home, have a stiff drink, and do some serious thinking. He was now going to be a father—news he'd just learned—which was the most important thing. All his decisions had to take that and Lonnie into account. Life was getting complicated. For now, he decided, he wouldn't say anything about his parents and the *Titanic* to Lonnie or his mother, not until he knew how he felt about it. Not until he believed it.

CHAPTER TWENTY
You're in the Army Now!

Boston, 1942

LONNIE SAT AT THE HEAD OF THE BED AND LISTENED CARE-fully to Owen. "What do you mean you accepted a commission? Why? How could you? I thought you were 4F."

Owen felt miserable, but he plowed ahead, hoping he could get her to understand. "I know. I am. They're making a lot of exceptions here, Lonnie. No basic training, and it's not like I'd be in the infantry. And…to be honest, they're not giving me much of a choice. I've talked to Army brass, the FBI, OSS, the whole damn group of them. They've made it pretty clear that I either agree or the lab at MIT will suddenly find it harder to get the funding they need."

"But why?" Lonnie said. "Why you? Why now?"

"It's top secret, but it's about my work with nuclear physics. I'll be working in a lab stateside. They probably won't even give me a gun, thank God."

"Oh, Owen!" Lonnie said, fighting off hysteria. "I don't know where to begin. This will turn our lives upside down. We are having a baby in just seven months. I like our lives here! And what about my work? Where is this new lab?"

"I don't know. Somewhere out west in the desert. We won't know the location until we arrive."

Lonnie was trying not to cry from frustration—she knew there was a war on, knew that husbands, fathers, brothers, and sons from all over the country were fighting and dying in foreign lands. But it still felt so unfair. Owen was supposed to be exempted from all that. She knew she was being selfish, but she didn't want the war coming into their little family any more than it already had. She'd already lost too many nights' sleep worrying about her mother in The Hague, where the Nazis were firmly in control now and had set up an informal command in Schaduwgazon.

She took a deep breath to steady herself. "When then? At least they've told you that?"

If it was possible, Owen looked even more miserable now. "About ten days. MIT has agreed to keep me on staff with a paid sabbatical while we're gone. And the Army will provide housing. And, uh, there's a hospital on base."

"A hospital?" she echoed. "So what? They're going to offer me a job now too? Working in an Army hospital in the desert?"

"Yes, that's what they said."

Her frustration was replaced with anger in flash. "Well, that's a great consolation prize," she said. "I was looking forward to actually practicing in my field until I couldn't anymore from the pregnancy. I'm guessing this hospital doesn't have a pediatric unit?"

Owen looked up at her with his big brown eyes filled with guilt. "You know they don't, nothing like Boston … but maybe they deliver babies," he said softly. In fact, her unit at Boston was renowned nationwide for groundbreaking treatment. "I'm sorry, baby. I really am. It's just…a lot of people are being called up, and now I'm one of them." He paused and swallowed hard. "There is one option. You can stay here in Boston while I go. A lot of men are away from their families right now. You can stay here and practice until you can't any longer, then come out to join me when it's getting closer to…the time." He gestured at her belly.

The first words that rose to her lips were an accusation that somehow Owen wanted to leave her behind and go off, leave her to fend for herself as she became more pregnant. But she bit them off before they could spill out. Her darling man was in front of her looking as miserable as a child who got caught breaking the rules.

"Owen, I have to be honest. This is a lot to take in. I shouldn't say anything more right now. Let's sleep on it. We can talk tomorrow."

That night, Owen held her until she drifted off, her mind spinning with anxious and angry thoughts. She was mad at the Army for dragging Owen into this, mad at the Germans for starting a war in the first place, and angry with herself for being selfish. And underneath it, she realized, she was scared: What if Owen was wrong? What if the Army did give him a gun and make him actually fight? In the darkness of the long night, that seemed like a real possibility. When she finally did drift off, her sleep was restless and filled with shapeless dreams.

The next morning, she was up early, and Owen found her in the kitchen making coffee.

"Good morning, sweetheart," he said, sitting at the small table watching her.

"Good morning, Owen." She put a mug of coffee on the table and sat down with him. "I've thought most of the night about what you said. You should have asked me before you accepted the commission." She held her hand up when he started to talk, "But I've accepted that you were in a difficult position. And I won't say I'm not upset about it. I don't want to move. I wanted to practice here and have our baby here in Boston, where we met, where we live. But…I know you did too." She stifled a small sob and powered ahead. "And I know that as much as I wished for these things, there's a war on, and the whole world is making sacrifices. So many people are giving so much more. And I also know that you're an extraordinary man, and they wouldn't have come to you if they didn't think you could help. So, I'm not going to stay here alone without you, Owen. I'd rather do almost anything else in the world, including emptying bedpans, than be away from you for one minute longer than I have to. If you have to do your duty, then I'll do mine. Right alongside you."

When she finished talking, both of their eyes were filled with tears. At that moment , Owen loved Lonnie more than anything in life. He drew her close to him and put his hands on her tummy, the one that held the child they would love more than life. This moment would be one he never would forget, he suspected a life-changing one, for not only this little soon-to-be family but perhaps mankind.

He wished he knew how to explain to her that it wasn't just about moving, wasn't just about having their baby on a strange base. It was also about the work itself and how he was desperately afraid of what they were about to ask him to do. But just like the news about his parentage and the *Titanic*, he couldn't burden her with that now. She was making a sacrifice for him, and he was grateful.

"Sweetheart, I don't know what to say," he said, smiling despite the emotions coursing through him. "We are entering unchartered waters and will make this journey an adventure. But I promise I will do my level best to make this right. And thank you. I don't know what I'd do without you."

"Hopefully, you'll never have to find out," she said.

CHAPTER TWENTY-ONE
It Ain't Boston

The Manhattan Project, Los Alamos, New Mexico 1942

WHILE BEING BRIEFED IN WASHINGTON, D.C., OWEN WAS QUIETLY SWORN *in as an American citizen. Three days later at Boston's Custom House and on the way to Hanscom air force base, Lonnie pledged her allegiance in front of a federal judge and became a citizen.*

Life at the base quickly settled into a routine. Being the newest physician, Lonnie was assigned the swing shift at the hospital but hoped to change to regular working hours as soon as possible. Her specialty, pediatrics was in low demand because very few babies were quartered on base. The chief of staff assigned her GP duties, so her day was filled with aches and pains.

Owen made good on his promise to Lonnie when he insisted on having a meeting with General Orley Miller, Commanding Officer of the Manhattan Project. Given Owen's reputation and the importance of his addition to the team, the general was all ears.

"Good morning, sir, I'm Captain Owen Miller."

"At ease, Captain. My adjutant tells me that you are just now arriving and had a personal matter to discuss."

"Yes, sir, that is correct."

"Well, Captain, get to the point."

"You see, General, I was recruited to join the project because of certain specialties I can bring to the table. At MIT, the War Department approached me, and, well, here I am."

"I'm fully aware of your background. The Department of the Army has made special efforts to keep you and your wife happy and comfortable."

"Yes, sir, and the quarters that is being provided are great." Owen was referring to a large Spanish-style villa just a few miles from the base. It came fully furnished and included Rosa, a live-in housekeeper.

"So, Captain, you are comfortable?"

"Well, yes and no."

The general looked past his half-glasses and stared at Owen: "You want more?"

"Not for me, sir, but for my wife."

"Oh, I see, happy wife, happy life. What does the little woman want? A new dishwasher or maybe one of those new ironing machines?"

"No, sir, nothing like that. You see, my wife, Lonnie, is a highly trained pediatric surgeon and was in active practice in Boston. She had to give it up when I was commissioned and assigned to Los Alamos."

"And that's a problem? Doesn't sound like one to me."

"Yes, sir. Lonnie is uniquely qualified and one of the few women in the country, maybe even the world to specialize as a pediatric surgeon, and she doesn't want to give up her work after seven grueling years of study. She has worked tirelessly and has distinguished herself."

"I see. Well, she can work here in our base infirmary. They are always in need of a good doctor."

"Lonnie is a lot more than a GP and putting her in a base infirmary would be like putting you in charge of the mess hall."

The general smiled and got the message. "Look, Manning, I not sure what can be done, but like they say, you're in the army now, and it is what it is."

Owen knew that if he didn't pull all the punches out now, nothing would be resolved. "Yes, sir, I completely understand, but you know us geniuses, we can't work when we aren't happy, it's much too distracting. And like you said, a happy wife is a happy life, and I'm pretty sure that's not going to be the case." He took a deep breath, not believing that he just threatened the highest-ranking officer he ever met.

"Captain, it looks like you are delivering a message. I think it goes something like this: if we don't find a way to make your wife happy, you'll be unable to give us a hundred percent?"

"That's pretty much it, sir."

The general was getting used to dealing with these thin-skinned, temperamental scientists from the start of the Manhattan Project. Dr. Oppenheimer, for one, was especially a prima donna. He insisted that the army paint his lab blue because he hated standard-issue green. It made him grumpy, so he said. When the post commander pushed back, he squealed like a pig and threatened to pick up his marbles and go home. Blue it was, three days later.

"Well, I hear you loud and clear. Let me see what can be done. I understand there is a rather sophisticated research hospital in Albuquerque, some fifty-eight miles from here; it's part of the University of New Mexico. Let me make some calls and see what I can find out."

Owen was visited by Major Peter Randle, his direct superior officer, two days later. The major informed Owen that the UNM was interested in talking with his wife to fill the chief of pediatrics position. Since the hospital was an hour's ride, the army would provide a car and driver. Lonnie was thrilled with the opportunity to be at a large teaching hospital and jumped at the chance.

Four months after Owen arrived at Los Alamos, New Mexico, he was promoted to military assistant to Dr. Robert Oppenheimer, director of the top-secret Manhattan Project. The team worked twenty-four-hour days with twelve-hour shifts.

Their work progressed rapidly, but they soon reached a significant roadblock. The excruciating standstill was the topic of discussion in a Wednesday-morning staff meeting. The project scientists and army brass filed into the underground bunker, which housed the main headquarters for the Manhattan Project. It was a grim, windowless room with virtually no décor; three-foot thick cement walls covered with blackboards, graphs, and maps all with pull-down shades to hide their content. A low clicking sound came from a section of the room filled with human computers, mostly men and some women, working with a variety of mechanical aids to perform numerical analysis of complex formulas relating to nuclear fission. The sophisticated analog computers, the size of typewriters, hummed day and night as a legion of data experts crunched numbers and solved mathematical equations.

General Miller, commanding officer of the project, opened the meeting with a question aimed at Dr. Oppenheimer.

"Let me see if I understand you, Dr. Oppenheimer. It seems that the project's critical elements are well on their way, if not already completed, and have passed quality control scrutiny. Am I correct?"

"Yes, General Miller, we are almost there. But we have a problem with the vessel. Nuclear fusion happens when atomic nuclei of low atomic number fuse to form a heavier nucleus, releasing significant energy. Our problem, gentlemen, is that we have not come up with a vessel that can tolerate the radioactive material without prematurely degenerating."

Owen listened carefully as Oppenheimer went into detail and was followed by two other team members, one a physicist and the other a chemical engineer. They mapped out the science and chemistry of the problem.

Owen waited for a pause in the conversation and addressed the elderly general, a full-framed man with an army whitewall haircut. "Excuse me, General," Owen interjected. "I have a colleague, an English civilian employed by Britain's Department of War. He is working on ceramic technology at Oxford in England. He attended MIT with me, and we pledged Kappa Sigma together. But most importantly, he's my best friend. His project is a joint venture with the U.S. Navy and the British War Office. They were working on payload issues not too dissimilar to ours. Last time we spoke, we discussed some breakthroughs they had with dymoceramic vessels associated with torpedo payloads. With your permission, I'd be glad to contact him and see if he has any further developments that would be of value."

"Any port in a storm, Dr. Manning. How do we get in touch with him?"

"I'll write and see what he has got to say."

The general walked over to Owen's side of the table: "Way too slow, Manning. And dangerous too. We have to suspect everyone. I'll have operations set up an overseas call on an encrypted line. You can qualify the value of his research's relevancy, and if that pans out, it may justify a trip over there to see what they have. I'll talk to Admiral Callaway after we discuss your call. He'll need to approve any inter-service coordination."

*****

Within thirty-six hours, Owen received orders. He was to be on a military transport plane heading to a top-secret British airbase outside of London, just beyond Oxford University. He was taken aback by the speed of this decision. Had he realized that he was going to be sent overseas and leave his beautiful and very pregnant wife he probably would have not made his suggestion. That night he told Lonnie what happened.

"What do you mean you're going to Europe? How could you? We are having a baby! Europe is a very dangerous place right now. My mother will tell you that firsthand. How did this happen?"

"Please Lonnie, calm down. I don't know exactly how it happened. Our project is at an impasse, and we need some outside expertise. I just mentioned that Winney could be helpful because of his work in the UK, and the next thing you know they put me on a plane."

Lonnie gave Owen an incredulous stare: "It was your idea?"

"No, no, not my idea at all! But since I knew Winney, they figured I would be the best one to go." Owen could tell by the look on Lonnie's face that he was in trouble.

Lonnie's fury changed to fear. "Oh God, Owen. By all accounts Europe is being destroyed. Thousands of people killed right in their own beds. You could be one of them! I don't want our child raised without a father … like both of us were. You can't go. No, you just can't!

Owen walked towards Lonnie and put his arms around his now sobbing wife. "Lonnie, I have no choice. It's an order. And besides, this could lead to the resolution of what's stalling the project. If we solve the problem the war will end, and everyone will have their husbands and fathers back home."

Lonnie pulled Owen so close that he could actually feel the baby's kicks. "Owen, I love you, and I don't what to be without you. You know I'd do anything for you but having you in harm's way is just too much."

"I know, my love. But hopefully this will help the Allies. I will do everything I can to come home safely—and soon—to you."

*****

The plane landed, and a bright red MG convertible pulled onto the tarmac, and the door flew open: "Hey, Duck, how the hell are you?"

"Winney, is that you?"

"Sure as shit is. Wow, look at you, a captain! I thought you were 4F?"

"I am, but they made an exception. And look at you, still a civilian."

"Yea, as long as I bloody can. When they told me you were arriving today, I volunteered to pick you up. So come on, let's hustle, my mates are waiting for us back at headquarters. Hop in. I got some good hooch in my briefcase."

"Nice ride. Is it yours?"

"A perk from the British government. They wanna keep me happy."

"Nice. All I got was this uniform and a decent place to live."

"Tell me about Lonnie, is she good?"

"Yeah, very pregnant at the moment, due pretty soon. She's working as Chief of Pediatrics at the University of New Mexico and doing a bang-up job, getting to do some surgery too. I'm hoping to get out of here as soon as possible so as not to miss the big event. She could have the baby early!

"Good thinking, Owen, I don't think she would appreciate you missing it. Come on, let's go somewhere and catch up and then figure out a way to solve your problem and get you back home."

Winney's MG streaked down the Bath Road, heading further away from London. Owen, tired from the transatlantic flight, was nodding off as the roadster turned off the main road and up a quiet lane and then onto a long, tree-lined drive.

"Where is this place, Winney?"

"It's a little place my father gave me last year. It's called it Ashton Hall, but I call it Love Shack. I bet you can't guess why?"

"I don't need to; I already know."

The MG came to a halt in front of a beautiful Georgian country home. It wasn't an original but an exact replica of one. The façade was freshly painted a pale cream color, which accentuated the dark wood-framed windows. On top of the third story sat four symmetrical dormers like a row of crows.

"How do you like it, Duck?"

"Pretty swanky; I'd say it's swell."

"I'm glad you like it. You know my home is your home, so come in, and Gertrude will take good care of you."

"Gertrude? Come on, Winney, I'm a happily married man and about to be a father, so I'll pass on Gertrude and all the rest of your concubines. "

Winney burst into laughter. "So would I. Gertrude is the housekeeper and came with the house, probably older than the house. Trust me, she's a daft cow, but she cooks like a Cordon Bleu chef. Wait 'til you see her; she's the size of Buckingham Palace, counting stables."

The friends walked into the manor house's great hall and were greeted by the portly housekeeper, who collected Owen's valises and scurried up the grand staircase. "There is a fire in your study, sir, and some fresh scones coming up right away."

"Skip the scones, Gertrude, but a bucket of ice would be lovely. Make it two; there is going to be some serious drinking going on."

By the time the clock in the hall chimed seven, Owen and Winney were on their fourth scotch and feeling no pain.

"Duck, do you know how lucky you are?" Winney said.

"Me, lucky? Yeah, but are you kidding me? You got it all. Incredible looks, a body like a Greek God, girls chasing you wherever you go, a bottomless barrel of money, at least a couple of mansions, not to mention a goddamn title, and to boot, you're a frigging brilliant rocket scientist—and you call me lucky? God!"

Winney took another gulp of his drink and patted the arm of the massive leather sofa, as to say, "if you only knew." In a slightly alcohol-induced slur, he opened up to his friend for the first time.

"It's not all that it seems. Sure, I'm lucky, one could even say blessed, but I'd trade places with you and a lot of other blokes too if I could."

Owen opened his mouth but could not find the right words and decided to just sit back and listen.

"I know this may seem ridiculous, but everything I am or have has been given to me. Sure, I made it to Oxford and MIT, but to me, that was child's play. It was easy and filled my time."

Winney took another slug. "After a while, I began acting the way people expected me to act. You know, running around, drinking, partying all the time, and not taking anyone or anything seriously, especially myself. I looked into the mirror every morning and shaved a pretty face, but one with nothing behind it, no character or meaning."

Owen saw the pain in Winney's eyes.

"When I was growing up, lots of people hung around me because I had a lot of stuff and access. But I had no friends. The truth be told, no one wanted to be around someone who was better-looking, smarter, and richer than them. Or someone like me who didn't have a sincere bone in his body and thought less of himself than they did of him."

Winney tripped over toward the butler's table and poured another drink, adding two ice cubes.

"You know you are my only real friend, the first and only one. Sure, there are lots of hangers-on and wannabees, but none worth a pound."

Owen blinked in recognition of Winney's compliment but said nothing. He realized that Winney was not only being cathartic, but well on his way to a massive hangover in the morning

"Look, I've said enough. But it feels good to get this off my chest. To know that at least one person knows that I know."

"Know what, Winney?"

"That I am a fraud. I have the depth of a sheet of parchment paper and can't hold a candle to the real people, people that count, people like you. And there are things about me that are… well, shameful, skeletons in my closet that haunt me." Winney sighed. "You know, when the war broke out, it was a time when men had to measure up, and I knew I could not."

Another moment of silence and another long sip. "Duck, you know why I'm not in the army?"

"Yeah, your father pulled some strings, and that was that."

"Right, but the reason he pulled strings was that I begged him to. I was afraid. Not in a cowardly way, but fearful that I would bugger it up and get somebody killed because I was so incapable of being a leader. You know, just being smart doesn't make you one."

"But you are making a contribution, Win. Your fantastic work in the lab, the scientific research you've done, all that counts."

"Not for me. Like I say, child's play, all that stuff is easy-peasy. It doesn't count, at least not to me."

"You got this all wrong. You are a great guy. Don't sell yourself short."

"I wish I could agree. My life is loveless and a sham."

"Don't say that. People love you; your parents do for sure."

"My parents love me because they have to; they are my parents. As a father, you'll find that out for yourself soon enough. Sure, I've been in lust, but never in love. What I'm talking about is the kind of love people earn through mutual admiration and respect. I've never known that, and let's face it, I don't deserve it either.

"But enough of my bellyaching." Winney rose from the sofa, looked around the stunning room and shrugged. "Look at this place, I don't deserve it, but I am what I am. Maybe someday I'll find the real me, one that everyone will like, and more importantly, one that I, myself will like."

Winney loosened his tie, unbuttoned the first two buttons of his Bond Street custom-made shirt, and changed the subject. "Look, Owen, you got a few days to get settled. But come Monday, we are going to a factory where we have a lab. So, take it easy until then. I promise you, from then on, it will be no bloody picnic, you'll soon see. Tomorrow I'll drive you to London."

CHAPTER TWENTY-TWO
MY TUB RUNNETH OVER

The Bismark Hotel, London

"OWEN, IS THAT YOU? I CAN BARELY HEAR YOU."

"It's me, sweetheart. I can hear you. Are you all right?"

"Yes, where are you?"

"Officially, I can't exactly say, but it's near where I bought you that locket on our honeymoon."

Lonnie instantly knew he was in London. Her mind raced back to those unforgettable two weeks when they explored not only London but each other. The stunning suite at the Ritz that her mother arranged as a wedding gift filled her memory. She recalled crowded London preparing for the inevitable, with most everyone in drab green military uniforms. Tourists still visited the sites, but a palpable sense of anxiety swirled in the air like a warning: "Beware, dark war clouds are forming."

Lonnie reminisced how she savored the luxury of silky, crisp sheets that were changed every day in preparation for a night of sheer ecstasy. The overwhelming feeling of excitement flooded her mind despite the gloomy atmosphere of impending war out-side on the streets. She remembered her sense of completeness when Owen made love to her and the lust she felt as he entered her willing and beautiful body time and time again. Owen loved her in every conceivable way, and she loved Owen so entirely it was impossible to describe.

A smile crept over her face as she remembered the commotion when the tub overflowed, and a frantic housemaid, followed by the enraged assistant manager, banged on their door: "Sir, there is something wrong. Sir, are you there?"

A key was forcefully inserted, and the door flung open, allowing an entourage of hotel staff to enter the room. Poor Owen was lying stark naked on the bed.

"What has happened? Madame." The maid covered her eyes, pretending not to see Owen's privates.

"Whatever do you mean?"

"It's the water, water everywhere. From the loo. Perhaps it's the tub!"

"Buggers, I forgot…I drew a bath. We just sat down for a minute and before you know it…well…"

"Well indeed," the assistant manager had indignantly snorted. "I know full well what was going on here. It would be appropriate if you two could get yourselves decent so I can send a couple of porters in to mop up this mess."

Owen covered himself. Sensing the manager's misconception: "We're on our honeymoon, and this isn't some sort of after-noon tryst."

"Your honeymoon! Of course, you are," the manager sarcastically replied. "I didn't come down in last night's rain." The manager clicked his fingers to signal a couple of porters waiting at the door. "Sort this out."

"Lonnie, are you there, sweetheart?"

Jolted back to the present, Lonnie pressed the phone to her ear. "Yes, darling, I'm here. I'm doing fine. Dr. Martalone says it is just a matter of days now. Can you come home?"

"Oh, how I would love that, but it's impossible. I am losing sleep over it. I am so sorry, sweetheart. I'm only just getting started on some pretty important things; I just can't leave. But I will be with you in my heart. Remember, you promised me a boy!"

"But what if it's a girl?"

"I'll love her as much as I love you. And I'm not worried, the next one would be a boy."

"Next one? Let's just get this one out of the oven and then we'll see."

"So, my love, how's it going in Los Alamos? Everything okay at the University?"

"Good…just fine. Do you remember when we first arrived and met Courtney O'Reilly? She's a counselor at the University now, and we have lunch most days. Her husband is a munitions expert here on base. We are getting to be pretty good friends. She hasn't said anything, but I suspect she might be pregnant too."

"I'm glad you have a friend you can rely on, especially with me gone."

Lonnie heard some shouting in the background. "What on earth is going on?"

"Oh, that's some of the guys. They came to pick me up for dinner. Winney is here too."

"Winney, how is he?"

"I'm not sure. We had a chat the other night and, well, I'm not sure."

"Maybe it's the war. Nobody is feeling jolly these days."

"Maybe, but I don't think so. I gotta go, darling. I love you, sweetheart. I'll be thinking of you. Now go and make me a proud papa."

"OK, and send Winney my love, I miss seeing him."

The connection broke before Lonnie could say her final words. She whispered them anyway into an empty phone: "I love you, too, and I'll be praying for you and Winney and all the men every night. Please come home."

Lonnie's call was not just one to say hello and when Owen hastily ended the conversation she was, in a way, grateful. What she wanted to tell Owen was that she had the oddest feeling that she was being observed when she walked the village streets outside the base and around the university campus. She carefully looked a number of times but just didn't see anyone. No, she thought, it was more of a feeling than a sighting. She was glad she didn't say anything to Owen. After all, he had his hands full over there, and besides, it was probably her overactive pregnant imagination playing tricks on her. In the end, she chalked it up to being jumpy about her soon-to-be delivery date and Owen being so far away from her.

CHAPTER TWENTY-THREE
DIVINE PROVIDENCE

OWEN FELT THAT WINDING UP IN ENGLAND WAS IN SOME WAY divine providence. London was only a few hours' train ride from Scotland, where he hoped he could find the missing pieces to the puzzle the colonel had unveiled when they met at MIT.

On Saturday morning, determined to find the truth about who he was, Owen rose at five in the morning, the sky still dark, and grabbed a cab to Victoria Station, to catch the 5:45 Royal Scotlander to Hamilton. Bomb craters in the streets made difficult going for the taxi to maneuver the roadway. As he rode through the city streets he couldn't believe his eyes. This city, which had welcomed him and Lonnie, and provided memories for a lifetime from their honeymoon, was now so surreal. Destruction was everywhere. A stale odor filled the air, one of burning debris and death. This was Owen's first time up close to the horrors of war on the civilian population. He wondered: would his work make him part of the problem rather than the solution?

"So, Guv," the cabbie asked, " Ever seen anything like this? Those Nazi bastards make every night a nightmare."

Owen, practically speechless, could barely respond, his voice a whisper. "No nothing like this."

The cab arrived at Victoria station, which was a shell of the building it once was.

He thought it utterly amazing that the trains could still run given the conditions, but with the British determination, they did.

Owen had done his research and confirmed that the Alkins clan originated in a place called Arbroath, which had no direct train service from London. After a while he stopped looking out of the window, or at least till he left London city limits. He couldn't bear to see what mankind was doing to their fellow mankind. At Hamilton, Owen changed to a local train and arrived in Arbroath around lunchtime. Several times his train was side-railed to allow military transport trains the right of way. Eventually the train arrived two hours late.

Arbroath was a picturesque seaside village where the sun shined and the air, unlike London, was so clean it smelled like freshly laundered linens. Owen thought it was a charming place, seemingly unspoiled by modern times and so far seemingly untouched by war. He strolled around the Common and peered into the shops. A butcher shop next to a greengrocer and that next to a general store framed the green.

Several souvenir shops sprinkled around the center featured almost authentic Scottish memorabilia. Owen spotted a little red tartan kilt in the window and made a mental note that if he had time, he would return and purchase it for his soon-to-be-born child. He laughed and thought it didn't matter whether the baby was a boy or a girl since a kilt worked for both.

That thought brought him back to the time Lonnie had told him that she was expecting, just before they left for Los Alamos. It was a frigid night in Boston, with light snow falling as Owen returned late from the lab, dog tired.

"Hi, sweetheart. Bitter out there tonight. More snow predicted, too."

"Hi, honey, I'm so glad your home. You're right, the weather is dreadful. I was worried about your ride home and the slippery roads. That old car needs tires, and God knows when we will ever get any because of the shortages."

"The roads are not what's dangerous; it's the maniac Boston drivers you have to worry about. You'd think they would know how to drive in the snow."

"Yeah, they should. Boston gets lots of it. You know this weather reminds me of when I was growing up in The Hague. We didn't have much snow, but the days were gray and cold, just like Boston in the winter. Are you hungry?"

"Nah, I grabbed a bite at the cafeteria—a dog and some fries. Yucky, but filling. Did you eat?"

"Yeah, at the hospital. It was a busy day but one of the best."

"Really, one of the best? Why's that?"

"Well, I went over to see Dr. Longworth, and he gave me some incredible news."

"You got that promotion! Wow!"

"No. Better than that."

"Come on, don't get me all worked up. Tell me."

"Well, he sat me down and said that Owen Manning is going to be a father."

"Who?"

"You, you dolt."

"Me? A father? Oh, my God."

Owen raced over and embraced Lonnie. "Wow, a father. I wasn't expecting that."

"No, silly, I'm the one who is expecting. Are you okay with it, I mean, having a baby?"

"No, not okay, I'm thrilled, excited, surprised, jubilant! I can't believe it. A father!" Owen grabbed Lonnie and waltzed her around the kitchen. "A father, holy mackerel. Wait till our moms hear that they're going to be grandmas! They won't believe it."

Owen and Lonnie lay on the sofa and watched the glowing fire in their charming Commonwealth Avenue townhouse. Lonnie nestled her head on Owen's broad shoulders. Their minds drifted as they wondered what the future would bring. Parenthood, the war… how would it affect them and their child? Things were not good. Thousands of young men were being drafted into service. Shortages and rationing were commonplace taking their vicious bite into the once-idyllic American society. The news reported that Europe was on fire and that the Germans were relentlessly pushing their conquests.

Life had been so good for them, and now it was getting even better with this exciting news. But dark clouds loomed. Was this the best time to bring a new life into the world? Who knew what the future held?

"It's going to be a boy, right?"

"I don't know, Owen, maybe not."

"I don't care, Lonnie, a girl is perfect, especially if she turns out like you. How could I not love her?"

Lonnie held Owen closer and spoke her thoughts. "I'm a little bit scared, you know."

"Of what? You're a doctor, and you deal with babies all the time. You know all about these things."

"Not that, silly. I'm scared of how our lives will change, and I'm worried that war is making everything upside down. I'm frightened about my mother over there, alone and surrounded by evil and treachery, and that she will never get to see our child and be a grandma, and then there's my job. How will I manage with a baby?"

"Your job? Don't worry about that. You don't have to work; we'll have plenty."

"But I *want* to work. It's my life, and I put far too much into it to walk away."

"Lonnie, there are no guarantees in life. But one thing you can count on is that whatever happens, we are a team, soon to be a team of three. Together we will face everything, you, me, and number three."

"How about number four?"

"Her too."

A car horn brought Owen back to the Arbroath Village Common and his mission at hand. After a short walk, he checked into the Seaforth. The Victorian-style hotel was situated directly on the ocean.

"So, sir, what's your fancy at Arbroath? Here for some sea air and a bit of rest?" the chatty porter inquired as he walked Owen to his room.

"Some of both, perhaps."

"Well, sir, I bid your mind. Arbroath is a quiet place, but we've had a bit of excitement as of late. Sad to say, not the right kind of excitement. You see, a couple of German aircraft visited our wee village day before yesterday. The road and Common were strafed by machine gunfire. Several Polish soldiers playing football on the Common were mowed down. Poor wretches, bless their souls."

"I suppose there is no escaping it anymore, anywhere. Things are getting pretty bad all over. London's a mess. Bombs dropping every night. Destruction is pretty widespread."

"Damn Nazis. Devils, all of them."

They arrived at Owen's room, a front one with a nice view of the ocean. "Would you be requiring a good restaurant and a recommendation for a pub, sir?"

Before Owen could answer, the porter continued: "It be the Bonnie Bee or the Thistle's Thorn for a foamy pint and then McTherstan's for a chop right from the farm. If it were any fresher, it would be baaaaaaaahing."

"Thank you. May I ask you a question?"

"Aye, what might that be?"

"If I wanted to know about the Alkins family, who would I ask?"

"Alkins? Well, you can ask just about anyone. There is a lorryload of them all over Arbroath. The lord mayor for one. If you go to the Bonnie Bee tonight, you'll probably run into him. He holds court on Saturday night, and he knows everyone's business."

"Thanks, I'll give it a try." Owen flipped the porter a quid.

"Mighty kind of you, sir. And don't forget McTherstan's. My cousin owns it. If you fancy meat, try the chop. Tell him Aslow sent you. He'll give you an extra pint if you do."

Later, the Bonnie Bee was identical to every pub Owen had ever seen. Dark, smoky, a bit smelly, and filled with mostly men of all ages, each one trying to consume as much drink as possible.

He walked past the dartboard and the snooker table and took a stool at the bar. The tables were attended to by a middle-aged woman who had more than a few miles on her odometer. When asked, she pointed Owen toward the table where the mayor and his cronies sat in animated discussion. Owen walked over to introduce himself.

"Good evening, sir."

"Aye, an American. You give that away the moment you opened your mouth."

"I guess so, sir. But I was wondering if you could spare me a moment or two. I'm here in Arbroath trying to find some information about me and perhaps my family."

"*Guím gach rath ort*—I wish you well—but as you can see, I'm a bit occupied here, giving my mates a lesson in politics."

Own decided to play the vanity card. "But Mr. Mayor, I'm only here overnight, and I am so anxious to learn more about my background. From what I hear, you're the authority on just about everything in Arbroath."

"You don't say. And who'd be spreading that manure? Probably my bonnie lass wife. She calls me a know-it-all."

The men around the table laughed and poked each other like a bunch of high school sophomores.

"The lady got that right," howled one of the drinking partners.

Another one piped in: "The way I hear it, the mayor's little lady wears the trousers on Fannybrook farm."

"And they suit her," yelled another mate, followed by even more laughing and poking.

"Well, I asked around, and that's the word. The mayor is the man to ask."

"You married, mate?"

"What? Why would that make a difference whether you talk to me or not?"

"It doesn't. But I have a wee bonnie lass granddaughter at home who would take a fancy to a pretty boy like you."

Owen turned bright red. "Oh, I see Mr. Mayor. But I'm married and about to be a father anytime now. So, you might say I'm out of the market."

"Too bad. All right, I'll give you five minutes. What's on your mind, lad?"

Owen spoke as rapidly as possible, thinking that the mayor looked like a man of his word and five minutes meant five minutes and not a second more. Owen explained that he suspected he was Gregory Alkins and that, some thirty years ago, he had been taken to America by his mother, a woman named Grace Alkins.

The mayor abruptly stood up. "You are a bloody lying son of a bitch. And I mean that. Bloody hell! You aren't Gregory Alkins no more than the man in the moon. Now get your arse out of here, or me and my mates here will trounce the shit out of you."

"But, sir, wait, I meant no harm. I don't understand why you are so upset."

"Like I said, you bugger, get your arse out of here—now!"

Owen realized that if he didn't leave, he would be physically accosted and possibly end up in the slammer since the mayor more than likely was the judge, jury, and executioner around here.

The confrontation cause Owen to lose his appetite, so he walked back to the hotel and found the porter mopping the floor in the modest lobby. "So, lad, an early night of it? How did you like the pub? Did you find the mayor?"

"Sure did. And he wasn't too pleased with me."

"Aye, he's pretty dodgy, especially after a few drinks; he's not the happy sort. And rightly so, he has much to be unhappy about."

"Why's that?"

"Well, a long time ago, there was a wee scandal here in Arbroath. The mayor's reputation was greatly tarnished. You see, almost fifty years ago, there was this bloke, one of the world's finest association footballers. He was capped three times for Scotland and later played for Queen's Park, our leading Scottish club. Injured at thirty-two years old, the bloke retired here in Arbroath even though a lot of the townsfolk didn't like his kind. He married a local, and they settled down and had a son who grew up here. The lad was an athlete like his father, but a wee bit unbridled."

"Interesting. So, I assume the mayor was one of those folks who didn't like the footballer and his family?"

"Aye, but not at first, he respected the player's talent, until..."

"Until what?"

"Well, the footballer, who was called Watson, Andrew Watson, and his son Joshua didn't fit in. The family lived out of town on a sheep farm and kept pretty much to themselves. But this Joshua lad was a stallion who liked the lasses and did a lot of oat-sowing with the locals, if you get my drift. You see, he was a strapping young fellow, and the lasses around here found him sort of exotic."

"Not the average kilt-wearing Scott, I take it."

"*Go díreach.* Yes. So, one night this Joshua got caught by the mayor with his trousers down behind the Bonnie Bee. As if that wasn't bad enough, to make matters worse the young lass in the doggie position with her knickers down around her ankles turned out to be none other than the mayor's sixteen-year-old daughter."

"Oh shit, I can see how that would be a poke in the eye with a stick."

"Aye, the mayor not only ran Joshua out of town but castigated his entire family."

"The mayor seems to be wound up pretty tight. He threw me out of the pub for no reason at all."

"Not a surprise, probably too much drink. You should have bought him a whiskey."

"I was just about to do that. But when I told the mayor I thought I was someone named Gregory Alkins, he exploded and called me a bloody liar along with a mouthful of other colorful expletives, many of them in Scottish."

The porter dropped the mop and looked into Owen's eyes. "Who did you say you were?"

"Well, that's it, I don't know for sure, but I believe I'm Gregory Alkins, and my mother Grace Alkins lived here years ago."

The porter let out a low whistle. "Gregory Alkins, you say?"

"Yea. You look like you saw a ghost. What the hell?"

"Well, young man, I don't think you're Gregory Alkins. You know, the incident we were just talking about with Joshua and the mayor's daughter, well, it produced a child. A boy named Gregory Alkins. The lass hung around Arbroath for a couple of years with her son and eventually took off for America. We heard sometime later she died in transit on that *Titanic* ship. The mayor has never been right since. I think if he ever found that Joshua, he'd string him up."

Owen reached for a chair and sat. "Sir, you said that you didn't think I am Gregory Alkins. I've done my research, and the facts line up. You confirmed Grace Alkins left Scotland with a two-year-old boy named Gregory. Further, you said that Grace was on the *Titanic*."

"Aye, but—"

"Let me finish. It was verified that a boy arrived in New York as an unaccompanied child. The steamship line records show that a Gregory Alkins traveled third-class with his mother, who was later reported lost at sea. In America, a check of the immigration records shows Gregory entering with a married couple name Manning, and well, I guess they just took the boy home and raised him as their son. If this is all true, then I'm very confident that I am Gregory Alkins. And as troubling as it may be, I guess that means that the mayor is my grandfather. And the way I see it, he's no Father Christmas."

The porter stroked his chin, shook his head, and hesitated for a moment. "Well, lad, I hate to contradict your theory, but it just ain't possible."

"Why? I just laid out the facts. They are indisputable. Look, I'm a physicist, and I know facts don't lie. So, why are you such a naysayer?"

"My dear boy, you haven't given me a chance to tell you exactly why you are not Gregory Alkins, then, now, nor ever will be. I'm one hundred percent positive. And I don't care how you stack up those facts, it just ain't so."

Owen was beginning to get peeved at the porter. "Okay, give me one good reason why you don't believe me."

"Very well. You see, I know Gregory Alkins's father was Joshua. And his father was the great footballer, Andrew Wilson, who migrated to Scotland from British Guinea to play professionally. I already told you that."

"So? Like you said, you already told me that story."

The porter took a seat in one of the old lobby chairs. "When the mayor's daughter had Joshua's baby, it was a village scandal and the mayor's biggest disgrace. That is why anything to do with that whole lot makes the mayor wild."

"But that doesn't disprove I'm Gregory Alkins."

"Aye, that doesn't, but this does. Young Gregory was the spitting image of his father, Joshua, even as a baby. Joshua and his father, who was from British Guinea, were colored, black as the ace of spades."

"What?!"

CHAPTER TWENTY-FOUR
The Facts Are Clear

The train ride back to London was a long one. Owen laid awake most of the night, and his mind raced between frustration and stress. He leaned back in his first-class seat, thinking that he didn't know if he was more unsettled about not getting to the bottom of his origins or that his mathematical mind had come to the wrong conclusion. Both pissed him off. Perhaps it was time to face the realization that he might never know the truth about himself.

"So, why does it even matter?" he rationalized. "Ellen Manning is the best mother one could ever want, and my father is long gone, nothing more than a vague memory. I should just settle for that and give up chasing ghost tales."

As he fell in and out of napping, he had the oddest sensation, as if someone were watching him. He looked around the crowded train. A few church ladies, a couple of kids, eight or ten old men, and the few odd businessmen probably on their way to Hamilton, where this train ended and he would transfer for the Scotlander to London. He figured in a few hours he would arrive empty-handed and be back ready to take on the challenging work ahead.

The train slowed as it entered Victoria Station. Owen grabbed his bag and walked to the back of the car, then stepped off. He stopped to pick up a paper at the newsstand, then turned and bumped into a short, stout man with a briefcase. "Pardon me, sir, my fault, sorry."

"Not a problem, Dr. Manning. I'm sure it was an accident."

Owen was taken back. "How do you know my name? Do I know you?"

"Let's say I know a lot about you. But that is unimportant."

Owen detected a slight accent but wasn't able to identify it. "I'm sorry, but I must be on my way, so please move on."

The stranger persisted and followed Owen as he walked through the crowded station. "Doctor, I have a message for you. From your brother-in-law, Hanz Weber. He sends his regards and wanted to let you know that Lonnie's mother is doing well."

Owen stopped dead in his tracks. "Listen, buster, you are upsetting me. Say what you want and be on your way."

"Very well, Doctor. Herr Weber is looking to introduce you to some gentlemen in London. They are interested in your work and would like you to share it with them. They will pay well."

"Are you serious?"

"Yes, deadly serious, Doctor. Herr Weber thinks that maybe your mother-in-law would appreciate it if you would cooperate. He fears for her health. So, my friend, just be prepared to meet our liaison on Thursday."

"I not interested. I won't even be in London on Thursday. Now get lost."

"Don't worry, Doctor, they will find you wherever you are."

Owen was rattled, feeling that his space had been violated and that he was clearly being targeted. He hailed a cab back to his hotel, thinking that he needed to tell someone about the encounter, but he didn't exactly know who.

"Good evening, sir," the desk clerk offered as Owen walked through the lobby toward the receptionist's desk.

"Good evening."

"I'll be begging your pardon, sir, but the tellie has been ringing off the hook for you. And there's a telegram as well. Here you go."

"Thank you."

Owen opened the telegram first:

> *Dearest Owen,*
>
> *Your little darling has arrived. Stop. A bit early, but sound as a dollar. Stop.*
>
> *All is well. Stop. Call me when you can.*
>
> *Your loving wife,*
>
> *Lonnie*

"OH MY GOD!" yelled Owen.

"Bad news, sir?" inquired the clerk.

"No, no, good news. Great news! I'm a father."

"Blimey, let me be the first to congratulate you, sir. Is it a chap or a lass?"

"Oh my God, she didn't say…how could she leave that out?"

Owen almost skipped into the lift and rifled through his phone messages. One from Lonnie, of course, two from Winney, and another one from his commanding officer.

Owen raced into his room and picked up the phone. It took a bit, but he finally got connected.

"Hello, honey, can you hear me?" he asked Lonnie.

"Yes, very well. It sounds like you are right next door. Sweetheart, I tried calling before the baby came, but I couldn't reach you. No one knew where you were."

"I'm sorry, but I popped up to Scotland."

"Scotland? Why?"

"I'll fill you in later, but first how are you? How is the baby?"

"We are both doing great. She's beautiful, just perfectly beautiful."

"She? She's a she?"

"Yes, dear, are you disappointed?"

"No, no, of course not. You just forgot to say what the baby was in your telegram."

"Oh, Owen, how stupid of me. I was so excited to tell you the news, I must have forgotten that detail. Are you okay with a little girl?"

"For sure, and now I have two beautiful women to love in my life."

"That is so sweet. Thank you. I was worried because I thought you wanted a boy."

"I'm thrilled with a little girl. God, I feel awful, I wasn't there for the big event. I'm so sorry, Lonnie, really sorry."

"I know, and we missed you. But it went so fast. We almost didn't make it to the hospital. It was a dreadful night, snowing so hard, almost a blizzard, which is quite unusual for Los Alamos."

"Wow!"

"Dr. Martalone was concerned at first because the baby was in a breech position. But Thank God, at the last minute, the little sweetheart turned and popped out. The doctor said, 'Like a champagne cork.'"

Owen teared up and sniffled. "I'm so proud of you, and her too. The little sweetheart, I like the sound of that."

"She's six pounds, nine ounces and perfect."

"A real bundle of joy! I can't wait to see her."

"And she can't wait to see you, and neither can I. It's been so long, and I miss you. So why Scotland?"

Owen decided not to go into details. He wasn't ready to expose Lonnie to this dark uncertainty in his life. He could barely rationalize it himself. "It's complicated, but I'll fill you in when I see you."

"Promise? You won't forget?"

"No, I won't forget. Promise."

CHAPTER TWENTY-FIVE
Help Wanted

The Netherlands, The Hague, Schaduwgazon

THE DUTCH GOVERNMENT HAD DECLARED NEUTRALITY TO no avail. After the Germans bombed Rotterdam, the States-General of the Netherlands, both the Senate and House of Representatives, met at Binnenbholf in The Hague to officially sign an official surrender.

The royal family, along with many government officials, fled to England two years previous to the surrender . Princess Juliana and her children continued from London to Canada, where she took residence in a remote villa. In a broadcast to the Canadian people, she proclaimed her loyalty to The Netherlands but now wanted to be thought of as a citizen of the world and make Canada her new home.

Things in The Hague were deteriorating. The city was crawling with Nazis and fellow Dutchmen who conspired with the enemy. Every government office had been taken over, and the Dutch population lived in fear. The Germans declared Arbeitseinsatz, a decree that required mandatory forced labor. All adult males were forced to work in German factories, putting their lives at risk not only because of the harsh treatment but because the factories were bombed regularly by the Allies. Those who refused to comply with forced labor went into hiding.

In dealing with the Jews, a roundup for exportation to camps was mounted. The remarkably accurate and comprehensive population records kept by the Dutch allowed the Nazis to identify and quickly apprehend thousands and thousands of Jews. Fostered by the Germans willingness to pay a bounty to Dutch police and informers who turned in Jews resulted in great success. Desperate Dutchmen sold their fellow compatriots out for money to buy bread due to severe food shortages and rationing.

Life was becoming more and more arduous. Lonnie's mother, Maria, was able to smuggle out letters and even a rare phone call to the United States.

"Hallo *lieveling*, it's Mamma. Are you well?"

"Mamma, it's you. They are letting you call?" Lonnie exclaimed.

"I'm calling from a secret place, on a phone that is not being monitored by the Germans. I was able to slip away unnoticed, but it probably will be the last time since I am under house arrest. My time is limited, so let me tell you what I want to say to you."

"Yes, of course, please."

"I'm doing well, as well as expected. Things in The Hague are deteriorating. The German army is everywhere, and no one can be trusted."

"Are you still at Schaduwgazon?"

"For now. At first, it wasn't too bad. I could leave to visit the doctor or to the market, but with a German escort. But they are beginning to tighten things up.

"The Germans have confiscated our home. At first, they were gentlemanly, but as time went by, they became insufferable. They were careless and had soirees with women, damaging the furniture. Drunken officers would actually urinate on Schaduwgazon's steps and have orgies on the front lawn, forcing local women to unwillingly participate. When they finished having their way, they would beat them like dogs, put them in vans, and take them away to who knows where."

"Oh, Mamma, how barbaric and horrible for you. I'm so sorry."

"Recently, they began inventorying and moving some of our artwork and valuable Oriental carpets, putting them into the landskeeper's house. I think they plan on looting everything."

"Mamma, don't be foolish, they are only things. Let them take what they want as long as they leave you alone."

"No. It isn't right. I objected, so they trumped up some charges. They said I had Jewish ancestry, which made me a criminal in the eyes of the Reich."

"Jewish? They just make things up? How absurd!

"Of course, these are false charges—they are simply awful to the Jewish citizens. and it's all madness. Besides, the only thing Jewish about me is that I love kugel. But like I said, I'm under house arrest. I'm a prisoner in my own house. They put me in the landskeeper's house with one of the maids. I am a prisoner for all intents and purposes."

"Where are Katrina and Hanz? Can't they do something?"

"I'm sad to say Katrina has left Hanz. But for a good reason. His radical views and conspiring with the Nazis made him intolerable. Hanz has become a violent drunk and a womanizer, fraternizing with the German officers. I even think I saw him out on the lawn at one of those…I can't even say what. Katrina feared he might turn her in to the Germans, for no reason other than to be rid of her. He took all her jewelry and some of mine too and sold it. After that, he beat her up. The swine. Luckily, she's fled The Netherlands and is in a safe place."

"What a beast! Why didn't Katrina take you with her?"

"She wanted to, but I couldn't leave. They wouldn't let me. I get the impression they think I might be useful. But for what, I have no idea. Lonnie, I sent some very special things of mine with Katrina. Things that Hanz didn't get his hands on. You should know, just in case."

"In case? In case of what?"

"Well, you never know. They are some things your father gave me years ago. But never you mind, dear. I'm fine, just fine."

Openly weeping, Lonnie knew her mother was anything but fine. "I'm so scared for you, Mamma. I fear I will never see you again, and you will never see our baby."

"Oh, sweetheart, I'm so sorry. But I pray this will pass, and these devils will go to hell where they belong. They reek of evil and are heartless occupiers."

Lonnie hung up the phone, shaking. "I must reach Owen. He'll know what to do."

When the phone rang late in the afternoon at Owen's hotel, he answered at the first ring.

"Captain Manning."

"Oh, Owen," Lonnie cried into the phone. "I had awful news from Mother."

"What is it? What's happened?"

Lonnie explained in detail her mother's dire situation while Owen listened carefully.

"Lonnie, this is serious, and I'm so sorry. I love your mother very much, and I am really sad to hear this news."

"Owen, is there anything you can do?"

"I don't know, let me think about it. I know some heavy hitters, and perhaps they have connections."

"Oh yes, please, Owen. Do whatever you can. When can you come home? I need you. WE need you."

"Not certain. We are getting into the thick of things here. I have to visit a lab on Monday. I'll probably know more then."

"Well, you tell that big-shot general or whatever he is that you are needed home and that the bloody war will just have to happen without you."

"I only wish. But don't fret, dear. I will be doing critical work. Something that counts. It very well may shorten the war. You'll see, but not just yet."

"The baby is crying. She wants to be fed. Your mother has come out to be with us. She is so wonderful. How lucky we are to have her, and now our baby has her as the perfect grandmother."

"I can hear the baby; she sounds very healthy. Go and feed the little sweetheart. And kiss her for her daddy and give one to my mom too. Oh, yea, two kisses for you."

"Good night, my darling. Be safe. I love you…and…"

"And what?"

"Please come home."

Owen ended the call and closed his eyes. He had missed one of the most important events in a man's life: the birth of his first-born. It didn't seem fair. But then again, he was not alone, given the millions of other men away from home serving their country. And then this business with his mother-in-law. What a mess!

His thoughts were interrupted when the phone rang. "Hello, Manning here."

"Duck, it's Winney. Where the hell have you been? The whole place has been trying to reach you."

"Oh, I popped up to Scotland, but I'm back now."

"Scotland, what the hell is going on up there? Found a little piece of lass…ha-ha?"

"Don't be a jerk. Does your mind ever get out of the gutter?" *Sounds like the old Winney I know.* "Look, I'll tell you about Scotland later. So, what's up?"

"The old man is putting the pressure on all of us. The boys here have come up with nothing, but they think this Brit up in Stoke-on-Trent has something, maybe a breakthrough. The high mucky-mucks in DC want us to get up there and find out if there is a viable solution, you know, to the problem. No details over the phone. We're leaving London tomorrow at six A.M., so get crackin'. We have military transport to take us, so just show up."

"Do you think we'll get our answers there?"

"Owen, like everything else in this war, it remains to be seen. And you'll be right there to see."

CHAPTER TWENTY-SIX
THE ELUSIVE LORD
SOMETHING OR OTHER

Stoke-on-Trent

THE TEAM FROM LONDON ARRIVED AT STOKE-ON-TRENT A couple of hours before lunch. They were brought to Huntington Arms, a local hotel where they checked in, and then were immediately transported to the Devonshire factory. It was a rambling complex of brick and limestone. Five massive smokestacks billowing white smoke were attached to the kilns that rose from the factory's roof like enormous fingers attempting to grab clouds. The long driveway ended at the administrative office. An elegant Georgian façade featured transom windows over an enormous paneled front door that was flanked by an intricate pediment and side pilasters. Some forty-feet high, a side-gabled roof soared. Applied to the building was a chiseled cornerstone: "Nominee Elegant: MDCCXXIV," meaning "In the name of elegance, 1834." Gold leaf letters carved into the detailed cornice above the door identified the company: Devonshire, Ltd.

Lieutenant Colonel Miller greeted the team and escorted them three stories down to a subterranean lab. He explained that the lab was underneath the Devonshire factory, where many experimental vessels are made and tested, and it ran independently from the china maker.

"Good morning, gentlemen. I'm Lieutenant Colonel Miller, Her Majesty's Royal Army, First Ordnance Division. These gents here are Lieutenants Locker, Pettieman, and Houser, all part of my contingent. The other chaps are Yanks. Lieutenants Levin and Markus. The bloke in the corner cubical is Dr. Hanover from the University of London, on special loan."

Major Linden, the ranking U.S. officer from London, introduced his team: "Gentlemen, this is Captain Manning, Lieutenants Smith and Kurtz, and Dr. Barrington, one of your own, an Oxford man." The team made the rounds with handshakes.

"So, let's have a start at it, then. We're in the conference room. Follow Sergeant Mayo."

Sergeant Mayo glided across the room and did not go unnoticed. She wasn't a day older than nineteen and filled out her uniform with great aplomb.

"This way, gentlemen," she said almost seductively. "I'll take you to the meeting room."

"Hey, Duck, how would you like to spread some of that mayo on your knockwurst?"

"Jeez, Winney, grow up."

"Something's growing all right…. She's a real pin-up!"

"Gentlemen," the colonel began, "our goal is to coordinate what you folks have come up with and what we have here."

"Yes, Colonel," replied Major Linden. "But there is the question of security. We will share what we can, but the rest will have to stay classified. We'll go on a need-to-know basis. I'm sure you understand."

"Right. Of course, Major, completely understandable. Same with us."

The men had talked for several hours when Sergeant Mayo delivered lunch.

"See these dishes? They're made right here," the colonel continued. "This place produces fine china for the High Street trade. When war broke out, the owner got a government contract to provide mess hall dinnerware. Like this. Pretty nasty, but utilitarian. If any of you are interested, there's a museum of sorts on the third floor. It displays all of the company's designs over the years…more than two centuries."

"Sound's riveting," mocked Winney. "Absolutely riveting. Maybe Sergeant Mayo could show me around after hours, being quite a dish herself."

"Dr. Barrington."

"Yes, Colonel. Please, it's Winney."

"We are here to win the war. To find a solution to something critical and defeat the Nazis. Our success means saving millions of lives and ending the carnage. So, I would appreciate it if you would stick to business and try to keep not only your mouth but your loins under control. This is no time for levity or wise arse remarks. Do I make myself clear?"

Winney sank into his chair, rolled his eyes, sipped his tea, turned to Owen, and mouthed: "Bugger him!"

Major Linden went on, "You see, Colonel, our project in New Mexico is ready to launch, but we are having trouble containing fissile material. There is a chemical reaction when it is placed in a steel vessel. The same problem with iron, aluminum, and copper. The best, but not satisfactory, was a glass-ceramic material, but it didn't last long enough before it started to degenerate."

"Go on."

"So, Captain Manning suggested we contact Winney here in London, who was aware of your work at Devonshire. Apparently, you have had success in developing some sophisticated vessels for torpedo payloads, and we were wondering if there was some kind of synergy."

"Well, Major, we'd be more than glad to help. What I can tell you now is that we have made a lot of progress. The owner of Devonshire is a brilliant scientist, Sir Nigel Dasher-Hornsby. His background is Oxford with a degree in advanced chemistry. After his father's death, he took over Devonshire Ltd. and grew it exponentially, making it UK's most sought-after fine luxury china producer. When the war broke out, the British War Office convinced Sir Nigel to share his expertise.

"He cut a hush-hush deal with the government, set up this research and development lab, and with his help, we were able to develop a ceramic formula that allows torpedoes to hold larger and more deadly payloads. Once we had the workable formula, the vessels were produced right upstairs, under the guise of making cheap military mess dishes. No one was the wiser.

"Still, the current vessels, as good as they are, really needed to be improved upon to assure 100 percent reliability. The team, with Sir Nigel's help, continued the research, and we were getting pretty encouraging test results. We reached a certain point in the development when Sir Nigel sort of went a bit dodgy on us."

"How do you mean?"

"I believe that he has figured out how to make the ceramics we need, far exceeding what we have now. And I'm rather sure it's something that could work for you too. One of our mates did a little snooping and got a glimpse of his calculations, which later disappeared from the files. Also, Sir Nigel's behavior seemed to change."

"Really? Is that why he's not here in this meeting? Are we dealing with a wacko? How did he change?"

"He didn't want to work with the team and insisted on doing everything by himself. Ran his own tests and did his own firings in the kilns. He wouldn't share any of the work product with the rest of us. Then, out of the blue, he decided to design and make china for himself. He worked nights and weekends in the factory."

The colonel continued the briefing: "It seems more recently that Sir Nigel's health hasn't been good. He's seemed to age dramatically and appears older than he is. He won't share what his doctors say, so we're in the dark. On top of that, we have a distinct feeling that our aims are now different. We briefed him about your interests and needs before your arrival, which I must say was met with lukewarm enthusiasm."

"Has he become a sympathizer? Does he have a family? What do they say?"

"As far as being a sympathizer, no, nothing like that. He's a true-blue Brit, and by all accounts, hates Nazis. But I think he realizes that our work, and yours too, could be and probably will be weapons that would decimate the earth and kill people on a massive scale not seen before. He is a gentle sort, on the soft side. Maybe Sir Nigel is torn between patriotism and humanitarianism.

"With respect to family, he has none that we know about. They…M16, that is…gave him a complete once-over. Trust me, MI6 checked him out two ways to Sunday before we put this installation here. His father, Sir Sidney, died years ago, and his brother was killed in an avalanche at St. Moritz in 1911. The old man left Sir Nigel everything, including a title as lord something-or-other. He never married, no kids, legitimate or otherwise. Just him, his business, his estate, and his staff."

"So do you think he will help us?"

"I honestly don't know what to make of the bloke. We think he knows a lot more than he lets on. We suspect that he probably has come up with some critical improvements to what we already have. If he has the formula, he isn't sharing it with us. Maybe it's in his head or hidden in Briarcliff, his house.

"So, he has it all figured out and is just holding back?"

"Possibly, Major. We have seen notes and experimentation that would lead one to that conclusion. However, as I mentioned, the notes suddenly disappeared, and testing stopped. Again, I think he's got something but is not forthcoming."

"Have you challenged him on this?"

"We are his guests here, and we must remember that. I think with what we already got and Captain Manning's fresh eyes, we might be able to pull the rabbit out of a hat, regardless of whether Sir Nigel participates."

Four days turned into six and then ten and then three months. Owen, Winney, and the team put in fourteen-hour days, returning to the hotel so exhausted they barely could eat. Los Alamos was all over them, telling them everything was ready to go, and all that remained was the vessel. Likewise, the British Home Office was breathing down Colonel Miller's back. Help from Sir Nigel wasn't forthcoming—he hadn't been to the lab since before Owen's team arrived and was totally disengaged.

Test after test yielded only 89 percent reliability, sometimes a bit lower. It wasn't good enough. Los Alamos demanded that the test results must be at least 96 percent reliable. Owen and the team wondered if they were ever going to meet those criteria.

Time was running out.

CHAPTER TWENTY-SEVEN
In the Name of the Father, the Son, and the Double Cross

As was her routine, Lonnie left her office at the university around four. After the baby was born, she gave up the car and driver that the army was providing, feeling that the fifty-mile drive home was a good time for her to unwind and have some time alone to sort out her day. Owen had arranged for a brand-new Ford convertible, one of the last to come off the production line before the factory was converted into making tanks. It was a Super 8, and she loved opening it up on the long straightaway cutting through the desert. On nice days, she retracted the top and enjoyed the open air blowing through her long blonde hair. It was almost cathartic. As she approached one of the rare crossroads, a car was stopped by the side of the road. An elderly man seemed stranded and perplexed. The Ford came to a roaring stop, and Lonnie called out: "Excuse me sir, are you all right?"

The man stared back. "Well, not really. I seem to be lost and—"

Suddenly the back door of the old black sedan opened, and a tall middle-aged man approached Lonnie.

"Good evening, Doctor. Lovely evening isn't it?"

Lonnie strained to see the stranger's face but did not recognize him. "Do I know you? Are you with the university?"

"No, Doctor, I'm not. And you are quite correct; you do not know me. But I know who you are and who you mother is, Madame Quackenbush.."

"You know my mamma?" A chill ran through her body. "What is it that you want?"

"I'm here to deliver a message, an important one. You see, we are here to make a bargain, more precisely, a trade."

"I have no idea what you are talking about. Trade what?"

"Your brother-in-law, Herr Weber tells us when his wife left Germany for Sweden, she took some very valuable gems that belonged to your mother and father. This was a crime since all valuables of the Dutch people were required to be turned in. The Third Reich needs funds for the war effort, and such priceless and valued gems would go a long way to build airplanes and tanks.

"Like I said, I don't know what you are talking about. Now get out of my way."

"Doctor, you don't seem to understand. What I am saying is that your mother's welfare is in peril. And the resolution of that is simple. You give us the gems, and she will be unharmed and allowed to go free. Free to see that adorable new baby of yours."

"Look, whoever you are, I have no control over any of this. I barely know where my sister is and if she even has these gems you speak of."

"That's no problem. We know where she is, and as far as the gems go, we know she has them; your mother told us."

"What? She told you that?"

"Well, not exactly. She told you, in a phone call, which she foolishly assumed was a secure line. Nothing is hidden from us."

Lonnie remembered the call and the conversation. "So why don't you go to Sweden and get whatever it is you want from my sister?"

"Sweden is difficult. It's a neutral country and getting in and out of there does not go unnoticed. So, it would be better if you went to Sweden and got the gems. You are an American now, and they are free to roam the world."

"You are insane. Go to Sweden, leave my baby? No, I can't do that."

"But you will, Doctor, unless you want your mother to be sent to a camp, one where very few survive, and life is most difficult, especially for the elderly."

"You wouldn't dare."

"Oh, but we would, and will. So, here's the plan, Doctor. You will go to Sweden, get the gems, bring them to The Hague and turn them in at Gestapo headquarters. After that you will be reunited with your mother and transported back to Sweden for your return home. Simple. Tidy."

"I don't trust you. How do I know you'll keep your word?"

"You don't, but as we see it, Doctor, you have no choice. Because the word that you *can* trust is that your mother *will* be sent to a very uncomfortable camp. Oh, and by the way, this mission is top secret. You will not tell anyone, or the deal will go sour and that can be disastrous for your mother. No one, not even your husband, your mother, or mother-in-law, and most specifically the authorities. You will have to leave on Friday; it's arranged."

"Friday? That's only a few days. I have to make arrangements. The baby, my job..."

"That's up to you to figure out. Just be in New York on Saturday, The Babylon Hotel on 57th Street. We will take care of the rest."

Lonnie was distraught by the time she approached her driveway. How could she just drop everything and go to Sweden? Much less not tell a soul. *What would Owen do?* She so wished she could sit and cuddle with him on the couch, having a brandy, talking about each other's days. From a simpler time. A time before the world went mad. She knew the evil German was deadly serious. If she didn't follow instructions exactly, her mother would be doomed. She thought about the gems and how they were meaningless if they could save her mamma's life. In her mind they were no more than glass, albeit glass that could purchase her mother's life. Lonnie unlocked the door rushed into the house and was greeted by their kindly housekeeper, Rosa. She had been a godsend to Lonnie without Owen around.

"Good evening, Doctor Manning. She just had her bath, and she finished the whole bottle about an hour ago."

"Thank you, dear, get some rest now. We'll be just fine."

"Then here you go ma'am." She handed the baby over to Lonnie. "I'll be saying good night now, see you tomorrow at 7:45."

Lonnie put the baby in the playpen and poured herself a large glass of wine She was unnerved and needed to figure out what to do. She picked up the phone and began to place an overseas call to Owen. He would know what to do. But she suddenly hung up. The phone was probably bugged, she thought. "They'll know I called him, and they warned me not to tell anyone."

Lonnie picked the phone up again, this time instructing the operator to call a long-distance number in New York. A cheerful voice on the other end answered: "Hello!"

"Hello Mother Manning, it's Lonnie."

"Lonnie? How wonderful to hear your voice. Are you OK? Is there something about Owen?"

"I'm fine." Lonnie lied. "And nothing new from Owen. He's over there working his heart out."

"And my darling little granddaughter?"

"She's perfect, just perfect, and she misses you. Look Mom, would it be all right if I came to New York and left the baby with you for a few days?"

"All right? It would be divine. When? And why?"

"On Friday, if that is OK."

"Sure, it's fine. Where are you going?"

"I have some university business to attend too, just a couple of days, and I'll be back."

"Absolutely no problem, dear. Does Owen know you're going?"

Lonnie panicked. She knew that Owen didn't speak with his mother very often because overseas calls were very limited and usually reserved for spouses. But in the rare chance he should call, his mother could say something.

"No, Owen doesn't know, but it's best he doesn't. I don't want him worrying about me traveling around. Let alone with the baby. It's just best we keep this between us."

"As you wish, dear....Mum's the word."

*****

The SAS airliner landed in Stockholm just before nine in the morning. A cab ride to the Grand Hôtel where she was staying only took a half hour. There was to be a message at reception with details as to where Katrina and she would rendezvous. It had been a long time since the two sisters were together, not since her wedding to Owen. Katrina had arranged to have a friend drive to the city and pick Lonnie up for the hour drive.

"Oh, mijn God, het is voor altijd! It's been forever!" screamed Katrina as the two hugged and kissed in front of a little cottage, now home to her. Katrina switched to English. "How is the baby? And Owen?"

"The baby is fine. She is with Owen's mother in New York. As for Owen, I only hear from him sporadically. He is on assignment."

Katrina knew better to ask where. "Come, make yourself comfortable. I'll fix some koffie."

"Thank you." Lonnie looked around. "Whose house is this?"

"The cottage belongs to a third cousin of ours, Luther van Linden. You don't know him, but Mother arranged everything when I left The Hague. He's a local estate agent, and he has access to lots of properties."

"It's lovely."

"Well, it's not what we are used to, but anything is better than being in The Hague living under those monster Nazis. You know, Hanz turned into the worst of the lot. He was a traitor to our people and became a sadistic cad." Katrina teared up. "He even beat me and stole all our money and most of the family jewelry. So, why did you come? It's so dangerous to travel. Even though Sweden is neutral, it could fall at any time."

"I came because I am being blackmailed. If I don't comply the Germans will kill Mamma and possibly me too. I can't leave my baby an orphan. They were so threatening."

"Hush, Lonnie, let's go for a walk. I trust no one, and even Swedish walls could have ears." The two sisters walked down the garden path, and Lonnie filled Katrina in.

"So, you are here to get the last bit of gems so you can buy Mamma's freedom? Does Owen know about this?"

"No, nor does anyone else, not even Mamma or you, until now. Do you have the gems they are talking about?"

"Yes. When I divorced Hanz and left The Netherlands, Mamma gave them to me for safekeeping. Hanz knew I had them and beat me blue trying to find out where they were, but I would not give them up. I know we would need them after the war."

"Well, Katrina, we need them now. To buy Mamma's freedom—and mine too."

"Of course. When I arrived in this village I made friends with the local minister. He offered to hide them in the church where they would be safe."

"We must retrieve them immediately, and I must take them to The Hague."

"Lonnie, do you trust those animals? Will they keep their word and let you both go after they get what they want?"

"I have no choice but to trust them. There is no alternative."

"Of course, you don't. When will you leave?"

"Tonight, if possible, just as soon as I can get on a plane. I must be back home before Owen finds out what I've done."

"And where will Mamma go?"

"She can't go to the United States. They are greatly restricting any European visitors for fear of spies."

"So where then?"

"I will try and get her here, with you."

"Oh my God, that would be an answer to my prayers. I miss her so, and I worry day and night."

*****

Fearful that a customs official or some rogue German soldier might steal the gems en route, Lonnie and Katrina camouflaged the smaller gems by painting them black, an old smugglers' trick, and then sewed them onto Lonnie's hat like beads, amongst the feathers and veil.

"Lonnie, there are these three large stones—too large for the hat."

"Yes." Lonnie thought for a moment. "You know I kind of remember Mamma talking about there being four. She said Papa called them the 'Quartet.'"

"*Ja,* I recall something like that too, but Mamma only gave me three."

"Hmm."

Katrina suggested that they cut open the large fur collar on Lonnie's coat and hide them deep within the collar. The stones barely fit under the pelts. As the two women hastily sewed they recalled the history of the stones. Their father, years ago, owned diamond mines in South Africa and during a dig in Botswana these extraordinary diamonds were unearthed.

Back then he decided never to disclose their existence, fearing they would create far too much attention and perhaps he would have a problem getting them out of Africa, so he quietly smuggled them out the country undetected by the government. What was so rare about the gems was their purity, virtually flawless. In Amsterdam his master cutter, recognized as the world's finest, created spectacular finished diamonds each one weighing more than 305 carats. Even then the stones were not only extremely rare, but priceless. The diamonds were put into his private collection stored in a safe at Schaduwgazon. When the war threat grew worse and Katrina left The Hague, their mother gave the gems to her in order to get them out of the hands of the Nazis. She told her that these gems would always ensure that they would provide for the family if necessary. Foolishly, Katrina had told Hanz about the gems when they were first married.

*****

The Hague

Lonnie landed in The Hague early the next morning, and two grim-faced Gestapo agents met the plane and escorted Lonnie to German headquarters now in the town hall.

"Doctor Manning. So good to see you. I'm Commander Blauder, at your service."

"Where's my mother?" Lonnie demanded.

"In good time, Doctor."

"Well, I won't have anything to do with you or anyone else until I see my mother."

"As you wish." Blauder yelled out to his aide. "Bring *die Judenschlampe rein.*"

Lonnie understood enough German to know that this Nazi was calling her mother a Jewish bitch. "Excuse me, Commander, though I detest your beliefs about Jewish people, I also want to say neither my mother nor any of our family is Jewish, so please don't refer to her as such."

"That is for the Reich to determine not you. The official records say your mother has Jewish blood and that is that. She will be treated like an enemy to the Reich."

Maria Quackenbush was escorted into the sterile office and offered a chair. "*Sitzen*, Frau Quackenbush."

Lonnie looked carefully at her mother. She seemed fine, although her eyes were deep and sad. They had allowed her to dress properly, and she did not have the infamous, horrifying yellow star sewn to her smart outfit. Lonnie raced to embrace her. "Mamma, are you all right?"

"Yes, *liebling*, Mamma's fine. I am worried that you traveled here during a war!"

The commander interrupted: "Yes, Doctor, your mamma is fine, as will be you if you cooperate. Let's get down to business. You have something for me don't you?"

Lonnie sheepishly looked at her mother. Up until now her mother had no idea about the

unwanted bargain she had agreed to. Her mother sat as Lonnie turned to the commander. "Yes, I have what you want here."

Lonnie took her coat off and ripped open the newly sewn stitches. The enormous diamonds fell into

her lap"And there is more?" inquired the commander. Sighing, Lonnie took off her hat and yanked off another dozen or so stones.

" Don't fool with me, Doctor. These are black."

"Only painted. Just take the paint off and you will see."

"How clever." The commander collected the stones, put them in a box but secretly placed one of the larger painted diamonds in his pocket.

"And now." Lonnie said. "We are free to go?"

Blauder laughed out loud. "You must be joking. We have far more important plans for you . You see, this entire gem scenario was just a charade."

Lonnie felt a chill pass over her.

The commander sneered, his eyes completely devoid of humanity. "Oh yes, we knew about these valuable stones and that they would go a long way to finance the war, but our real objective was to get something far more valuable than diamonds. You see, Doctor Manning, what the Reich really wants is not what you and your mother had, but what your husband has."

Lonnie covered her mouth in horror. "My husband? What does he have to do with this?"

"Everything." Blauder turned to the soldier standing guard at the door. "Sergeant, escort these ladies to Schaduwgazon. They will be kept there under house arrest for the time being. And sergeant, be careful with them—they are our secret weapon to win the war!"

CHAPTER TWENTY-EIGHT
MAY DAY, MOTHER'S DAY

I T WAS A WEDNESDAY EVENING, AROUND 10:30, AND OWEN SAT at the bar having a solitary nightcap. He wanted to be alone after more than twelve grueling hours at the lab. He longed to get home to be with Lonnie and the baby.

For the first time in his life, Owen felt sorry for himself. He was usually so optimistic about everything. His life had been charmed, and even though school had been hard work he sailed through a doctoral at MIT despite his disability.

Dyslexia, for some, could be crippling, but for him, it was what drove him to achieve—more like a daily challenge than a hindrance, a challenge that he competed against and was determined to beat.

And then there was Lonnie and how that wacky Mama Lucia had set them up. It sounded like a romance novel.

Adding to Owen's melancholy was the lack of success at the lab. Up until now, failure was not in his vocabulary. He and his team were discouraged, however. To date, the lab tests had been encouraging but were still not able to meet the demanding expectations. The pressure for a breakthrough was mounting. What irked Owen was the chance that a possible solution created by Sir Nigel was being withheld. It could make a difference. So much depended upon their success. If such information existed and it was valid, he and the others could pack up and go home— mission accomplished.

Owen ordered his second drink and continued his lament. It seemed to him that the day in that conference room when the lieutenant colonel had told him about his fake birth certificate signaled the beginning of a new phase in his life, one of considerable uncertainty.

"Bartender, another, please." His third.

Cupping the glass in his hands, almost in a prayerful way, Owen closed his eyes and tried to imagine what would come next. A fellow dressed in a postman's uniform entered the barroom and made his way toward the empty stool next to him. "Anyone sitting here?"

"No, be my guest." Owen noticed the man did not have a British accent and thought it odd that a postman would be a foreigner.

"Thank you, Captain Manning."

That voice … he had heard it before. Where? And then he remembered: Victoria Station. This was the guy who bumped into him.

"What do you want?" he said. "I told you I would have nothing to do with you."

"Oh, but Captain, you surely will. You see, there's a certain elderly woman in The Hague and her beautiful daughter, oh yes, I believe she is also your wife, both very precious to you. Am I not correct?" The Postman paused and then answered his own question: "Of course, I'm right. So, these women would be quite indisposed if you are less than cooperative with us. Do I make myself clear, Captain?"

Owen was stunned: "What do you mean my wife is in The Hague? She is in the United States with our baby!"

The Postman chuckled. "You may think so, but she is not. She is with her mother, and they are guests of the Third Reich. We can be very persuasive when we want to be—and a little thing like offering to send her mother to lovely accommodations in one of our work camps seemed to be just the inducement we needed."

Enraged, Owen jumped up from the bar stool and grabbed the Postman by the neck. "If you harm either one of them I'll..."

Struggling to get free the Postman spurted out: "It would be most unwise to hurt me, after all, I'm here to help you save your wife and her mother. If something happens to me, well, Captain, I'm afraid you will never see them again."

"How do I know you really have them?"

"Well, call your mother in New York. She has your daughter while your wife went to Sweden and then to The Hague. You see, it was all planned out. It's amazing really. We all *have* a mother. They seem to be a weak spot for most people. And now the lovely doctor is our guest until you give us what we want."

"Look, I told you before, I don't have anything you want."

"Let us be the judge of that. We know a lot about your work and would like the opportunity to review it. That's all we ask."

"I've got nothing for you!" Owen abruptly pushed his drink off to the side, turned quickly, and started to walk away from the intruder.

"Captain, don't be foolish. Something might happen to your wife, and her poor, frail mother. The lack of steady food supplies—it's weakened some of the already pathetic drains on our society. And I suppose I shouldn't say—but indeed I shall—that we can even reach all the way to New York where that pretty little girl of yours is. We made that *very* clear to your wife through our contacts in New York. Could you live with that the rest of your life? … I think not. It's up to you. I'll be in touch. Meantime, I suggest you make some copies of your notes and those of your colleagues too."

Owen, anxious to escape, rushed up to his room. As he mounted the stairs, he recalled Lonnie's calls and letters. She was becoming more and more desperate about her mother's well-being. Europe was on fire, and the Nazis were capable of anything. And somehow, some way, they managed to lure Lonnie to The Netherlands, which seemed inconceivable. And now they were holding her hostage. He reached for the phone and called his mother.

"Hello?"

"Hello, Mom, it's Owen."

"Of course it's you, only you and Lonnie call me Mom, and you surely don't sound like her."

Not wanting to alarm his mother, Owen carefully questioned her: "Do you have the baby there with you?"

"Why yes. How do you know that? Did Lonnie call you?"

Owen ignored the question. "So where is Lonnie"

"Oh, Dear, she didn't want to worry you, but she is on some kind of thing for the university. She wasn't very specific, and I didn't want to pry; you know, to be a good mother-in-law that's a no-no. She said she would be back for the baby in a couple of days. Dear, is there a problem?"

Owen lied. "No, no problem. Just surprised that she would travel during wartime and not tell me first."

"As I said, she didn't want you to worry. The world is crazy right now, and it was only for a couple of days, so she just went and that was that."

"Look, Mom, security these days is very tight. I work on stuff that is highly sensitive and therefore under great scrutiny."

"What are you driving at Owen? I don't understand."

"Nothing, nothing. But do me a favor, and don't let the baby out of your sight. Promise me."

"Of course, I won't. Owen, you are really beginning to worry me."

"There is nothing to worry about, really, Mom. Everything is fine. I've got to go now. Kiss the baby for me, and one for you too." Owen hung up.

*****

Owen paced his small room all night, back and forth, eventually ending up in the old overstuffed easy chair in the corner. He put his head in his hands and cried. He was for the first time in his life frightened, frightened to death. Everything that meant anything to him was at risk. He cursed the day he agreed to work for the Army. If he had stayed safe and sound at MIT, none of this would have happened. He knew his instincts about the war were right. Killing never is justified, but then again . . . is it? So much is at stake, and when the enemy is Godless and ruthless isn't fighting back survival? But this was no longer a case of moral outrage or righteousness. This was about saving his family. He needed help and knew he could no longer keep these threats secret, and he was obliged by law to report any enemy contact to the military police. Failure to do so was nothing short of treasonous. But if he did, it surely would not bode well for Lonnie and her mother. He thought it ironic that there really wasn't anything of real consequence to give these Nazi operatives, even if he wanted to—there were still missing pieces.

Owen had a sleepless night. Trapped between two loyalties, he tossed and turned, trying to figure out precisely what to do. He knew he could never forgive himself if he lost Lonnie, life would not be worth living. And for his little darling girl, to grow up without a mother was nothing short of unthinkable. He knew what having only one parent was like.

But then there was the unfathomable alternative, that of being a traitor—that too would never give him a moment's peace for the rest of his life.

About an hour before dawn, he could not lay in bed another moment. Restless and exhausted, Owen walked down the long hall to the loo for a shower. He had to be at work in a couple of hours, which made him even more nervous. Being so close to the material these operatives were after would make the temptation greater.

"Good morning, Owen, sleep well?"

"Not a wink, Winney, how about you?"

"Like a bloody baby. I hit the bed and was out until my clock woke me out of a sweet dream, including a rather raunchy romp with a particular Sergeant Mayo. Quite a bird, that Mayo, at least in my dreams." Winney looked at Owen. "Mate, you look like shit. What's wrong with you?"

"Nothing. Nothing. Just didn't sleep well."

After lunch, Owen walked around the factory's grounds, needing to get some fresh air and think. He walked into the main entry of Devonshire Ltd and admired the magnificent building. Someone had spent a lot of time and money making this a showplace. Intricate moldings adorned the coffered ceilings, and large murals, obviously painted by exceptional artisans, covered many of the walls. Some were iconic British pastoral country scenes and others of historical London landmarks from different centuries. Two remarkable chandeliers centered in the room seemed to be made of fine china, probably crafted at this very factory.

Signs directing visitors to the company museum led Owen to the third-floor showrooms. There, massive glass cupboards displayed three centuries of Devonshire's craftmanship. He strolled amongst the displays, marveling at the intricacy of the designs, quality of the workmanship, and attention to detail. Owen felt a strange affinity to all of this; something down deep spoke to him. It was an odd feeling, him being a man of science and never having much exposure or interest in art and particularly not fine china. He laughed to himself, thinking back to his college apartment and how he ate most meals on mismatched dishes his roommate had pinched from MIT's cafeteria.

Owen paused in front of one of the cabinets and read the placard: "Special edition commissioned by the War Department for the High Supreme Command Mess, London 1910." Something flashed in the back of his mind. Was it the date, 1910, which coincidently was the year he was born? No, that wasn't it. But what? He read it a third time, stopping on the words "the War Department."

Owen rushed back to his room to find his address book. He couldn't quite remember the name he was looking for but knew he had written it in the book years ago.

"What was that name?" he said out loud. "Did it start with a C? No, not C."

He frantically paged through each tab, starting with A. When he got to S, the name popped out at him: Henry Louis Stimson, Secretary of War, United States Department of War. A plan formulated in Owen's mind as he sprinted back to the lab and commandeered the conference room, where he knew a secured phone line would allow him to make one of the most critical calls in his life.

It was early morning in Washington, DC, when the phone rang. "Good morning. War Department. The Secretary's office, may I help you?"

"Yes, this is Owen Manning from MIT. I'd like to speak to Mr. Stimson, it's important." Owen hoped using MIT would refresh Stimson's memory.

"Is he expecting this call?"

"No. Well, yes, sort of. Mr. Stimson said to call anytime I needed to talk to him."

"And you are, again?"

"Nobel Prize winner Owen Manning, from MIT. I know he will remember me."

The receptionist noted the incoming line and recognized that it was a number that the Secretary only gave out to particular people. "Very well, I will see if the Secretary is available. One moment please, Mr. Manning."

The phone was picked up a few seconds later: "I knew I would hear from you someday, and I was dead right—as usual. How are you, Manning?"

"Sir, I'm speaking to you on a secure line, so no one can hear us, I assume."

"You assume correctly, Manning, doubly secure. The number you called is also a War Department high-security line, so I can assure you we are alone. So how are you, young man?"

"Not well, not well at all. I have a horrible problem and need your help." Owen filled in Stimson on how he was now a commissioned officer, doing critical work for the Los Alamos project and the dilemma he was facing. When he finished, Stimson exhaled a deep breath into the phone.

"Wow. Let me get this right. You said you haven't shared this with anyone?"

"No one. At first I was alarmed but foolishly ignored the bribe, later followed by threats, hoping everything would go away. When you, in your own mind, know you would never accept such an offer, you almost dismiss it. Plus, I know there are much more urgent issues right now to bother someone about a bribe I immediately turned down. When this guy approached me last night and renewed the threat, I knew I was in over my head. They have my wife, Lonnie, and her mother under arrest on trumped-up charges. They are virtually prisoners. If I don't give them what they want, who knows what they will do. They are ruthless animals. I may never see either of them again. And what's worse they have made veiled threats against my infant daughter who is in New York with my mother."

"Where are your wife and mother now?

"At Schaduwgazon, my wife's ancestral home in The Hague. A while back my mother-in-law told my wife that they moved her from the manor house. I think they are being detained in the landskeeper's quarters, where they have stored a lot of the valuable art and Oriental carpets stripped from the manor, assuming to later loot."

"Look, Manning. I'm going to try and help, but it could take some time," Stimson said. "We have credible informants, and there is a measurable and effective underground in The Netherlands. I will find out what the best way to handle this will be. Until then, just hold on."

"Sir, I'm risking a lot on this, literally life and death. By doing the right thing and contacting you, I rejected an easier alternative, perhaps a safer one."

"I can appreciate that, Manning. But you made the right choice. Your country expects nothing less. I will do everything in my power to make this right. But do not, I repeat, do not give those bastards anything, understand?"

The secretary hung up, and Owen, now soaking with perspiration, once again put his head in his hands. "God, I hope I didn't just sign their death warrants."

Schaduwgazon was a beehive of activities for the local SS and high-ranking Nazi officers, making it virtually impenetrable. Since their invasion, the Nazis had infiltrated all levels of government in The Netherlands. The U.S. Department of War, now firmly allied with Great Britain, had established a sophisticated underground network throughout the European continent.

Via the highest of channels, Secretary Stimson contacted his counterpart in London. His call ended with his strong warning: "So, Mr. Secretary, do you understand what is at stake here? Captain Manning has knowledge and access to some of the most critical secret information necessary to end the war. If we don't help him, blackmail could tempt him to become a traitor to save his family. There is a fine line between duty and self-survival. This is a choice neither you nor I would want to make."

"I bloody well understand, Secretary Stimson. This will get our personal attention and have the highest of priorities. I will have a start of it as soon as we terminate this call."

"Thank you, Mr. Secretary. Time is of the essence."

*****

The Hague

At first, the Dutch resistance had a slow start, but after increasing Nazi-backed police harassment and the almost daily exportation of hundreds of Jews, the movement snowballed. The Dutch communists were the first to effectively organize and establish a network of cells. As the Nazis tightened their grip, more groups committed to the movement. Churches of different denominations, as well as independent militias, joined the resistance. Eventually, the resistance movement became an integral part of fighting German occupation and provided valuable assistance to the Allies. Its ranks included Dutchmen—and women—of all walks of life—schoolteachers, clerks, shop owners, and clergymen of many denominations. Their efforts were mainly nonviolent.

The resistors met secretly and planned strategic acts against the Nazi occupiers. The British War Department knew that over 300,000 people had been hidden by the local landlords and caretakers. Churches led the effort to find exits for the persecuted Jews. It was dangerous work—if they were caught, perpetrators were lined up and shot by the Gestapo and their homes were burned after being emptied of any valuables.

Despite their noble efforts, many members were betrayed by Nazi sympathizers and executed almost daily in public. Their families were corralled onto trains for the three hundred–mile journey to Sachsenhausen, a concentration camp in Oranienburg, just outside of Berlin. Individuals were culled from the line and beaten beyond recognition in front of their families. Infants were wrenched out of their hysterical mothers' arms and smashed against walls while Nazi officers stood by and laughed as the babies' heads split open and their brains sprayed their mothers and fathers.

Packed into boxcars like livestock, the cars meant to carry 40 were often jammed with more than 145 people. The train ride alone took hundreds of lives, and by the time the prisoners arrived in Germany, many of them were sick, dazed, and confused.

Hours after the British War Office Secretary's phone conversation concluded, the code name May Day, Mother's Day was assigned, and the British counter-espionage office made the necessary contact in The Hague. On the ground a day later, four members of the Dutch resistance were briefed, and a plan was set into place. It was a simple one, General Waverly, chief of MI6 in London, quickly gave it his blessing.

Twenty-five-year-old Aart Van den Berg, a strapping young resistance fighter, took charge of May Day, Mother's Day. He and three of his compatriots hatched the scheme. A phone call to the Nazi officer in charge at Schaduwgazon was made. Aart, who had studied medicine at Ludwig Maximilian University in Munich before the war, explained in perfect German that a high-ranking Nazi officer had demanded confiscation of several Oriental carpets and pieces of art. The orders supposedly came from Field Marshal Heinz Wilhelm Guderian. Assurances were given that proper paperwork would be provided at pick-up time. Aart's authoritative manner and bureaucratic demeanor convinced the junior officer.

The resistance had become experts at forging papers. Hundreds of fraudulent passports for Jews leaving the country were produced, as well as other "official Nazi" documents and bogus orders. The work's quality was so expert that it was almost impossible to discern the counterfeit from the real.

Three days after Owen's call to Secretary Stimson, a shiny black Mercedes lorry bearing a sign that read "Antique Transportes, Ltd." drove down the long tree-lined drive and entered Schaduwgazon's massive gates. The lorry was accompanied by a motorcycle with a sidecar carrying Aart Van den Berg dressed as a Nazi major. His impeccable command of German and military bearing made the impersonation totally plausible.

Two armed German riflemen stood guard on each side of the entrance, and a sergeant approached the lorry.

"Halt!"

Aart jumped out of the sidecar and answered the menacing sergeant. In perfect German, he said, "Heil Hitler! I am Major Hendrick, and these men are antique tradesmen and are here to pick up some special art items for Field Marshal Guderian." Handing the sergeant the orders he continued: "I am here to insure all goes as ordered."

The sergeant looked on his clipboard, verified that a pick-up was expected, and carefully examined the orders. "*Ja.*" Aart knew this meant, *yes, they look in order.* The Nazi walked away from the lorry and shouted to his men to open the van.

Aart signaled to the workmen, and one of them jumped out of the lorry and raced back to open the doors. He said, "Empty—just my helpers."

The sergeant handed the papers back and nodded. He had okayed them to proceed.

The Mercedes, followed by the motorcycle, started down the final part of the driveway and parked to the right of the front entrance. Schaduwgazon was now draped with Nazi flags and swastika placards. Aart and the men dressed in tradesmen overalls walked into the main hall and presented their orders. Captain Carl Schuman, the young officer in charge of Schaduwgazon's security, was summoned.

"Heil Hitler, I am Major Hendrick, here are my orders, Captain."

Taking the orders, the captain returned the salute: "Heil Hitler, Major. Ah, yes, we have been expecting you. We had the call."

Aart replied, *"Danke, Kapitän,* we were told the items are in the landskeeper's house. Where might that be?"

"Just over there. The men may pull the lorry up to the back door."

"Danke, Kapitän."

The men climbed back into the lorry and slowly pulled away. The landskeeper's house was not being guarded since it was within the gates of Schaduwgazon.

The team had picked four P.M. to arrive, a time when many troops would be winding down for the day. Two workmen accompanied by the masquerading major walked to the door and knocked.

"Good evening, we are here to pick up some art items. Is Frau Quackenbush available to advise us?"

"Yes, she is here," the elderly housekeeper said. "Please wait, and I will fetch her."

Lonnie's mother walked down the narrow steps and into the small, dark foyer. "May I help you?"

"You are Maria Quackenbush, yes?"

"Yes, I am."

"And your daughter, Dr. Manning. Is she here?"

"She's in the lounge. What business do you have with us?"

"We understand there as some rugs and certain artworks being stored here. May we see them?"

"Why?"

Aart walked toward Maria and whispered in her ear. She recoiled, not wanting to have this Nazi come any closer to her. Aart grabbed her arm and pulled her closer. "Don't be afraid. We are here to get you both out, just follow instructions. We must be quick."

"What? I don't understand. You're a Nazi…. And."

"Please, madame, it's not what it seems, I'm not a Nazi. I'm with the resistance. Your son-in-law Captain Manning sent us. His message is, 'He enjoys wearing the diamond cufflinks you gave him as a wedding gift. And that Lonnie and you are needed home. He wants you to meet the baby, so go with these men.'"

Maria immediately knew they were legitimate as only Owen would be able to give that message. Briskly, she walked the men to the storage pantry next to the kitchen.

"In there are the rugs and the paintings."

One of the tradesmen was carrying four long, hollow metal cylinders. Two of them had a contraption that resembled a snorkel mouthpiece. "Madame, we have to make this fast. Call your daughter, she must come with us too."

Lonnie arrived in the pantry. "What's going on here? Mama, tell me."

Aart whispered to her: "We are going to roll you up in these rugs and carry you out of here. It will not be comfortable, but it's the only way."

"Inside of a rug? We'll suffocate."

"No, that's what this cylinder is for. You put this piece into your mouth. It will allow you to breathe."

"I don't know if I can do that. I'm frightened," Maria cried.

"It's the only way. You will have to trust us. We've tested this many times."

"I don't know."

Lonnie immediately comprehended the situation. "Look Mamma, these men are here to save us we must listen. Do what they want…it's the only way."

Aart opened his hand: "I have pills here. It's a sedative that will put you in a very relaxed state. Take it. It acts quickly, and we will get you rolled up and out of here. Once we carry the rug with you inside of it to the lorry, we will cut it open and hide you under the floorboards; there's a secret compartment. It won't be more than a couple of minutes, and you'll be out. I know you can do it. Trust us."

From the kitchen window, Maria could see a German soldier heading towards the back door. It was not uncommon for the young soldiers to stop by and get some fresh baked sweets grudgingly provided by the housekeeper who hated Germans for their cruel treatment of the Dutch, especially the Jews.

"They're over there." The housekeeper motioned to the young soldier as he came into the kitchen. "Help yourself."

Lonnie, Maria, and the housekeeper exchanged worrisome glances, restraining themselves from expressing their true feelings about these German soldiers and their bold entitlement. They weren't worried that Aart and his men were in the other room since they had permission to be there. However, whenever a German was near, there was always uncertainty about what could happen. Nazis were known to shoot non-Germans just because they felt like it or because they didn't like the way they looked or dressed.

The soldier filled up a small container with half a dozen freshly baked krakeling smothered in sugar and cinnamon, paused, and said, "*Danke*, ma'am, *danke*. You got *kaffee*? Ya?"

"No *kaffee*, all out. Now be gone with you."

The soldier hesitated another moment, peered around the room as if he were looking for something, paused, and asked, "You maybe got some gingerbread in the pantry, *ja*?"

Maria's heart stopped as she gripped Lonnie's hand

The housekeeper walked between the soldier and the pantry door: " No. No

gingerbread, maybe next time. Now be gone with you!"

Grabbing another krakeling, the soldier popped it into his mouth and said: "*Guten nachmittag*, Frau Housekeeper, soon, until next time…. And don't forget your promise…gingerbread."

*****

Captain Schuman returned to his desk after seeing the van drive towards s the landskeeper's quarters. After a pause, he had a start at a stack of paperwork that had been piled on his desk since yesterday. His aide stopped at his desk.

"Sir, a cup of *kaffee* perhaps?"

"That would be *wunderbar*."

By the time the coffee arrived, the captain replayed in his mind the encounter with Major Hendrick and the Dutch workmen. As he pondered, he did not recall mentioning the artwork and carpets were stored in the landskeeper's quarters. In fact, no one knew that, so he wondered how the major did. At once, an alarm sounded in the back of his mind. Was there something irregular about this? Were this major and these workmen legitimate, and if not … The captain abruptly jumped up from his desk and shouted: "Stop those men! Sound the alarm."

A loud siren blared, and a half-dozen infantry soldiers rushed to Schaduwgazon's front steps and took their positions. Three German shepherds and their handlers appeared out of nowhere and were commanded to patrol the area.

Schuman and the soldiers rushed towards the landskeeper's quarters and burst open the doors. The bewildered housekeeper appeared from the kitchen, her apron covered in flour followed by her faithful little dachshund

"What's this? What do you want?"

"Where is Madame Quackenbush and Dr. Manning?" demanded the captain.

"I don't know, sir, they were in the garden a little while ago. But I've been in the kitchen baking and haven't seen them since."

Captain Schuman grabbed the old woman by the neck and drew her close to his face. "Listen, you Dutch bitch. If you are lying, I will kill you on the spot."

"Sir, I'm not lying. I don't know anything."

The captain didn't believe her. He knew this woman was a loyal servant and would lie to save her mistress. "I'm going to count to three. If you don't tell me where your mistress is, I will shoot you and that dog of yours dead. Do you understand?

The housekeeper shuddered and lost control of her bladder, defiling the marble foyer floor. "Sir, I beg you, don't kill me. I know nothing!"

Captain Schuman was having none of this. He pulled a Luger from his belt, cocked it, and fired it once. The gunshot echoed through the house and the small brown dog exploded as the 9mm bullet hit its tiny body. "Now, woman, tell me where they are *immediately!*"

The housekeeper could not believe her eyes. How cruel these Germans were to kill an innocent animal. She was truly unaware of precisely what happened and where her mistress and Lonnie were. "Sir, I know nothing, please, spare me."

Before the housekeeper could get the last word out of her mouth, the captain fired the second round directly into the weeping housekeeper's heart. "You lying Dutch bitch. You are a traitor to the Reich. Go to Hell!"

He nodded toward his men. "Take her body and put it in the trash for all to see. Now search everywhere!"

Soldiers spread out and began searching, some running down the long tree-lined drive leading to the gates. German shepherds fiercely barked and pulled at their chains, leading the pack to Schaduwgazon's entrance.

Aart Van den Berg was sitting in the motorcycle's sidecar presenting his papers to the guards, who had just searched the lorry finding nothing except the artworks and rugs.

An approaching sergeant yelled as he raced towards the gate: "Stop that lorry. Halt."

The gate guards could not quite make out the order and hesitated. Then, realizing what was going on, the guards reached for their weapons. Aart, figuring out the situation too, pulled his revolver, shot the two approaching guards, and ordered the lorry driver to get out of there.

The resistance driver slipped into gear and raced away. Two German motorcycles raced after them but were stopped when one of Aart's men opened the back door and tossed a hand grenade at their pursuers. A spray of rogue shrapnel pierced the driver's side of the van as it sped off.

CHAPTER TWENTY-NINE
You Better Watch Out!

Germany's high command in The Hague was enraged when it was discovered that Maria and Lonnie Quackenbush were snatched from right under their noses. They were crucial pawns in the plot to coerce Owen Manning into stealing vital information about America's nuclear program.

Germany's nuclear ambitions started in 1939 but were short-lived because of the rise of the Wehrmacht, a reorganization of the military that combined the army, navy, and air force. A nuclear project, dubbed Uranverein, or German for the Uranium Club, had only achieved modest success in building a nuclear reactor. In September 1939, Germany invaded Poland, and many of their skilled project physicists were drafted into the Wehrmacht and otherwise deployed, leaving the Uranium Club to wither on the vine.

Nazi spies in the United States bits were aware that America had made significant progress on a "secret weapon." They had been eavesdropping on dozens of American scientists, including Owen, for a long time, picking up and pieces of intelligence. The Third Reich was desperate to steal any information about this so-called secret weapon. German spies were aware of some sort of stumbling block in the development of the weapon and that a team of Americans had been discreetly dispatched to the UK. After the disappearance of Maria Quackenbush, Hanz Weber was soon summoned to the command headquarters in The Hague for a high-level meeting with the Gestapo officer Dinkendorf.

"Heil Hitler, Herr Weber."

"Heil Hitler, Major."

"Herr Weber, please sit down. We are more than distressed at the disappearance of Frau Quackenbush and her daughter. They took them from right in front of us. How could that happen?"

"Let me assure you I have no idea and had absolutely nothing to do with it. As you know, I reported Frau Quackenbush's connection to her son-in-law, Owen Manning, a Nobel prize-winning scientist in the hope that he might be convinced or blackmailed into giving us sensitive information."

"I see, Herr Weber. And exactly why should we believe you had nothing to do with this? How do we know that you were not behind the disappearance of the Quackenbush women? Playing both ends. She is your wife's mother, and Dr. Manning is your sister-in-law. How do we know that you were not an accomplice in the kidnapping to keep in good favor with your wife?"

"I assure you, I had nothing to do with it. Katrina and I are estranged over politics. She's a Jew lover, and I couldn't stand another moment with her. I hear she is living in Sweden with a relative. If anything, I would seek revenge for her foolishness and disloyalty to the Reich. As for me, I am a loyal party member and have proven it many times. Remember it was me who not only told you about Captain Manning's work but also told you about the priceless jewels being hidden in Sweden These are not the deeds of dual allegiances. "So, how have you managed with getting the information from Captain Manning?"

"We have planted informants wherever he goes. In fact, he is currently at a location just outside of London, which turns out to be very interesting, a curious coincidence."

"How's that, Herr Weber?"

"As you can imagine, in my business, coincidences rarely happen. Our people have also been keeping an eye on another scientist, one Nigel Dasher-Hornsby, a Brit. He's a dummkopf aristocrat, but from all accounts, a brilliant chemist. Oxford-trained. We have him and his plant under surveillance and have instructed the Luftwaffe to refrain from bombing the factory. Our sources tell us that they, including Manning and the Brit, are working on something that could prove vital to the Americans and their secret weapon."

"Go on."

"Captain Manning and his associates visited the plant some months ago. He came directly from the States, where he was working on some secret projects. We suppose that his work in the United States is somehow connected to his factory visit and Sir Nigel. Otherwise, why would he just show up to some sleepy village and a factory that makes china?"

"What kind of work are you talking about?"

"We are not sure exactly, but it has to do with some kind of chemical formula. We can assume this is correct since both Captain Manning and Sir Nigel are both experts in chemistry and physics."

"Chemical warfare?"

"No, sir, nothing like that. Something to do with making bomb components, we think. One of our operatives contacted Captain

Manning in Stoke-on-Trent, just outside of London, where Sir Nigel runs the factory. We were attempting to blackmail him if he didn't give us what we want. Later, we concocted the scheme to lure his wife, giving us incredible leverage over the good captain. Either he'd played ball, or he'd never see his wife and mother-in-law again. But now—"

"Exactly, Herr Weber, now what?"

"We were waiting for a break, but our strategy is no longer viable without Frau

Quackenbush and Manning's wife. We lost all our leverage."

"This is a very good yarn, Herr Weber. But the people in Berlin aren't happy, and that's a major understatement. If we find you had any part in letting these women slip away, things will go badly, very badly, for you. You will pay the price."

"But I had nothing to do with that....I swear."

"It really doesn't matter. We need to have someone pay for this blunder, even if it's a scapegoat. As a starter, the careless captain who allowed the escape is currently spending time at hard labor in a camp. He's lucky we didn't shoot him."

"I know our scheme has gone haywire, but we still have spies in place, and if we learn that Captain Manning has the valuable information, we will simply steal it from him."

"How, Herr Weber?"

"We have our ways, trust me. If he gets it, we will have it too. It could require some strenuous convincing, maybe even bloodshed if necessary."

"You better be right, Weber."

Hanz left the meeting with a good deal of trepidation and immediately contacted his cohorts in Berlin.

CHAPTER THIRTY
THE PATRIOT

OWEN WAS ON FIRE. HE COULDN'T SLEEP OR EAT, AND CERtainly, he could not concentrate on his work. Mr. Stimson had promised he would do everything in his power to save Lonnie and her mother....Nothing, not a word so far.

Owen contemplated the possibility of going through with the blackmailer's demands. If the army were to abandon him in this time of desperation, should they deserve his loyalty? After all, he was barely an American, a status just recently bestowed upon him when he signed on with the army. But the second that thought formed in his subconscious, he dismissed it. He knew citizenship required loyalty and sacrifice. But was the price too great? For God and country, he took an allegiance, but what about his precious little family? He thought, yes, gladly I'd give my life, as a patriot, but my family's lives ... that's entirely a different matter.

"Damn this war. It is making us all less than human." His work, he thought, was another mutually exclusive choice Let the genie out of the bottle with unfathomable destruction, or stay true to his principles and the preservation of mankind? The price was too great, for either, he thought.

On the fourth day, the call finally came. It was from the Department of War.

"Captain Manning,? This is Norvel Jakubowski, Undersecretary here at the department."

Owen held his breath. "Yes, I'm Captain Manning. Tell me. Is there word?

"Yes, sir, there is. A very brave group of resistors were able to penetrate Schaduwgazon and extradite both your wife and her mother."

Owen fell to his knees, tears running down his cheeks, and softly mouthed, "Thank God."

"Your wife is on her way back to the United States and will be there by tomorrow. She wanted to go to New York City."

Owen knew why she chose New York. . the baby was there.

"As for Madame Quackenbush, you know she is a patriot. She was personally responsible for financing the rescue of Dutch citizens. She gave most of her wealth to this cause and saved thousands … artists, intellectuals, professors, Jews, and everyday folks who were deemed enemies of the state. A noble woman indeed."

Owen grew impatient. "No, I was unaware of her benevolence. But please, tell me. How is she? Where is she?

"Well, Captain, the news is not good."

Tiring of this political double-talk, Owen demanded. "Tell me!"

"Sir, Madame Quackenbush was rescued from her home, but during the ensuing escape was injured by shrapnel from a grenade. Her condition was serious, very serious, and …"

"And what…Tell me, man."

"She was brought to a makeshift hospital because the Germans had control of all the medical facilities in The Hague. Every attempt was made to save her life, but the available medical treatment was very limited. And..." Jakubowski paused.

"And what?" again demanded Owen.

"Well, sir, I'm afraid that is where things get foggy."

"What do you mean foggy?"

"It was clear that Madame Quackenbush was unable to travel with your wife. Over her great objections, Dr. Manning was convinced to leave the country immediately, and she did. She said for the sake of her baby and husband."

"Go on, Mr. Jakubowski." Owen thought getting the story was like pulling teeth.

"Your wife was smuggled out of the country and, like I said, was put on a plane, a military one, for New York. Our intelligence sources say that hours later the brave resistance leader, Aart Van den Berg and his men were apprehended, mutilated, strung up in the public square, and used for target practice by the Germans until they were unrecognizable.

Owen shook his head in disbelief. "God, animals, the lot of them! But Lonnie's mother?"

"Well, we are not quite certain. In the confusion, somehow Madame Quackenbush was moved, and we have no further information. We are assuming the worst since her condition was so grave, it is hard to imagine that she would survive such an attempt. It is possible that other resistance members moved her body to save it from public humiliation, and to give this woman, considered a saint by many, a decent burial. This is not uncommon."

Owen held his hand over the phone's mouthpiece so Jakubowski could not hear his low sorrowful groan. "Does my wife know?"

"Not this. She of course knows her mother was injured but nothing more.

"Oh, I see." Owen knew that Lonnie would be beyond devastated to learn this tragic news. She and her mother were as close as a mother and daughter could be. And to lose her under such awful circumstances, with freedom within their grasp made it even more bitter. He also could not imagine her pain once she found out the Nazi monsters so mercilessly treated her rescuers.

"One more thing, Captain."

"Yes?"

"Mr. Stimson told me to inform you that your wife, who clearly has a keen mind as a doctor, was able to provide detailed information on the operations at Schaduwgazon. She memorized names and ranks. As this war drags on, this information could prove helpful. She was incredibly courageous, sir."

Owen thanked Jakubowski for the call and the life-saving efforts of all concerned. His thanks were sincere, but he dreaded what was to follow.

The call finally was made. Ellen Manning answered.

"Hello."

"Mother, it's me. Are Lonnie and the baby there?"

Ellen dropped her voice down to just above a whisper. "Yes they are both here."

"What has she told you?"

"How she tried to buy her mother's freedom but was double-crossed. And how her mother was seriously wounded and could not leave with her. The poor child is distraught. She is worried sick about her mother and so ashamed to have tried this misadventure without telling you, but she was lured and tricked. Owen, Lonnie just came into the room, and I know she will want to talk to you."

Lonnie grabbed the phone and burst into tears. "Oh Owen, I've made a mess of things. Poor Mamma, I had to leave her, so injured. But they made me. I had no choice. And she, herself, insisted I get out of there."

"She was right, Lonnie. It was for the best."

"Owen, Owen, I'm so upset. I don't know what's happened to her. Can you find out?"

"Lonnie, I heard from the War Department, someone high up. They were the ones who arranged the rescue after I spoke with them."

"I thought so. I knew you would do anything you could to save us. So, what did they tell you? Anything about Mamma? About our rescuers?"

Owen took a deep breath. "The news it not good. It seems that after you left they caught the men who rescued you from Schaduwgazon."

"Caught? Oh God, Owen, does that mean…?"

"Yes, they were executed, but they did not capture your mother. Local sources seem to think they moved her, but there is no word other than that."

"Well, that isn't bad news? Is it?"

"The fact is, Lonnie, the authorities are assuming that the extent of her injuries, coupled with her age… "

"What are you saying?"

"They believe her injuries were likely fatal, my darling."

"Fatal? She died?"

"That is the official thinking. They feel the resistance moved her body so that the Nazis could not dishonor her. You know she was considered quite the patriot, giving enormous funds to the resistance and saving thousands of lives. She was a hero."

Lonnie was inconsolable. "Oh, Owen, it's all my fault."

"No sweetheart, not at all. In fact, you risked your life to save her. The Germans lured you to The Hague, held you prisoner so that they could get me to give them top secrets in exchange for you and your mother's freedom. But it was a sham. In the end they would have killed you both after they got what they wanted from me. It's just the way those bastards act."

All of this was too much for Lonnie. "Owen, I must hang up. I feel faint. Please come home. I need you. The baby needs you. Please."

Owen's heart was breaking. He needed to be with his wife to ride out this tragedy. But he knew he could not just up and leave even if he wanted to. Duty demanded he stay the course. "Lonnie, I desperately want to be there, and if I could I would. But, you know as well as I, that it's impossible."

"I know, of course. I know, darling. But it hurts so much."

The called ended in tears on both ends. Owen knew he must get this job done in England and get back to Lonnie as soon as possible.

CHAPTER THIRTY-ONE
DRESS RIGHT

Colonel Miller's Office

"COME IN, CAPTAIN, HAVE A SEAT. I HAVE BEEN WORKING ON the enigma that is Sir Nigel. He is an odd guy, soft-spoken, and hard to read. Eccentric too. One thing for sure, though, he hasn't bought into the program. I'm positive he could be more than helpful if he wanted to. I meet with him once or twice a week as a courtesy. Lately, I noticed that his health is deteriorating. He hasn't been to the lab in months."

"Colonel, do you think he has what we need, the missing data?"

"Not sure. I know we talked about this before, and even after all this time, I'm just not sure. I continue to share our notes and findings with the old man, but the way he reacts, I get the feeling he sees something we don't. Or maybe something is missing. He nods and smiles but doesn't say a word." Miller shook his head in frustration. "I think we need to get whatever he is holding back before it's too late."

"How do you propose doing that?"

"I don't know. But I thought that maybe if you two met and hit it off, he might open up to you. You know, a fresh face, eager and willing. I know he likes and admires Americans. And meeting a Nobel Prize winner would impress anyone."

"Colonel, I'll do what I can. But don't get your hopes up. I'm no miracle worker. They didn't give me the Nobel for that. Whenever you want, I'll show up, bright-eyed and bushy-tailed. I'll try some good ol' American charm on him."

"Thanks, Captain. I knew I could count on you. I'll set it up ASAP. Try not to come off too Army, if you understand what I mean. On another matter, I understand from the way higher-ups that they helped out your wife and mother-in-law."

"You know about that? How? I just heard about it a few hours ago myself."

"Of course. The Department of Defense liaison in London passed on a message for you. Apparently, Secretary Stimson himself wanted you to know that your package was picked up and delivered. I have no idea what that means, but apparently, I didn't qualify in the need-to-know department and was given no further explanation other than it involved helping your wife and mother-in-law."

"Wow, he came through. This gives me a renewed sense of confidence in our bureaucracy."

An impressed looked crossed over the colonel's face "You know the Secretary? Like personally?"

"We've met, but how should I put it? We don't belong to the same clubs."

"Well, Owen, I better watch my Ps and Qs around you. You've got connections."

"Don't worry about it, Colonel, I've probably had my first and last encounter with Mr. Stimson."

*****

Briarcliff Manor House

Sir Nigel reluctantly agreed to have the American for tea. Marshall set it up in Briarcliff's study for four P.M. on Friday afternoon. Owen opted to wear civilian clothes, hoping to appear less military.

Owen had packed lightly when he came from the States. Thinking his stay would be only a week or so, he had brought only essentials and had no suitable civilian attire. He ventured down to the village High Street and found a haberdasher. The shop was elegant and pricey, obviously catering to a posh clientele. A bell clanged as Owen entered the dark-paneled shop. Bolts of fabric hung on the walls, and rows of antique-looking showcases housed gloves, ties, and ascots. As he approached the sales counter, he tripped over a display of walking sticks, sending half a dozen of them scattering across the floor. Owen quickly picked them up and replaced them properly.

An impeccably dressed salesman glared at Owen and gave him a rather condescending greeting. "Good morning, sir. How may I assist you?" Then he said, "Do you not see well, sir?"

Owen mentally translated that into, *What are you, blind?*

Mustering up as much dignity as possible, Owen walked closer to the counter and said, "I know this is a bit short notice, but I was wondering if you had anything off the rack. I don't have time for a custom-made suit, so I was hoping that maybe you have something readily available?"

"Ah, an American." This was said in a much more welcoming tone. Owen smiled broadly. "Yes, I am an American, is that a problem?"

"No, not at all, sir. In fact, we Brits owe a lot to you Yanks. Without you, I'd be selling lederhosen, and we'd all be speaking German."

The clerk looked Owen over from head to toe. He figured Owen was six feet five, with broad shoulders, a trim waist and very fit form. A perfect size forty-six, long.

"Well, sir, you may be in luck," the clerk said. "You see, I have two lovely suits, probably just the right size. They were custom made for a young chap who recently fell on hard times. Gambling, I heard. He left a deposit but never picked them up. People say he has left the area. Would you like to try them on?"'

"Great! It looks like this could be my lucky day! I'd love to try them on if you don't mind."

"Of course, sir. Here they are, two beauties, one a blue serge, an all-time standard, and a fabulous gray pinstripe, cashmere blend. Mr. Milton, the gent who ordered them, is a dashing sort and from an aristocratic house. Poor sod, he was always in some sort of difficulty, either money or women, sometimes both. He needs me to sew a lock onto that zipper of his and throw away the key. From what I've heard, it was hardly ever up."

Owen was getting the picture; this shopkeeper was a busybody.

The clerk buzzed around Owen like a social butterfly. "So, sir, the suits. Are they for a special occasion?"

"Not really. I have a business meeting up at Briarcliff."

"Briarcliff ! So, you know Sir Nigel? He's an odd duck, if I must say so myself. Lives alone up there in the Hall, with barely a friend or visitor. You know his old man, Sir Sidney, left him everything, the china factory and all the land and money. Sir Sidney, a bad lot, ran around like a dog in heat."

Owen tried to ignore the idle gossip, but the clerk went on.

"But Sir Nigel, has a good reputation, at least with the workers. Generous and kind Even buys expensive clothing for his butler…. Imagine, fifteen pounds for a butler…like I said he is a generous old coot."

"That's nice, now about the suits."

Disregarding the change of subject, the clerk continued: "He's a confirmed bachelor, you know. Rumors had it that he almost married somebody, I think in Italy, or maybe it was the south of France, whatever. But that kettle of fish never boiled. Probably cause he was expected to marry his own kind, or maybe he was just not the marrying kind, but who knows?"

The clerk rolled his eyes and continued: "Sir Nigel keeps to his knitting, running the factory, and managing his land. And speaking of the factory, lots of comings and goings there. It seems odd that so many of His Majesty's soldiers are in and out of that place, and all they do is make dishes. Bloody well! Is that something you're involved with?"

Owen ignored the question and disregarded the idle local gossip. "I don't know which suit I prefer."

"Well, try them both and see which one you fancy."

Owen picked the blue serge to try first. When he emerged from the dressing room, the clerk clasped his hands together and gasped, "You look drop-dead gorgeous. The suit looks like it was made for you. And, like you said, you are in luck. You see, Mr. Milton dressed to the right, and obviously you do too."

Looking in the mirror, Owen had no idea what the clerk was talking about. "You say dressed to the right? I don't see any difference."

The clerk, clearly amused, tactfully attempted to explain the world of custom tailoring to this American, who obviously had never stepped foot into a haberdashery.

"You see, sir, when we craft the trousers, we make the crotch a bit larger on the side that you dress. This makes for a more comfortable fit. In well-tailored trousers, no one should be able to see on which side, shall I say, nature has favored you."

Owen stared at the mirror, turned right and then left and then right again, trying to figure out if this guy was putting him on. "Are you kidding me? People actually worry about stuff like that over here?"

"Indeed, sir. It's all about the details. It is a matter of craftsmanship and personal appearance. You know, style is essential, but comfort is critical."

Still unconvinced, Owen took another quick look into the mirror. "I'll be damned."

Owen, in the end, decided to take both suits. He thought they would be a great souvenir of his time in the UK, and besides, his haberdashery experience made for an excellent story.

"If I could suggest, sir, a bit of tuck on the jacket, full cuffs on the trousers, and I'll remove the embroidered name in the lining, replacing it with yours. I can have them ready in the morning. May I deliver them, or will you call for them?"

"I'm at the Huntington Arms. Please send them."

"As you wish, sir, they will be there promptly at ten A.M. Will you be settling up now, or do you want to open an account due at the end of the month?"

"Now is fine."

"Thank you for your business. And, sir, God bless America."

CHAPTER THIRTY-TWO
STROKE OF GENIUS

MARSHALL PREPARED THE TEA IN THE LIBRARY JUST BEFORE four P.M., and Owen arrived precisely on time. He wore the blue serge suit with a tie he had picked from the haberdasher's case. It was a school tie from Leicester College, a posh men's university. Owen chose it because he liked the blue and white stripes. Unknown to him, wearing an official school tie was a faux pas. Only good old boys who attended public schools were entitled to wear them. The haberdasher had not only ignored the blunder but talked Owen into another tie, this one from Cambridge, for the gray pinstripe.

The enormous library was filled with awards and decorations collected over the decades by Devonshire Ltd. Photographs of King George and Queen Elizabeth sipping tea from golden Devonshire china cups were framed in a montage, next to a certificate bearing a royal crest. Owen leaned closer and read the inscription:

A Royal Warrant

By Appointment to His Majesty, The King

Supplier of Fine China and Dinner Service

A massive portrait of the late Sir Sidney caught Owen's eye. It graced a prominent place above the ancient stone mantel. As he studied the painting of the previous Lord of Lancaster, it seemed to him that Sir Sidney was looking down upon him in a condescending way.

Owen muttered, "Who the hell is that mean old coot?"

Overstuffed furniture invited the avid reader to settle in and enjoy a good book from one of the many first editions carefully cataloged and stored on the shelves. He walked around the stunning room and contemplated what it would be like to be surrounded by such splendor for one's entire life and then thought, "Not for me."

He caught a glimpse of himself in a large Georgian mirror. "Not bad," he thought. "I look like a million bucks in this get-up. I wish Lonnie were here to see me." Lonnie, he thought, the poor thing. She was depressed over the loss of her mother, and he felt like he was so much of a heel that he was not there in her time of need. Owen knew she was in good hands when she decided to extend her stay in New York as his mother's guest. Surely his mother would do everything humanly possible to help Lonnie through her grief and be with the baby.

His thoughts were broken when Marshall appeared at the door with Sir Nigel holding the servant's right arm. The old man not being that old looked frail but not desperately ill. Nigel walked into the library and put on his glasses just as Owen turned away from the mirror.

"How do you do, Sir Nigel? I'm Owen Manning, and I am so pleased to meet you."

*****

Owen was back in the colonel's office by 4:30.

"So, you're back early, how did it go?" the colonel asked.

"Well, Colonel, you won't believe what happened."

"Let me guess, the old man loved you so much he gave you a briefcase full of secrets."

"Not exactly, Colonel. I only wish. Quite the opposite."

"Yes, I'm all ears."

"So, I walked into this room right out of Buckingham Palace and waited for the old man to come down. I was all decked out in this British blue serge, hoping to make a good impression."

"Well, you do make a good impression and look quite the English aristocrat…quite dashing."

"Yeah, that's the look I was going for, thinking that Sir Nigel would relate. You know the Brits love all that hotsy-totsy fancy-dancy stuff."

"Stop stalling. What happened?"

"Well, the old man's butler escorted him into the room. I introduced myself as Owen Manning. Then Sir Nigel walked a few steps toward me and put on his glasses, took one look at me, and bloody collapsed right in front of me. I couldn't believe it. The guy at the haberdasher told me I looked drop-dead gorgeous, but I didn't actually take him seriously."

"So, he's dead? Sir Nigel is dead?"

"No, no, I was just kidding about dropping dead. But he did pass out cold. I helped the butler carry him upstairs to his room and put him into bed, and then we called the doctor."

"So, he's not dead?"

"As far as I know, no. I think maybe he had a stroke."

"Oh, shit, now what? If that old man dies, we'll never get that formula."

Another week went by, and the team made little progress. The testing results still read in the high eighties, not good enough. Early on Saturday morning, the phone rang in Owen's hotel room. He looked at the clock and thought, "Crying out loud, it's not even eight, and the one day I get to sleep in some fool has to bother me."

"Hello, Manning here," he answered.

"Good morning, sir, this is Marshall at Briarcliff."

"Who?"

"Marshall. Marshall at Briarcliff."

"Oh, hello. How is the old…I mean Sir Nigel doing?"

"Well, sir, he's quite weak. He had a stroke and is just now coming around to speaking, although slightly impaired."

"I'm so sorry to hear that."

"Right. Sir Nigel has asked to see you."

"Me? What on earth for? Last time he saw me, he had a stroke."

"Well, sir, if you could come by Briarcliff, Sir Nigel will explain."

"Explain what?"

"Please, sir, just come. Please. I don't think he has much time. You would be so kind as to indulge him?"

"Very well. Would this afternoon be convenient?"

"Yes sir, most convenient. Shall we say at two o'clock?"

This time Owen didn't wear the blue serge but showed up in his uniform. Marshall answered the door and asked him to wait in the great hall. While waiting, Owen looked around, wandering from room to room. He arrived in the dining room and thought it looked fit for a king. A large breakfront cabinet filled one entire wall between two doors. Owen walked over to get a better look at its contents. It was a set of the most elegant china he had ever seen, more beautiful than anything at the factory showroom. Centered on the shelf was a large bowl covered with intricate patterns in vibrant jewel-tone colors. It was quite different from the other china, with a more contemporary and less formal look. It was what an art connoisseur might call *objets d'art*.

Owen was startled by Marshall, who had quietly crept up behind him. "Excuse me. Sir Nigel will see you now."

"Good. Thank you."

Pointing to the breakfront, Owen asked, "By the way, these pieces are really genius. I assume they were made here in the factory?"

"Yes, sir, they were. Designed by Sir Nigel himself. The china has never been used, and the large bowl was the latest piece he made—just before you arrived."

"I see. It belongs in a museum, I'd say."

"Now, sir, if you will follow me? Sir Nigel is waiting."

The men walked up the double-spiral staircase and paused at the top landing. Owen looked down and whistled. "Some digs."

He was here only as a courtesy to a dying old man and had no idea why this guy insisted on seeing him. The possibility of Sir Nigel giving him the missing formula seemed slim, but it was worth showing up just in case. They reached the master bedroom door, and Marshall knocked.

"Come in," Sir Nigel said in a slightly slurred, barely audible tone.

Owen walked in and got a good look at Sir Nigel. There seemed to be an aura surrounding him—one of peace and altruism. His slurred speech was soft but deliberate. His eyes showed deep emotions. Owen had a sudden affinity toward the frail man.

Sir Nigel directed Owen to sit. "Marshall, pull a chair up, close to the bed for Mr. Manning." Then he corrected himself. "Pardon me, I should say Captain Manning."

Sir Nigel closed his eyes for a moment to collect his thoughts, then opened them and said, "I want to talk to you about something very important."

"Yes, of course. The formula?"

"Bloody hell, not that. Just sit still and listen to me."

"Yes, sir."

"When I walked into the library, the day I first met you, I couldn't believe my eyes. I was so stunned that my body just shut down. The doctor said I had a traumatic episode, which provoked a stroke."

"I'm so sorry to hear that, sir. But I can assure you, I had nothing to do with it."

"But, lad, you had everything to do with it."

Owen, entirely baffled, began to think that the stroke had affected the old man's cognitive abilities. Rather than argue, he chose to sit and just listen.

"Marshall?" Sir Nigel said.

"Yes, sir?"

"Hand me that picture and that album sitting on the nightstand." Sir Nigel took the picture, framed in an old-fashioned silver frame, and handed it to Owen. "What do you think?"

Owen examined the picture, then looked up in shock. "Where did you get this picture of me? How did you get it? Are you playing some kind of joke on me? I don't recall this photo."

"Be still and listen to me. That is a picture of my older brother, Prescott. An amazing likeness wouldn't you say, Captain Manning?"

"Your brother? Where is he?"

"He's long gone, killed in 1911. God bless his soul. But you can see how much you look like him."

"Yes, it's a rather remarkable resemblance."

"Maybe more than just a coincidence." Nigel coughed, and Marshall rushed to adjust his pillows and give the old man a sip of water. "Show me your feet. Take off your shoes and socks."

"What the hell are you talking about? I'll do no such thing."

Sir Nigel, clearly getting not only aggravated but fatigued, pushed Owen. "Look, just do an old man a favor. I don't have long, and this is important not only to me but also to you."

"Goddamn it. You are nuts. I'm leaving."

Owen moved toward the door, which Marshall was now blocking.

"Captain," Marshall said. "Please just do what Sir Nigel asks."

"Look, this better be good. And if I do this, then you owe me big time."

Owen untied, removed his army-issue dress shoes, and took off his wool socks. He had always been self-conscious about his feet, and exposing them in public was very humiliating, but he thought it would be for the greater good: getting the old man's secrets. "There, are you satisfied?"

Sir Nigel rose from his pillows to look. "Thank you." Handing a picture album to Owen, Sir Nigel said, "Look at these pictures."

Owen took the album and carefully examined the pictures. Two things jumped out at him. The first was the handwritten names and dates under each of the photographs. The captions, some with jumbled and others with reversed letters, were clearly written by someone with dyslexia.

"Sir Nigel, who wrote these names?"

"I did, years ago. Look carefully, can you see anything else?"

Owen instantly knew what the old man meant and nodded in disbelief.

"I see."

"The child in the picture is almost two years old there. It was taken by the sea in 1911."

Owen looked at the three or four photos of the young boy and exhaled incredulously. "His feet! They are just like mine! Who is this boy?"

"The boy is Lawrence, my nephew, who disappeared on the *Titanic* in 1912. And the man in the picture frame is his father and my older brother."

A jolt ran through Owen's body. His mind and heart raced. How could this be? Had the stars lined up to grant him the gift of knowing who he was? The very thing he had been seeking ever since that chat with the colonel at MIT? The idea that haunted him most nights before he fell asleep? Owen was barely able to mouth the words: "The *Titanic*, that's the ship my mother crossed on so many years ago. Holy cow, this is too bizarre to believe."

Marshall looked at Sir Nigel, who was clearly exhausted. "Captain Manning, I think it would be good to let Sir Nigel rest for now. Please come back tomorrow, and he will see you again."

Reluctantly, Owen agreed to end the meeting, realizing that the sickly man was spent for the moment.

"Very well. You can bet your ass I will be back and get to the bottom of this. I'll be back tomorrow night after work at 7:30 sharp. He better be ready to clear this up."

Owen didn't sleep much that night. He replayed the scene in Sir Nigel's bedroom over and over in his mind as he tossed and turned. After the disastrous trek to Scotland, which discredited his first theory about his past, Owen had resigned himself to give up seeking his true identity. Now something as unbelievable as Sir Nigel's narrative seemed outrageous. He wasn't ready for another let-down should this old man be wrong or devious. But if there was really some kind of connection between his own mysterious past and these pictures of Sir Nigel's family, he wanted to know. Owen couldn't wait till tomorrow.

CHAPTER THIRTY-THREE
Thanks, But No Thanks...

The day at the lab was excruciatingly long. Owen could think of nothing other than his upcoming meeting with Sir Nigel. Finally, around five o'clock, he went back to the hotel and tried to rest, eventually dozing off. The phone rang abruptly waking him.

"Hello?"

"Sir, begging your pardon, this is Richard at reception. It's seven P.M., and you asked to be called."

"Right. Thank you." Owen rushed to change into a fresh uniform and was out the door to Briarcliff, arriving precisely on time.

"Good evening, Captain," Marshall said. "Please come in. You are expected."

Owen looked the tall, distinguished, good-looking butler over, thinking he must have been a lady killer back in his day. He seemed so poised and cultured, much more than one would expect from a servant. And one thing for sure, he was devoted to Sir Nigel, never more than a few steps away.

"Thank you, Marshall."

Sir Nigel was in good spirits, sitting up in his huge mahogany four-poster bed. "Come in my boy, come in. We have much to talk about."

Sir Nigel, more carefully this night, went over dates and events—from the marriage of Owen's biological parents to the avalanche that killed his father, to the fateful journey across the Atlantic that ended in disaster. Owen revealed how the military, in delving into his background, had discovered his birth certificate was faked. Between the two halves of the story, Owen—and Sir Nigel—were now certain of his identity.

The evening flew by as Nigel spoke of the family that Owen never knew. He admired pictures of his biological father and beautiful mother and his parents' wedding album. He shared with his newly found uncle how wonderful his upbringing had been, how he had been so treasured.

"I am so glad, my boy. It would have killed me to think you were raised as unhappily as I was." Sir Nigel related the good and bad of his days at Briarcliff and how he had worked so hard to build the family's business and run a fair and just Briarcliff estate.

Owen listened intently. This man, an uncle he never knew, spoke of a family he never knew. A distinguished father, a courageous mother who refused to let her only child be imprisoned for life and dominated by his tyrant grandfather. A warm glow filled him as he continued listening. At last, he had found something that was long lost and desperately sought: his ancestry.

The tall clock in the hall struck ten, and Nigel yawned.

"I see you are tiring, so I should go," Owen said.

"Perhaps. I don't have the get-up-and-go I used to have. But will you promise me that you will come back? Maybe the day after tomorrow? There is so much more. We have decades to catch up on."

There were three more visits before the last. With each visit, Owen became more and more attached to his aristocratic old uncle. They spoke of so many things: Sir Nigel's love of art, his caring and generous ways, and the trials and tribulations of his life. The aristocratic gentleman spoke of his concerns about war and achieving peace, and his philosophical worldview, which actually was not too dissimilar to Owen's own private philosophy. Owen filled in the years and ways of his life—about his wife and his new daughter he had yet to meet, of the loss of his beloved mother-in-law at the hands of the wretched Nazis. He told Sir Nigel that he had no recollection of Agatha, his real mother, or his father, Prescott. Nor did he remember the ill-fated crossing on the *Titanic*. None of this.

Tears came to the old man's eyes when he heard more of Owen's happy childhood and his professional accomplishments, especially the Nobel Prize. How proud he was of this long-lost nephew. And how sad it was that he had missed this marvelous man's life. But the most significant pain came from the realization that he had such a short time left to share with Owen. All those years wasted and wondering.

Eventually, Nigel's conversation came around to something he wanted to clarify. By now, the men had formed a bond, one that transcended friendship and approached kinship. They sat in Sir Nigel's room, chatting and reminiscing. Although Nigel wanted to call Owen by his real name, Lawrence, he did not. It was Owen's decision that he remain Owen.

"Owen, I have a question for you. You have been so kind to me with your visits and good wishes, but I was wondering if they were sincere or just a ploy to get what you and your colleagues want."

Owen looked at the old man and decided to give him his honest answer. "Well, in the beginning, that was my strategy. Be nice and talk you into giving us the formula. But I must now be truthful and tell you that although it would mean a lot to me, and so many others, to have the information, my motives for being here now are strictly personal. You have become a very important part of my life now. I've told my wife about you, and she wishes she could share these moments with you… with us."

"Oh, Owen, thank you for your honesty, and more so, thank you for telling me how you feel. It means the world to me and makes this ill man happy and content."

Owen walked over and sat at the foot of the bed and grabbed Sir Nigel's hand. "I've come to think of you as the father I never really had. The one I never got to see grow old, and the one who never got to see what I have become."

Sir Nigel, deeply touched by Owen, remained silent for a few moments, then said, "Owen, I know you are upset that I am reluctant to help provide the missing formula that you so desperately need."

"Yes, but as I said, wanting time together is why I'm here now, not that."

"I'd like to explain how I feel, which will give you some insight into my position. I harbor this profound moral dilemma deep within. Choosing peace but at what price? Knowing that my formula could pave the way to develop weapons of such magnitude that they would scar the Earth forever, annihilating perhaps millions of fellow innocent human beings, is morally repugnant to me. And if such weapons ever got into the wrong hands, the world could be held hostage by unprincipled tyrants. I am well aware of what those types of people are, my father was one. I realize that if I give up these secrets, victory and peace would be at hand sooner rather than later. But at what price? Is the price too high? Do the means justify the end? Would this be an ill-gotten immoral peace?"

Owen had no easy response—he remembered before going to Las Alamos, he had many of the same thoughts, and perhaps still did. Everyone knew what they were doing would change the world if it were successful. Bombs that could level cities and kill millions. But then again, he remembered the cold look in the German's eye as he threatened him in that barroom and the whispered stories of trains full of people crossing the continent to certain death. Finally, he said, "I can't say if the peace would be immoral, or if we're doing the right thing at all, honestly. But I do know that if we don't do it, they will."

*****

One Week Later

Owen arrived at Briarcliff to be greeted by Marshall, who looked worried. "He's expecting you, please come through."

"Is he all right?"

"Sir Nigel is...well, you'll see for yourself."

The men walked up the grand staircase, and Owen noticed the sadness in Marshall's eyes. When they arrived at Sir Nigel's bedroom door, Owen heard voices and looked at Marshall quizzically.

"It's his solicitor, sir. He arrived at seven."

Marshall discretely knocked and swung open the solid oak door. "Sir, it is Captain Manning."

Sir Nigel rose his head from the pillows. "Come in, come in, please. Sit over there. This is August Sanders, my solicitor. August, this is Captain Manning."

Sanders, a man slightly younger than Sir Nigel, extended his hand to shake. "Nice to meet you, Captain." He then turned to Sir Nigel and nodded. "I bloody see what you mean."

Owen looked over at Sir Nigel. He was paler and frailer than just a week ago.

"Sanders has been with me since I took over the factory. He's the corporate counsel. But he is here tonight in the capacity of my personal solicitor and executor to my estate.

"Now, gentlemen, let's get down to business. I asked Sanders here this evening to memorialize the meeting and my wishes. As you know, I'm not well. The stroke has pretty much immobilized me and taken its toll on my body. Each day is a little more complicated than the day before. My doctors are not optimistic, to say the least. But tosh with all of that. Be assured, gentlemen, my mind is intact and rational."

Owen, feeling a tinge of pity for his uncle, thought, *As frail as he is, he's still in the game.* Out loud, he said, "I'm sorry, Sir Nigel, it's a misfortune."

"Sanders, recap for the record what we have journalized. I am too indisposed to do it myself."

"As you wish. Captain Manning, your real name is Lawrence Dasher-Hornsby, and the man in the painting in the library was Sir Sidney, your grandfather. Sir Sidney had two sons, Nigel and his brother Prescott, heir to Briarcliff and the title of Lord of Lancaster.

"Prescott and his wife Agatha were your birth parents. Your actual birthday is October 9, 1910."

Sanders fumbled through his nearby briefcase, "And here is your actual birth certificate and baptismal record as supporting documentation."

Owen took the papers and, for reasons he could not explain, trembled. "I see, thank you."

Sanders continued reading from the journal: "In December of 1911, Prescott was a victim of an avalanche in St. Moritz. His body was never found. Your mother, Agatha, returned to Briarcliff and to the intolerable conduct of Sir Sidney and needed to escape his tyrannical behavior and dominance over her and you. Agatha feared he would ruin your life, as he had so many others. By all accounts, he was an unfaithful husband, a cruel and vindictive father, a ruthless predator, and a shameless philanderer."

Sir Nigel coughed, and Marshall rushed to his side with some water. "Go on, Sanders, the rest of it."

"Agatha, your birth mother, took you and raced to America for freedom, but in a split-second, fate stepped in and erased their lives at least that was what the family assumed for many years."

Owen already knew a lot of this, but having it so matter-of-factly spelled out was impactful.

"When word came that you and your mother were lost, the world ended at Briarcliff. Sir Sidney turned into a madman. He took his grief out on everyone, especially Nigel, who never measured up to Sidney's expectations. You see, he was the spare, and Prescott was the irreplaceable heir.

"Sir Sidney mounted a massive search for you, but there never was any evidence one way or the other whether you were alive or dead. Eventually, Sir Sidney gave up not only the search but on life. He handed Devonshire over to Nigel lock, stock, and barrel, even though he clearly felt Nigel was unworthy and incapable of filling Prescott's shoes. His Lordship became a reprobate, combing the countryside for conquests."

Nigel stopped for another coughing jag and more water from Marshall. "Don't stop, Sanders…"

"When Sir Sidney died, by British law, Sir Nigel succeeded Sir Sidney and became Lord Lancaster, inheriting all that came with it. This is when Nigel learned something terrible from his mother. Sir Sidney was not his father. It explained why he mentally and physically abused Nigel for most of his life."

Nigel leaned up in his bed. "Let me finish. What I really inherited was a life of living a lie. Not just the lie about not being his true son, but many other lies and personal demons. So, Captain Manning, you have stumbled into a fate you never could have imagined. You are the true Lord Lancaster, and all that you see here is yours. I have only been a bastard custodian."

Owen sat speechlessly. What was this old man telling him? How could any of this be real? As he contemplated the enormity of this new reality, he weighed the impact it would have.

Finally, he said, "Look, sir, I didn't come here to trade in my life for yours. I came here to help my country solve a problem and find a formula that would save lives. So far, that hasn't happened. If you want to give me anything, that's what I want…the formula. As for the rest of it, no, it's not for me. I have a wonderful life as Owen Manning. My wife and my daughter love Owen Manning, not some obscure aristocrat called Lord Lancaster living in a faraway land. So, Sir Nigel, thank you for allowing me to learn who I was, but I am perfectly happy for who I am. It suits me well."

"Excuse me, Captain Manning," the solicitor interrupted. "You do understand what you are declining. It's a vast inheritance and an incredible legacy. It is an immense fortune, an empire with millions of pounds, thousands of hectares of land, priceless antiques, a successful company, Devonshire Ltd., and so much more. You are the rightful heir. It is all yours. I advise, no urge, you to reconsider your decision. You will be a wealthy and powerful man. And you would be the rightful heir."

"Thank you, Mr. Sanders. But I am already a rich man. Rich with the things that mean the most to me. Mere treasure in a faraway land has no value to me. I was raised as an American and have no intention of being anything other than an American. I want this for my daughter and her children to follow. So, again, I respectfully decline."

"I see, Captain," said Sir Nigel. "I give you credit for standing up for what you value. It's something I've never dared to do. I was always too weak or too scared or too humiliated."

Sir Nigel looked around the room. First at Owen, then at his solicitor, and lastly at Marshall, who stood behind him.

"Mr. Sanders, take this down. It shall be a codicil to my will. I want Captain Manning and you to witness what is my final decree, indisputable and irrevocable."

"Very well, Sir Nigel, I will comply with your wishes."

"Let's make a start of it." Sir Nigel dictated to Sanders: "I, Nigel Dasher-Hornsby, known as Lord of Lancaster and member of the peerage at the House of Windsor, acknowledges a flawed assumption to the exalted title. I further acknowledge that the true heir is Lawrence Dasher-Hornsby, known to others as Owen Manning. He, after many efforts to dissuade, now abdicates his claim to title and estate know as Briarcliff. This state of affairs leaves the title and realm of Lord of Lancaster without an heir.

"Therefore, I hereby bequeath upon my death my entire estate, absent any title as precluded by English law. This bequest includes all real and monetary assets, including the enterprise know as Devonshire Ltd. to my faithful Marshall."

Sanders paused in his writing and asked, "Excuse me, Sir Nigel. For the record, what is Marshall's last name?"

"Marshall. That is his last name."

"I see, sir. Then for the record, what is Marshall's first name?"

"His first name?…it's James."

CHAPTER THIRTY-FOUR
Bowl Gazing

Sir Nigel peacefully passed away two days later. When Owen learned of his passing, he was saddened. Clearly, the two men had formed a bond, not just their God-given blood bond, but a relationship based on mutual admiration, respect, and empathy.

Owen lamented, "The poor old guy was morally caught between a rock and a hard place, deciding between the lesser of two evils as he saw it. Maybe in time, he would have come around and seen it in another way. But for now, he took his secrets to the grave, something that could have saved lives." Owen, in one respect, envied his uncle's courage and conviction, and wished perhaps he could have the same luxury.

The hotel desk clerk rang Owen's room. "Captain Manning, there is a gentleman here to see you. Shall I send him up?"

"Who is it?"

"The gentleman says his name is Marshall. Mr. James Marshall."

"Marshall? Oh, yes, have him come up."

Moments later, Marshall knocked on the door.

"Excuse me, Captain, but I would like to have a word with you."

Owen walked over to the makeshift bar. "Of course. Please sit down. May I fix you a drink?"

Settling into one of the lounge chairs in front of the small coal fire, Marshall placed a package next to him. "Drink? No, nothing for me, sir."

"Don't mind if I do, do you?" Owen paused, trying to find the right words. "Please accept my deepest condolences on Sir Nigel's passing. I know you were dedicated to him and surely will miss his presence. Now, to what do I owe the pleasure of this visit?"

Owen took the chair across from Marshall. He assumed that Marshall probably spent most of his life in domestic service. From what Owen had observed at Briarcliff, Marshall was totally devoted to his late Uncle Nigel. He figured Marshall to be about the same age as Nigel, yet he looked so much younger and certainly was in a lot better health.

Marshall began: "On Friday, Sir Nigel is being laid to rest. Just before he passed, he made two final requests."

"I see. I assume these requests have something to do with me? And let me remind you, I have already turned down any inheritance."

"Yes, sir, that was made clear. But these requests are a horse of a different color and do have something to do with you, very much so."

"Okay. What are these requests?"

"Before I begin, I want to say something about how incredibly magnanimous you are concerning Sir Nigel's estate. Of course, I had no idea that when you declined Briarcliff and all that goes with it, Sir Nigel would bequeath it to me. Even now, I not sure how this could happen, but I do know why."

"I suspect, Marshall, one can only assume that it is a well-earned reward for being a loyal servant for all these years. Undoubtedly you were dedicated to him, and I guess he felt it was a just reward."

"It is a bit more complicated than that. But I think you should know why your uncle would do such a thing. When you declined your inheritance, along with the title, there would be no proper heir. Yes, I understand that you do have a child, a daughter, who would normally be next in line. However, under English law, something called primogenitor, only males can inherit from their fathers. Thus, she would not qualify.

"Sir Nigel was entitled to leave his property and wealth to anyone, so he chose me after you declined. But titles cannot be bestowed. So, without a proper heir, the title of Lord of Lancaster will be in abeyance."

"Is there more? If so, please continue, Marshall."

"Yes, sir, there is more. More in the way of explanation that I wanted to bring to your attention. Something that would clarify your uncle's actions. Nigel's father, Sir Sidney, and my mother, shall I say, did business together—a filthy business at that. She was the proprietor of the Primrose Cottage, a place of ill repute that Sir Sidney visited regularly. From a young age, I was expected to work there and was compelled to engage in some clearly sordid behavior. Often I was forced to perform acts against my will and frequently physically abused by men who paid my mother for the pleasure.

"Sir Nigel and I had a chance encounter at Primrose many years ago. We were both young boys. I was nineteen, and he was just turning eighteen years old. Nothing actually happened, but his visit did not go well. I thought nothing of it because, as my mother would often say, her patrons would come and go. I never got the pun until much later in my life.

"Months after our first contact, Sir Nigel made it a point to run into me in the village. Although coming from entirely different worlds, sort of the prince and the pauper, we learned that we had things in common, including how miserable our lives were and dark demons, mine exploited by my perverse mother for money, and his beaten out of him by his alcoholic sod of a father."

Owen wondered why Marshall felt that this information was of importance to him, but he politely listened.

"Soon, our friendship became more, much more. We would meet in secret in the village whenever we could. Sometimes in the middle of winter, I'd sneak up to Briarcliff, and we'd rendezvous in the secluded hunting lodge. For hours we would sit in front of a roaring fire and put away our misery and intimately share...." Marshall blushed, stumbled, and stopped. "I think you get the picture. When we were older, in July each year, Nigel would arrange passage to the South of France where we would summer at a rented villa. Naturally, this was all very secretive. No one ever knew, especially Sir Sidney. When we sunned ourselves on Paloma's Saint-Jean-Cap-Ferrat's private beaches, it broke my heart to see Sir Nigel's scarred and disfigured back from the brutal horse whippings inflicted by his monstrous father."

Owen sensed that Marshall's soul-bearing was becoming painful. "Do you want that drink now?"

"Perhaps. I'm feeling a little scared. I've never been so honest with anyone. Baring one's soul is not easy; it takes its toll."

Marshall seized the offered glass and took a healthy swig.

"Things were going well for years. During our summers in France, we made a life as equals, befriending total strangers, many of them artists and musicians. Of course, when we returned to Stoke-on-Trent, I resumed my subservient role in the village."

"You stopped working for your mother as a…well, whatever they called it?" Owen almost blushed.

"Of course. My mother and I stopped seeing each other after I was horrifically violated by three perverse clients who took their pleasure. They had their way with me, and I was seriously injured. But far more damaging was that they stole my dignity. I resolved that night that I would no longer be a whoremonger's son, allowing her to sell me at Primrose Cottage like some cheap commodity. So, I ran. Sir Nigel sought me out and found me bleeding and hiding in the wood, only a blink away from suicide. If it weren't for his care and generosity, I could not have survived. He supported me, arranged for medical treatment, and made me feel worthwhile. He saved me from a living death and quite literally saved me from self-destruction."

Marshall, clearly distraught, took another swig and continued. "When Sir Sidney died, Nigel became Lord Lancaster. He was finally free from his oppressive father. He asked me to come and work at the manor so we could be close. I trained to be a butler. We lived a cat-and-mouse life, ensuring the domestic staff and factory workers never got drift of our relationship. Nigel fitted his dressing room next to his bedroom with a cot for me. He explained he wanted someone nearby should he require something in the night."

Owen interjected: "I saw that cot when I visited. I thought it odd, but nothing more."

"Well, Captain, there was whispering from time to time, but we were discreet and did the best we could."

Another swig and Marshall continued.

"I am telling you all this because I wanted you to know that Nigel's generosity toward me was more than just that. I wanted you to know that his worldly goods are going to the only living person who loved him. I thought you would like to know that."

Owen sat speechless, not knowing exactly what to say. So, he said nothing and took a big gulp of ten-year-old scotch. Marshall broke the silence.

"But I have digressed. I mentioned when I arrived here that Nigel made two final requests. The first was that you do his eulogy. You are his only living relative, and he felt it was only proper."

"Excuse me, Marshall. I don't think I'm qualified to deliver a eulogy for a man I only just met. I know so little of him, that is to say, nothing other than what he spoke of and what you just told me, and I certainly don't think that would make good material for a eulogy, do you?"

"Of course not. What I confided to you must never go anywhere." Another sip. "But I think Nigel would have been a wonderful uncle. He loved your father dearly and lamented his death. Later, when you were assumed lost, he despaired even more. As soon as he learned who you were, he insisted on leaving you everything."

"Which I don't want," Owen reiterated.

"But, Captain, that is not the point. This isn't about material wealth. It is that he thought of you as family, and it is family who should commend his soul to the grave with a proper eulogy."

"Look, Marshall, this whole deal is daunting. I can't—"

"Captain, stop. Please do not decide right now. Sleep on it. The funeral is on Friday. Lots of time to mull it over. Please."

"You know, Marshall, you should be the one doing this. You were a special person in his life. You said you loved him, and I must assume it was mutual."

"Please, we could not speak of love, much less show it. Until tonight, I never spoke of it to anyone. If I dare do a eulogy, it would confirm the whispering and tarnish Nigel's reputation in many people's eyes. No, never. It wouldn't be fair to his memory. So, please, just think about doing it. Like I said, you are Nigel's only living relative, and it would have pleased him so much if he knew you agreed to his last request."

Owen nodded and murmured in frustration. "Ah."

"Now for the second request. Nigel asked that I give you this box. He didn't really explain why he wanted you to have it. There is a note, however. It may be enlightening."

"What is it? You must know."

"Yes, I do. I packed it up myself. It's a bowl, part of Nigel's exclusive collection. One of a kind, as far as I know. He never allowed anyone to touch it. I don't know the significance of the gift, but Nigel was adamant that you have it as soon as he passed away."

Marshall swallowed the last bit of his drink. "And now, sir, I must go. I have fulfilled my promise."

"I see. Well, thank you. And, Marshall, don't worry, you have my promise of confidentiality. What we discussed will remain between you and me. Obviously, my uncle cherished your relationship. It sounds like you were the only person who really cared for him."

"Captain, I can tell you are Prescott's son. You see, I knew him too. He was a gentleman, as are you."

"What are your plans, Marshall?"

"I'm not sure. I will honor Nigel's wishes and run the estate. There will be resentment and criticism from many, but I shall do my best. As for the factory, I'm sure it will have to be dealt with, but probably not by me. It's a task way over my skills."

Marshall rose to leave. "May I shake your hand, sir?"

"Of course. It's my pleasure."

"Thank you, Captain. I only wish Nigel could have lived longer so the two of you could have become closer. And that he could have met your wife and daughter. You know he was a kind and thoughtful man—one who lived a complicated life. And think about doing the eulogy. Nigel desperately wanted you to do it. Now I bid you good night, Captain."

Owen poured himself another drink and walked over to the bed, where he placed the square box. It didn't weigh much but was rather large, wrapped in brown paper and tied in ordinary twine. On a label, Owen's name was written in a rather elaborate scroll along with the words: "Very Fragile." The brown paper peeled off easily, and a beautiful sateen presentation box was revealed. Embossed on the top was the name "Devonshire, Ltd." The lid was fastened by a gold-brocaded frog. When Owen opened the box, he saw a large china bowl securely placed within the fitted interior. He recognized it immediately. It was the bowl from the massive breakfront in Sir Nigel's dining room.

Owen raised the bowl out of the fitted box and saw an envelope, also displaying the trade name Devonshire Ltd. He opened the envelope and unfolded the thick bond stationery embossed with the family coat of arms atop. The handwriting was not the same elegant script on the label and obviously written by someone with an unsteady hand.

> *My dear Owen,*
>
> *The unpredictable way we were reunited was nothing less than an act of destiny. I am sorry that we will never have the opportunity to get to know each other as family. Your father, my brother Prescott, was a marvelous person. I loved him dearly. Your mother was not only wonderful but wise to take you away from Briarcliff.*
>
> *I send you this one-of-a-kind Devonshire piece that I designed solely for myself.*
>
> *I made it just a few weeks before you arrived at Stoke-on-Trent. It is not only beautiful but telling. May peace be your legacy, for it surely will not be mine. God bless you,*
>
> *Faithfully your loving uncle,*
> *Nigel*

*****

Saint Auburn's Episcopal Church, Friday

Nigel's funeral was a sad and lonely affair with just a handful of attendees, mostly staff and business acquaintances. As with most peers, a King's representative was dispatched to represent the Crown. The service was held in a small chapel on Briarcliff's grounds. Large vases of white gladiolas were placed on each side of the ancient altar. They were Nigel's favorite and came from the estate's greenhouse. Marshall had personally picked and arranged them just the way his "Master" preferred.

The altar, dressed in traditional black and purple colors, indicated a state of mourning. Sir Nigel's flag bearing his coat-of-arms was placed over the casket, along with a single white rose. A high Episcopal requiem Mass was celebrated by the Right Reverend Morris Longchamp, parish vicar of Stoke-on-Trent.

Father Longchamp climbed the steep steps of the intricately carved pulpit and addressed the congregation: "My brothers and sisters in Christ, we are here to honor the life of Lord of Lancaster, Sir Nigel Dasher-Hornsby. This morning, I am pleased to ask Sir Nigel's nephew, Captain Owen Manning, to present the eulogy."

As Owen walked slowly toward the podium to the left of the pulpit, he turned to Marshall and gave a smile of capitulation, acknowledging that, in the end, he did the right thing.

Toward the end of the service, the congregants offered each other the sign of the peace. For Owen, it was especially poignant. Perhaps his uncle was at last at peace. But he could not say the same for the world, which had clearly gone mad.

Sir Nigel's remains were carried to the graveyard surrounding the church. The small group of mourners followed, led by Owen. Marshall hung back and walked with the other servants, as what would be deemed appropriate despite the importance he played in Nigel's life. Nigel, as his mother had, left precise instructions not to be buried next to his father. Instead, he chose another plot at the opposite end of the graveyard overlooking Devonshire, Ltd.— a plot with a single remaining open space. A modest headstone was placed on the grave with an epitaph that was authored by Marshall.

Sir Nigel Dasher-Hornsby—Lord of Lancaster
Briarcliff, Trent-at-Stoke
Someone who shared so much and asked for so little
A scientist, an artist, and a man of peace
Requiéscat in páce.

After a small luncheon at the manor house, Owen returned to the lab. The team was still spinning their wheels, clearly stymied by the lack of success.

"Hey, Duck, I've had enough for today, how about a pint?"

"Sure. I'll meet you back at the hotel. Oh, Winney, I'm not in the mood for a party, so come alone. Okay?"

"Sure thing, Duck. I get it. See you in an hour."

After a couple of pints, the friends decided to have an early bar dinner, choosing the house specialty of Guinea hen pie with hardy turnips.

"You know, Duck, if we don't get this puzzle solved pretty soon, we will be the biggest losers ever to come out of MIT. I can see the reunion banner: 'Duck and Winney lost the war.'"

"Yea, but I think we are so close. If we can only find that missing piece."

Winney polished off the last bite of his Guinea hen pie. "Well, if that old man didn't die on us, we probably could have eventually gotten it, even if we had to bully it out of him."

"What makes you so sure he even had something, Winney?"

"I don't know. But I had a feeling he was holding out. The old man almost seemed frightened to work on it. The old sod had notes; some of the mates saw stuff, remember? Buggers to him to go and croak on us." Winney stopped. "Sorry, Duck, no disrespect. I forgot the geezer turned out to be your uncle. Who would have ever imagined that? Bloody hell!"

"I'm turning in, Winney. I'm beat. See you in the morning."

Owen returned to his dreary room and placed a call to Lonnie. They spoke for twelve minutes, the allotted long-distance time. He tried desperately to cheer Lonnie up; not only did her mother's death still lay heavily on her but the loss of those brave young men who saved her saddened her still further. As usual Lonnie asked: "When are you going to come home, sweetheart?"

"Soon dear, soon." He only wished. The call ended with tears and kisses after which Owen walked down the hall for a quick shower. The water, by English standards, was surprisingly hot and pounded on his tired body. He thought: "When the hell is this going to be over?"

He yearned to return to his life with Lonnie and the daughter he'd never seen. He missed the close intimacy of their marriage, Lonnie's soft, willing body next to his and the unbridled passion they shared. If only that crazy old uncle of his had relented and given them the missing link, assuming he even had it.

Owen returned to the room, and the large box sitting in the corner caught his eye. "I wonder if Lonnie will like that bowl? It's pretty and certainly valuable." He opened the fitted case and lifted the bowl out, noticing how delicate it was. The colors were so vibrant, despite the bowl being somewhat translucent. *Kinda masterwork*, he thought.

Owen placed the bowl on his dresser and laid back on his bed. He contemplated how different his life could have been. British aristocracy, he laughed out loud, a Lord of the Realm. Just like in a storybook, for crying out loud. But he was comfortable in his choice to pass on it. He thought that all of that wealth and power never brought his uncle much happiness. Perhaps the old adage was true: money can't buy happiness. It certainly didn't buy very much for Uncle Nigel. He smiled when he remembered Winney's version of the old adage: money can't buy happiness, but it allows you to look for it in a lot of places. What a piece of work, that daffy Brit.

With his gaze fixed on the bowl, he relaxed back on the bed. Nigel was not only a brilliant chemist but a very talented artisan. He decided that Lonnie probably would like the bowl. Maybe they could put it on a mantle when they got one someday. He closed his eyes as his mind wandered. The patterns on the bowl swirled in his subconscious. Then in a moment of recognition, he sprang from the bed, raced over to the dresser, and grabbed the bowl. He rotated it and traced the design with his finger.

"What is this? They are all mixed up, not just geometric shapes, but letters and numbers and hard to make sense of them." With closer examination, Owen realized that he could make sense out of them because they were backward and sideways and upside down. His uncle had suffered from dyslexia just as he did. The design was not just a design but an equation that was clearly readable to another dyslexic.

Uncle Nigel's gift was more than a priceless bowl. It was the formula that everyone thought his uncle took to his grave.

Owen wondered, "Why would the old man give this to me, knowing I could figure out what it was. He was hell-bent on the consequences should his formula result in what he thought to be genocide. Perhaps he didn't have the courage to step up and relied on me to make what he felt was a wrong choice."

Dumbfounded, Owen reached for the phone. "Ring me through to Dr. Barrington's room."

"Ciao, Barrington here."

"Winney, it's me, Duck."

"Duck, I thought you made an early night of it. What's up, do you want to party?"

"No, no chance. But you're not going to believe this, the old man came through big time."

"What are you talking about?"

"My uncle Nigel. He gave it to me."

"I thought the old sod died? Are you seeing ghosts, or maybe a little too much hooch?"

"No, no. Look, tomorrow we will go to the lab and check it out. I'm sure that the crafty old guy wanted me to have it at the very end, and he found a way."

"Right. Well, if this isn't one of my cockeyed dreams, then I'll see you in the morning, and we'll have a look-see. It's late, I need my beauty sleep; now go to bed."

"Is that a girl I hear in the background?"

"Yea, it's my mother, you sod, she came to tuck me in, now go to bed."

Winney slammed the phone down, and Owen hung up. But he wasn't the last to leave the call.

Special Agent Moyer, a German scout across the street from Owen's hotel, pressed the stop button on a recorder. Moyer was charged with the responsibility of wiretapping the contingency that came up from London to work at Devonshire.

The scout immediately contacted his handler. "Herr Schmidt, this is Special Agent Moyer. We may be in luck. I was eavesdropping on Manning. In a conversation, he was quite excited about some kind of breakthrough. He wasn't specific, but it could be something important, maybe something we want."

"*Wunderbar*, Herr Moyer. Well done. I hope it turns out to be something of value. Now we will have to find a way to get it."

Owen rose at 6:25 the next morning, and as was his routine, he went for a run. The village streets were deserted and shops shuttered. He ran past the butcher, an estate office, and then a bakery. As he made the turn onto the High Street, a dark sedan pulled up beside him. The doors opened, and two tall men approached him.

"Captain Manning, We'd like to talk with you, if you please."

From the accents, Owen knew this was trouble. "*No*, I am not pleased. Look, I'm on my run, and I'm not interested in talking with anyone, especially you. And for your information, you got nothing on me. My wife is safe and sound in the States, and my dear mother-in-law is gone, may she rest in peace."

"We are well aware of that. It was a most regrettable blunder on our part. But that doesn't mean that you are not at risk. Perhaps an unfortunate accident might befall you. Something toxic that you eat, or maybe a careless driver along the road as you take your run could make your kid fatherless in a blink of an eye. And you think your family is safe in New York? Do you know how many Germans live in New York City?...More than 200,000, and let me assure you, Herr Captain, many of them are loyal to the Fatherland, and others have relatives within our reach in Germany—useful pawns. So don't go thinking you and your family are out of our reach. And remember, we had you wife once. It could happen again, and this time there will be no rescue."

Owen once again felt threatened but would not allow these thugs to see it. "I told you that you better get lost. I want nothing to do with you."

"Well, Captain, if you don't want to have one of those accidents I mentioned, or a mishap to your beautiful wife and young daughter, I suggest you show up this evening at nine. We have a farmhouse just outside of the village. It's called Holly Hill Farm and not very hard to find on the Old Farm's Road. You won't be able to escape us. It will be a pity if your lovely young wife becomes widowed and your little baby, fatherless."

The black sedan drove away, leaving Owen in a cloud of exhaust.

CHAPTER THIRTY-FIVE
THE HOMESTRETCH

SHAKEN BY THE ENCOUNTER WITH THE GERMANS, OWEN returned to the hotel, showered, and reported to the lab. There, he and the team assembled in the secure conference room to discuss Owen's discovery.

Colonel Miller started: "From what you have said so far, it looks like you have come across something important. Start from the beginning."

"Yes, sir. I was exhausted and lying in bed, trying to relax. I have a condition that requires me to keep a keen focus most of the time. It can be exhausting, so to rest, I let my guard down and allow my mind to roam freely."

When Owen finished relating his discovery, the colonel asked: "So it was in code? Something no one would typically pick up on."

"Not exactly a code, sir. Like I told you, Sir Nigel was dyslexic, so he put his formula on the bowl in raw form; in other words, without trying to correct his writing. A non-afflicted person would not really make much of such writing, thinking it to be random scribbling or jibber-jabber, especially if it were cleverly incorporated in a pattern or some kind of design, which is precisely what Sir Nigel did on the bowl.

"When I realized what I was seeing, I immediately transcribed it into regular characters and numbers. It appeared to be a formula. I have it here."

Owen handed a yellow pad to the colonel.

"Captain, are you certain this is the missing formula we were so desperate to get from Sir Nigel? The one we were unable to convince him to give us?"

"Yes, sir. I believe it is the missing part, and I think we will have the elusive answer we are seeking."

"Why are you so sure?"

"For a couple of reasons. First, Sir Nigel made a serious attempt to hide this formula using a rather unique method. Why would he do that unless he had something important to protect? I am a physicist and have considerable chemical engineering experience. My training tells me that the transcribed formula is directly related to the work we have been doing for months. It fits. With it, we will be able to reconstitute the elements and produce the kind of material needed to cast a vessel that will meet Los Alamos's needs. I'm just plain sure of it."

"Fantastic, Captain. We will begin the tests immediately. If our results are satisfactory, Los Alamos will be thrilled to hear that we may finally be in the homestretch. Well done."

*****

Holly Hill Farm

Owen arrived at Holly Hill just before nine wearing civilian clothes and carrying a black satchel, one like a diplomatic courier uses to transport documents. The farm was easy to find—just about everyone in the village knew Holly Hill, an old farm in disuse. He had a knot in the pit of his stomach. By any measure, he felt scared to death. He really never wanted to do this, but in the end, he had no alternative. He prayed that this whole thing wouldn't explode in his face and could not wait till it was over.

Owen walked to the door of the small farmhouse and opened it. No one was there, and a single candle burned on the old rickety dining table. Walking in a bit further, a rat ran across his foot, and he jumped back in revulsion. A stale odor hung in the room like the decrepit drapes half hanging off their proper rods. Not a sound, apart from the slow drip of filthy rainwater that had accumulated on the roof and was leaking from the ceiling. He thought: "Where are these bastards?"

When he saw an envelope on the table, he grabbed it. The envelope bore his name, so he ripped it open and read the typed note within: "Behind the small barn."

This made Owen even more nervous. Changing the location probably meant he was being observed. Perhaps looking to see if he was alone. There were two barns on the farm. The little one sat on top of a small knoll some four hundred yards away from the farmhouse. It was a bit of a climb, and the ground was wet and slippery. More than once, he fell to his knees as he rushed toward the barn. By the time he reached the well-worn barn door, which was slightly ajar, he was a bit winded. Or was it just his heart beating so fast, mirroring the controlled panic he felt.

"If this goes badly, I'm a goner."

Owen thought about his family and how he was doing this to protect them.

"Captain Manning." A thug called Stephan with a thick German accent called out from. within the first stall. "Did you bring what we want? I hope so because if you haven't, well…things won't go well for you."

Owen peered in. His view was partially blocked by a large sedan parked in the middle of the barn. He moved slightly to the left and saw the shadowy figures of four men. One was sitting at a table with his back to the door; the other three stood.

"Yes, it's all here. But I'm afraid it is well beyond your level of comprehension. Very technical, something only a physicist or chemical engineer would understand."

"Not to worry, Herr Captain. We have an expert sitting here to confirm the authenticity of what you brought. The satchel, please, just drop it on the table."

Owen complied, and the spokesman for the group struck a match, which lit up the darken barn momentarily. The man ignited an old oil lamp on the table, and the room came to light.

Owen walked over to get a better look at who was at the table, the supposed expert. What he saw defied reality.

Sitting at the table was Winney Barrington, his best friend.

"What the hell are you doing here?" Winney said.

"I might ask the same of you?"

"Owen, I'm here because I have no choice. You see, these bastards have the goods on me. Remember when I told you I had skeletons in my closet. Well, the Gestapo did a lot of digging and found the worst one. You see my mother's father was part German, some great-great uncle was a part of the royal family. He had a really splendid place he called Wunderbar Ruhe—Wonderful Rest—just outside of Wiesbaden, a spa town some forty kilometers from Frankfurt. As a kid we went there every fall for Oktoberfest and again for the holidays.

"It was the October I turned eighteen, and after way too much beer and schnapps, Eric, a townie, and I were got caught doodling some milkmaid. Her father went bonkers. When I returned to Wiesbaden for Christmas, the farmer confronted me. His daughter was pregnant, and he wanted me to marry her. Christ, she was only sixteen. I told him there was another bloke, Eric, involved, we both did her, and there was no way to know whose kid it was.

"There was no reasoning with this chap, and he pulled a knife and threatened to cut my willie off if I didn't marry his daughter. It came to fisticuffs, and the farmer chased me and tripped on a rug, falling down the stairs and ending up dead.

"In order to cover up a real scandal, my grandfather paid off the family handsomely, and he never told my parents. As for the girl, I never knew what happened or if the baby was real, or if it was mine or Eric's."

"So, when these Nazi bastards confronted me, I caved. More than caved, I betrayed my country. They concocted a much more damaging and perverse version of the story, and I didn't want this bogus version of the incident to confirm to my father that I was genuinely a cad, a worthless coward. And what about you? What are you doing here?"

"I'm here because my Uncle Sam asked me to come."

"What? Who?" Winney looked at Owen, and Owen looked back. It was a look of "don't ask, you'll see."

"Look, gentlemen." Klaus interrupted. " I don't care why you are here. Now, let's get down to business." He opened the black satchel and pushed the papers in front of Winney. "Take a look, is this what we want?"

Winney looked up at Klaus and said: "Don't rush me, Kraut. This stuff is not for kindergarteners, and I need a drink before I look at anything." Winney pulled out his pint-size flask, unscrewed the shot-glass cover, and filled it to the brim. He leaned over and spoke to the full glass: "I'll be right with you, sweetheart; Daddy needs to take a look at something."

Owen, listening and watching, couldn't believe his ears. Winney was actually having a drink in the middle of all of this espionage. He thought, "We might get killed, and he's having a drink, calm as a cucumber."

"Well, hurry up, Barrington!" Klaus shouted. He turned to the other two men and barked, "You two go outside and keep an eye out. I don't trust either one of these guys; they may not have come alone."

"What a break," Winney thought as he rifled through the pages. When the other two thugs were gone, Winney asked Owen to look at the formula on page seven. "Look here, Owen, I think there is a mistake." Taking his pen, he began to write in the margins using binary code, the language of scientists: "Go along with me. I'm going to get us out of here."

Winney waited for the opportune moment, and it finally came. Klaus was leaning against a side door just behind the table. "Hey, Kraut, come here, look at this."

Klaus walked over to the table, and Winney lifted the shot glass and tossed it into Klaus's face. Klaus was taken aback, but before he could scream out, he collapsed.

Owen was frozen in shock while Winney bolted from the table. "Get in the bloody car," Winney mouthed. "They left the keys in it when we arrived."

The two men jumped into the old Morris Minor, fired it up, and roared through the barn doors. The two German lookouts were stunned and unable to get off a single shot.

*****

Devonshire Lab

Around midnight, Owen and Winney showed up at the lab. They had unfinished business with Colonel Miller.

"Come in, gentlemen. … Quite a night."

"I'd say, sir. One, I'm not too anxious to re-live," Owen replied.

"You've done your countries proud, congratulations. We've got those two Nazis outside the barn and are rounding up a lot more of them as we speak. We've had our eyes on them for a long time, but up until now, and without your help, we had nothing on them. You both took a great personal risk and are heroes. Manning, you will be written up for the Bronze Star and you Barrington, the George Cross, UK's highest civilian award. Your country owes you a great debt of gratitude. Now go back and get some rest; you deserve it."

The two men drove back to their hotel quarters in complete silence, both trying to figure out what had just happened. When they entered the hotel, Owen asked, "Hey Winney, let's have a drink; I want to talk to you. I have a lot of questions."

Winney scratched his head. "Right, I got some questions too."

"I'm going first. If you don't mind me asking, Winney, what the hell was in that flask?"

"Ha, ha," Winney laughed. "It was a concoction that some of the guys in MI5 cooked up for spies. I wasn't sure it would work, but I took the chance and used it full strength, and the Kraut dropped like a lead balloon." He paused. "Now it's my turn. Owen, why would you give the Nazi bastards our secrets? It's not like you."

"They had my wife and mother-in-law detained in The Hague, threatening to kill them. I had no choice but to play ball. There was a rescue attempt, and we got Lonnie out, thank God, but in the escape my mother-in-law was mortally injured.

"I'm sure noticed that the material I gave them was mostly old and pretty much disinformation. I worked with Army Intelligence, and tonight was a sting. We just made it look like I was going to be a turncoat, but never would.

"Winney, how did you wind up in that barn, and did you know I would be there?"

"Like you, the Krauts approached me. They were tracking all of us assigned to high-profile military projects. They needed someone to authenticate stolen top-secret documents that were being provided by another leading scientist."

Winney continued, "They told me that they would blackmail me about the milkmaid incident in Germany years ago."

"So that story was true, not just bullshit?"

"Sad to say, it was true and embarrassing, but not nearly as bad as what the Krauts cooked up.

"When I refused to play ball, the bastards said they would enhance the incident and make me look like a complete pervert by changing the official report to read that the victim was not the milkmaid but her underage brother who, after I allegedly assaulted him, was committed to an asylum. Further, they had German sympathizers in London, one of them my roommate at college, who would sign affidavits with similar stories, all untrue, but which would ruin my reputation and could land me in jail— you know diddling men is illegal here in the UK. I spoke to a couple of mates in MI5, and they agreed to set up the sting to catch the turncoat scientist as well as the German operatives he was collaborating with. They also set me up with the knockout juice.

"Did you know the scientist was me?"

"Not a clue."

The two men sat for a long time not saying a word until Owen decided to call it a night.

"Good night, buddy. It's been one of those days."

"Yea, Owen, one of those days, for sure."

Owen turned to leave the bar and paused; "Hey Winney, you know what I just realized? You are a genuine hero."

Winney grinned. "I suppose I am, mate."

CHAPTER THIRTY-SIX
MIRACLES DO HAPPEN

THE NEW INFORMATION WAS A BREAKTHROUGH, BUT IT WAS going to take several more weeks, perhaps even a month or two before it was ready for Los Alamos. Testing and verification, along with refinement, were all underway at Stoke-on-Trent. Owen was growing increasingly restless and dreamed of returning home. To appease his uneasiness, the American Command in London agreed to allow Lonnie and the baby to come for a short visit. It was arranged to be in neutral Ireland, a place exempt from German bombing. Officially the trip was positioned as a VIP visit by Dr. Lonnie Manning, an International Red Cross pediatric surgeon. She would tour hospitals, lecture at the University of Dublin's School of Advanced Medicine, and visit rehabilitation facilities for war-injured victims.

Owen was delighted with the concession and couldn't wait to break the news to Lonnie in a late-night phone call.

"Hello, sweetheart, it's me."

"Me?" Lonnie teased. "Could you be more specific?"

"Darling, stop. I have some wonderful news."

"You're coming home …. At last!"

"No, sorry honey, I wish I were. That won't be for another few weeks. But the news is almost as good. The high command has granted permission for you and the baby to come to England for a visit."

"England? Aren't they dropping bombs over there? As much as I am dying to see you I don't want to actually die to see you, bombs withstanding."

"No, don't worry. The visit will be in Ireland. Officially they are a neutral country, and the Germans aren't committing acts of war against them."

"Ireland, isn't that part of the United Kingdom? How could they be neutral?"

"Don't ask me, but they are, truly. The Army doesn't make mistakes like that."

"And the baby?"

"She can come too. It's all arranged. A commercial flight to Dublin, first class."

"When?"

"Next week, Thursday. Are you game?"

"Owen, I'd travel to Mars to be with you. And our little girl has yet to meet her handsome brave father. By the way, the army wrote me a letter. They are giving you a Bronze Star. How wonderful, but for what?"

"For having the neatest desk and sharpest pencils."

"Stop, tell me the truth." Lonnie was so delighted to hear Owen was back to his playful self.

"I'll explain it all when you get here. It will be great pillow talk."

"I think not. War stories don't make for good pillow talk. And besides that, I don't think there needs be much talking at all."

"So, until next week, I love you so much and long to see you and that little precious girl of ours."

The Douglas DC3 took off right on time. Lonnie had traveled from NY to Liverpool with three fueling stops and twenty six hours of traveling. In Liverpool she immediately changed flights to Dublin. Aer Lingus was only a few years old but already had established regularly scheduled flights to a half dozen cities in Europe. Being an Irish airline, their airplanes were permitted to land in Nazi-occupied countries, providing one of the few neutral transportation alternatives.

Owen's trip wasn't so easy. At the last-minute a three-star general bumped him from a military transport plane going to Dublin. Determined to get there, he boarded a train in Stroke-on-Trent and traveled to Liverpool where he transferred to a ferry. The trip was long, hot, and uncomfortable, taking more than twelve hours. To make matters worse, the first-class sections on both the train and ferry were sold out. But it didn't matter. He was on his way to one of the most important rendezvouses he would ever have. Periodically, his heart raced as he thought of seeing Lonnie again, and their baby for the first time. *Sure,* he thought, *I've seen pictures of the baby, but seeing her in person, holding her and kissing her is something I have been imagining since the day she was born.*

Owen still harbored guilt about not being with Lonnie when she gave birth. Not being able to take that midnight feeding or change that stinky diaper as bad as it might be was something he would have treasured.

And, of course, there was Lonnie. His love for her was immeasurable. How long had it been since he held her in his arms? Since he tenderly kissed her? And since he made love to her? Far too long, and in fact, it was almost like a distant memory. He was almost nervous as he contemplated their first night together after all this time. Maybe she would be too? He fantasized that maybe they would be like honeymooners, all shy and anxious. Who knew? But he was soon to find out.

The train arrived in the Dublin Town Center. The gray day would normally put a damper on anyone's spirts, but not his. He was on the way to see the love of his life and meet the daughter he never knew.

"Dublin Arms, driver, and make it snappy."

"Right Gov, snappy it will be, but it cost you an extra bob or two."

Lonnie was already checked into the hotel, showered, and changed. The baby lay sleeping in the bassinette next to the full-size double bed. The little darling had traveled well and slept a good part of the trip. Lonnie worried about the time change and if it would create havoc with the baby's schedule. For the third time, Lonnie looked into the mirror over the makeup vanity and plumped her hair. And for the third time she sprayed Owen's favorite perfume about her neck and shoulders. She worried what she would wear for the reunion and finally settled on the same dress she wore when they visited his mother in New York for the holidays, some years ago. Owen loved it, and she loved that he did.

Hours passed as she waited. Owen didn't say exactly what time he would be there, but she knew, come hell or high water that he would. The friendly porter delivered tea about four along with a warm bottle of milk. About halfway through the bottle came the knock on the door that she had waited for so long.

Lonnie rushed to the door with baby in arms and flung it open. "Owen, Owen, my darling, Owen, It's you. I can't believe my eyes; we are finally together.

Owen eyes welled with tears as he looked at Lonnie and his precious little girl that he had waited so long to see. Taking the baby from Lonnie's arms he held her high into the air trilling in circles. "She's gorgeous, absolutely gorgeous."

*****

Three days later

As part of the arrangements, Lonnie was to visit a number of facilities. In the morning, she visited St Patrick's Hospital, where she toured the intensive care pediatric ward and was introduced to the chief of staff, Dr. Keeley.

"It's an honor to meet you Dr. Manning. Your reputation precedes you."

"The honor is mutual, Sir. I am thrilled to be here."

"We have arranged a full day for you, Doctor."

"That's wonderful. I look forward to it."

*****

Owen stayed in the hotel with the baby, the two of them now inseparable. With a little help from a hotel nanny, everything was managed.

Lonnie's tour continued until lunch after which she was driven to the University of Dublin's Medical School. She was invited to give a lecture to all the third-year interns specializing in pediatric surgery.

Lonnie ended speaking about four: "So doctors, I commend you for your dedication and sacrifice. Yes, I say sacrifice, because all of us have sacrificed and will continue to have to sacrifice. Being a physician comes with intrinsic and nonnegotiable sacrifice. You all know exactly what I mean. And with the war, we will be called upon to treat the most difficult and challenging cases. It is why we are physicians, to heal, to do no harm, and to do the work of the almighty. Thank you for your kind attention. I bid you adieu and pray that God will guide you in this journey called healing."

The dean of medicine, Dr. Mickman raced to the podium and shook Lonnie's hand. "Thank you, Doctor, that was inspirational. We are most grateful. And now, I am told we are to take you to your final stop on today's visit. It's called The Cottage, and it's just around the corner so we can walk. They will be serving tea just about now."

"What an enchanting name."

"Yes, it is. It's called that to make the patients feel at home. Most of them, many of them children, are victims of the war, coming from all over Europe. They have suffered serious injuries from bombs, shrapnel, and gunshots near or to the head. It is amazing how well so many of them are doing and some are well on the road to recovery. The place is run like a home away from home. Many of the patients, those who are capable, pitch in and help run the place. Some help tidy up; others sit with the more infirmed, while still others help the cook, prepare meals, and bake."

"That sounds like a marvelous program. I found that the sooner you can get patients doing everyday things, the sooner they become independent and healthier."

Dean Mickman and Lonnie walked the short block to the Cottage. It was a lovely, large old home that had Tudor accents amongst the stucco facade. The entry hall was welcoming and nothing near institutional.

"Come in, Doctor. I want you to meet some of the staff. They do an incredible job here."

Lonnie shook hands and smiled as the dean introduced half a dozen or so dedicated doctors and nurses.

"So, Dr. Manning, what do you think of our little Cottage?"

"I think it is one of the best ideas I've seen in a long time. Treating patients in this kind of environment makes all the sense in the world. It's homey, healthy, and healing. My highest compliments."

"Thank so much. Your praises mean the world to me. Now, come let's enjoy some tea. Some of the patients have prepared a special tea, with a somewhat international flavor, given their ethnic diversity."

Lonnie walked over to the tiered tea table with an empty plate. The small sandwiches, cookies, and tarts all looked delicious. But what caught her eye was a plate neatly stacked with a familiar cookie. "Why look at these," she said to the Dean standing next to her. "They remind me of something my mother and our housekeeper made years ago."

"Do they?"

"Indeed. They are called krakeling, a favorite Dutch sweet."

"Well, I am happy you like them. I'll introduce you to the baker who makes them, who is recovering from a loss of memory most likely caused by the horrific injuries sustained at the hands of the Nazis. The patient has made marvelous progress, although still has a way to go. Wait here." The dean headed toward the kitchen. "I'd like you two to meet."

Lonnie smiled, and the dean went to collect the baker. "Here she is. Dr. Manning, meet Maria. She's the one responsible for the cookies."

Lonnie dropped the plate she was holding and gaped at the woman. "Mamma?"

CHAPTER THIRTY-SEVEN
THE PEACE WE ARE GIVEN

Alamogordo, New Mexico, July 1945

THE SUN HAD NOT YET RISEN AT 5:30 A.M. WHEN THE COUNT-down reached its end: "…, 5, 4, 3, 2, 1, ignite."

The switch was thrown, and high atop a steel tower, the first atomic bomb was detonated. Among the hundred or so observers were Owen and Winney, who watched a mammoth light flash from the tower, followed by an intense heatwave that withered everything within miles. Then a deafening sound painfully penetrated ears although they had been blocked with plugs. The boom echoed throughout the valley as a hellish ball of fire ascended into the dawn sky. A giant mushroom cloud billowed miles into the heavens. The destruction was breathtaking, stunning even to the most seasoned of scientists who were caught off-guard.

An unsettling feeling fell over Owen as he watched. This was the moment he had both dreaded for years and yet worked hard to achieve. He had always known they were working to unleash unbelievably destructive power but seeing it in real life was terrifying. He imagined the effect this would have on a city, the devastation.

And while he knew this would end the war and probably save millions of lives, what then? What would happen after the war was over, and this destructive power was unleashed on the world?

Owen remembered his uncle's words of warning and caution while he was in England: "Such a weapon in the wrong hands is dangerous to mankind. Is the price for peace worth the risk?"

He mulled over this dire caution each day as he and his team worked feverishly to complete and test their work. The results were better than expected, and Owen knew that soon he would be on his way home. But the gnawing reality that tormented his conscience was that he and his uncle were the ones largely responsible for expediting the ability to change warfare and annihilate vast numbers of mankind in mere seconds. Sure, he rationalized, it was a team, a large team's effort, but without Sir Nigel's formula and his own role in delivering it to the army things could be different.

Winney turned to Owen, who had the strangest look on his face. "What's up, mate? You look like you just saw the devil."

"I think I just did."

Owen wondered if God would ever forgive him for his role in this assault against humanity or if he could forgive God for allowing man even to imagine it. But regardless of what God thought, Owen knew without a doubt that he and he alone could never forgive himself. He had hoped his work was a way to finally end this war that consumed every corner of the globe and cost so many so much. Owen knew that Sir Nigel's unique bowl revealed the secret, but as the envoy of it he was solely responsible for what would follow. This reality haunted Owen, knowing that it could be the beginning of the end. But for now, he was resigned that it was the peace we are given.

The End

Epilogue

THE MANHATTAN PROJECT ENDED IN A FIERY BALL. ON Monday, July 16, 1945, the first atomic bomb was tested in Alamogordo, New Mexico. Spectators, mostly scientists and a few VIPs, hunkered down in a bunker some six miles away. They witnessed the mushroom cloud and intense light rising some forty thousand feet into the morning sky. The power was that of some twenty thousand tons of TNT. The launching tower, as well as everything in near proximity, was vaporized. Observers were stunned: the power exceeded even the most exaggerated projections. Dr. Oppenheimer was said to be so awestruck that he didn't speak for an hour.

The A-bomb, as the team of physicists and chemists dubbed it, harnessed the power of atomic energy in a way never before conceived. There were actually two different types of bombs. One was called the Little Boy, a uranium gun-type bomb, and the other was called the Fat Man, a plutonium implosion bomb. Both delivered an unprecedented and unimagined payload of destruction. The War Department had planned to drop the first bomb on

Germany, but by the time the weapon was cleared for deployment, the Germans surrendered, leaving just Japan in the war.

The United States faced a critical decision: whether to embark on a lengthy and expensive campaign to bomb and fight a land war to defeat Japan, or the unthinkable alternative of dropping the A-bomb and forcing a quick surrender by the Imperial Japanese armed forces. But at what cost? There was palpable negative sentiment toward Japan and its army, which was known to be especially barbaric toward American POWs. That, coupled with the deep resentment for the 1941 sneak attack on Pearl Harbor, made the decision to drop the bomb less agonizing for many. There were unchartered waters with many questions and few answers.

President Harry Truman was said to have spent many sleepless nights trying to justify what was being described as a potential holocaust. He was a moral and religious man, which made the decision even more difficult. Days of splitting headaches and stress plagued Mr. Truman before his decision.

In the end, Japan forced the president's hand by flatly refusing the ultimatum made in the Potsdam Declaration demanding unconditional surrender and clearly spelled out that Japan faced imminent danger, which would result in "prompt and utter destruction." On July 26, 1945, President Truman, urged by his military advisors, chose to alter history.

At 2:45 A.M. on August 6, 1945, the *Enola Gay*, a Boeing B29 Superfortress bomber named after pilot Colonel Paul Tibbets's mother, took off from Tinian Island in the Marianas. It was on the historic mission of dropping the first atomic bomb. The chosen target was Hiroshima.

After reports of the incomprehensible devastation of Hiroshima, President Truman ordered American aircraft to drop explicit, detailed leaflets written in Japanese on three more major cities that were targeted to be destroyed: Kokura, Niigata, and Nagasaki.

Still, even after the bomb destroyed 90 percent of Hiroshima, and repeated warnings were issued to the leaders of Japan and the Japanese people, a surrender could not be arranged.

Three days after Hiroshima, a second mission targeting Nagasaki was launched. Together the two bombings killed between 129,000 and 226,000 people, most of whom were civilians. The destruction was unfathomable. Following the attack, tens of thousands of people died from radiation-related illnesses. Six days after the bombings, Japan surrendered, and on September 2, 1945, aboard the *USS Missouri* anchored in Tokyo Bay, a formal end of the war was signed.

What happened next:

Hanz Weber changed his name to Moshe Hidlemen and managed to pay his way out of The Netherlands via Spain, landing in Argentina, South America. He married a peasant girl, who, like Katrina, he abused and bullied. Years later, his true identity was discovered by a team of Jewish Nazi hunters, apprehended at his remote farm, and returned to Germany. He was tried, convicted as a war criminal, and sentenced to life in prison. During his incarceration, he was compelled to compile and categorize thousands of Nazi photographs of the vile atrocities committed in the concentration camps Never once did he utter a word of remorse.

Five years into his imprisonment, he was found dead, which was determined to be suspicious.

James Marshall settled into Briarcliff after Sir Nigel's death. He ran the estate and became a popular member of the community. Devonshire China was sold off to an Irish conglomerate called Waterford, and the factory continued to employ many locals making luxury goods.

Late in life, Marshall met a much younger French man, and they took a fancy to each other. Discreetly, Marshall purchased a secluded villa in Provence and spent many years there with his "young man." At his death, Marshall's body was interred next to Sir Nigel in the single grave reserved for him. Marshall left Briarcliff and the associated fortune to a home for abused young boys.

The Mothers ...

For many years Ellen Manning enjoyed her life in New York. She spent most of her time volunteering for the Guggenheim museum and St. Elmo's church. One of her favorite accomplishments was fixing up her granddaughter with Mrs. Kelly's nephew, a budding television personality. Owen remained devoted to his mother and called every other day. On her ninety-third birthday, while on the phone with Owen, Ellen Manning peacefully passed away.

After the war, Maria Quackenbush left Ireland and immigrated to the United States. Owen pulled some strings to expedite the process. In 1959 Maria returned to The Hague to claim back Schaduwgazon. The Germans had spared the grand mansion, and it remained intact. Katrina joined her mother in the United States with her new Swedish husband, Lars. Lonnie was not mistaken when she thought her father had four, not three, priceless uncut diamonds. When Maria returned to Schaduwgazon she retrieved the missing stone hidden behind an oak panel in the library.

At a Sotheby's auction, the gem fetched more than 17 million dollars which Maria graciously shared with her daughters and numerous refugee charities. On Christmas eve, at her beloved Schaduwgazon, seventeen years later, Maria Quackenbush peacefully passed away while sitting in front of a roaring fire enjoying tea and krakeling, her favorite sweet.

Winney (Winthrop Barrington) left civil service immediately after the war. He married, once, twice, but the third time was the charm. His first wife was a West End actress he picked up in a club. She was a "showstopper" in the looks department but had the brain of a tick and the morals of an alley cat, as he liked to say. Wife number two was more or less an arranged marriage. It was set up by his aristocratic father. Nearly five years Winney's senior, Lady Gladys Lawson managed to talk Winney into a marriage that barely lasted the time it took to draft the divorce papers. Francis was wife number three. Winney met her on a transatlantic Queen Elizabeth crossing. She and her parents were assigned to his table in the first-class Queens Grill. Francis was nice looking but nothing like the glamorous beauties that Winney typically gravitated towards. After years of chasing beautiful but shallow women, Winney realized that someone like Francis had far more to offer than carnal knowledge. She was fun, bright, and genuine. They married, but the couple never produced an heir.

Owen and Lonnie Nine months, almost to the day, after Lonnie's visit to Ireland, she delivered twin boys. Lonnie felt that these precious twins would be a memento of their renewed love after so long a separation. The boys were named Prescott II after Owen's birth father and Nigel II after his uncle.

Ironically, by some seven minutes, Prescott II, Manning's older twin, melded into a personality quite unlike his namesake. In the late 1960s, he became active in the peace movement and joined the Peace Corps after graduating from Yale. His twin, Nigel, also developed into quite the opposite of his pacifistic namesake uncle. At eighteen, he was appointed to West Point, commissioned an infantry officer, and years later became a three-star Pentagon General. Neither of the twins suffered from dyslexia or had syndactyly.

After the war, Owen returned to MIT and worked on dozens of projects, becoming a world authority in the rapidly evolving field of computer sciences. It took years for him to reconcile his role in the war, but in the end, he understood that peace through strength could save the world from mutual destruction.

Lonnie resumed her medical practice at Mass General, working for more than 25 years, and became an acclaimed surgeon. The couple retired to Lake Winnipesaukee in New Hampshire, and Owen joined the IBM Board of Directors.